JENNY DENT lives and
beauty and variety stron   ... ...
writing. She has been writing across genres all her life and has
published, among others, several contemporary crime novels.
A Death on the Home Front, set in rural Cumberland in the
aftermath of the First World War, is her first historical novel.

Born in Wolverhampton, Jenny is a football fan and a season
ticket holder for her beloved Wolves FC. A Geography and
Earth Sciences graduate, she spends the rest of her spare time
reading, gardening, and enjoying the landscape around her on
foot or by bike.

Follow Jenny on X/Twitter @

To Liz

Best wishes
Jenny Dent x

A DEATH ON THE HOME FRONT

JENNY DENT

NORTHODOX PRESS

Northodox Press Ltd
Maiden Greve, Malton,
North Yorkshire, YO17 7BE

This edition 2024

1
First published in Great Britain by
Northodox Press Ltd 2024

ISBN: 978-1-915179-45-6

This book is set in Caslon Pro Std

*This book was inspired by, and is dedicated to, the men who
survived the Great War only to live with its
memories and consequences.*

*In particular, it is for my grandfathers, Peter and Charlie, and my
great-uncles Durward, Jack, Jim, and Teddy – especially Teddy
who, like his namesake in this book, went to war as a young man,
came home uninjured but traumatised, and spent
the rest of his life in an asylum.*

CHAPTER ONE

MERCY

Clinging to the fringe of the crowd gathered on the village green, Mercy stared towards the western horizon, searching for the Penrith bus. Around her, friends and neighbours gazed in the opposite direction, hands shading their eyes as they peered into the June sun and waited for the return of their last hero.

No-one ever seemed to want to let Frank Holland go. Perhaps that was why the army had been so keen to hold on to him for a full eighteen months after the end of the Great War, but today, even Frank was due home. Waterbeck was ready to welcome the last of its sons safely to the fold, and Mercy Appleby seemed the only one who felt any apprehension.

Behind her, the crowd shuffled impatiently, forming and reforming. 'There it is!' shouted someone, but the flicker they'd seen in the shimmering morning sun was a mirage or a mistake, and no bus appeared. The small crowd — about a hundred and twenty people, the population of the village plus a few strays from round about — shuffled around the triangular village green. Someone had unearthed a cache of paper flags left over from the victory celebrations and Lady Blanche Waterbeck, in an afternoon dress especially tailored to match the bunting strung along the frontages of the mellowed red sandstone cottages, was busy distributing them among the children. The vicar, his white cotton vestments billowing in a teasing breeze, stood by the side of the road, peering over his glasses towards the east while the ten village men who'd been to the front and come home again shuffled into a loose military formation. Agog with excitement, the village waited for Frank to arrive.

'Here it comes!'

This time there was no mistake. The distant rumble of an engine, the glint of sun on metal, forewarned them.

'Old bugger took his time.'

'Lads, lads! Line up the parade!'

Mercy wrinkled her brows. From amidst the bevy of cheering, flag-waving children, she saw Blanche look up. Her expression, belying the wild-west whoops of encouragement with which she was geeing up the youngsters, betrayed anxiety. Blanche was more than twenty years Mercy's senior and many social strata above her, but the two had spent the war taking on the work of their menfolk and over the years this forced companionship had turned to an unusual friendship. Whatever her personal feelings, Blanche would do her duty as doggedly as the men of the village had done theirs.

Blanche slipped herself free of the children, or almost so. Sally, Mercy's toddler, clung to the hem of her dress and followed her out of the crowd. 'Mercy. Do stay.'

She wavered. Who didn't love a party? 'I'm going to see Teddy,' she said after a moment's hesitation.

Blanche's discomfort showed. 'I know it seems a little… vainglorious.'

'It's not that.' But it was part of it. She thought of what Teddy might have said, echoing her own reservations. A parade, he'd have sighed, shaking his head. Do they think nothing's changed? 'He can't be here and I don't want him to feel left out,' was her final response.

'At least wait to welcome Frank home.'

'Mama,' said Sally, pleadingly.

She was tempted by her little girl's appeal, but no. She would not be a part of this dark celebration. 'Oh, sweetheart, I can't. I have to do something really important. I have to go and see Daddy and tell him how much you love him.' To Blanche, she turned an apologetic smile, but she resisted the invitation to slip back into the crowd. 'I need to give Sally to my mother. I don't want to miss the train.' And she wasn't dressed for a party, her olive green outfit strictly utilitarian, though the smartest she possessed, her straw cloche hat unadorned by either summer or fabric flowers.

'Of course.' Blanche hesitated for a while longer, as if she'd like to insist. 'Come along, Sally. Take you to your granny just now and you can see Mama when she gets home.'

It was a beautiful June day, but the clear blue of the sky behind the ridge of Blencathra in the west disguised a chill in the air. Clutching her bag in front of her with both hands, Mercy hugged Sally goodbye then turned decisively away, scowling once more along the road as the single-decker black motorbus lurched towards them and coughed to a halt, belching out a dark cloud of smoke. The door opened on the far side, then the vehicle rocked a little before setting off for Keswick and, as it drew away, the smoke cleared and there he was. Frank Holland, army kitbag over his shoulder, his lean figure appearing from the smoke like the genie from the lamp and with a broad smile illuminating his craggily handsome face, had come home.

'Frank!'

He dropped the bag as his mother, launching herself across the grass in an uncharacteristic show of emotion, hurled herself into his arms. Following her, the villagers surged forwards, the women to embrace him, the men to shake his hand. Next to Mercy, Jane Freeman jumped up and down, clasping her hands in front of her in sheer joy. 'He's back! Isn't it wonderful, Mercy? All our men are back from France. All of them.'

'Another one for you to get your claws into,' came a muttered voice from the knot of women beside them.

'Aye, and you'll try your Tom's patience once too often,' supplemented another, but if Jane heard, she didn't care enough to answer. Instead, she flung herself forwards and took her turn, greeting the homecoming hero with a squeal and a kiss, full on the lips.

That was typical of Jane. She never cared what people thought of her. A few years earlier Mercy might have been muttering with the rest of them, distrustful of Jane's free and easy nature, and giving her man a telling-off for being too obviously impressed by the young woman's assets, but these days Jane was no threat to Mercy's marriage.

Fortunately, Frank had no wife to screech her displeasure at him, but Jane had a husband, and he didn't look too pleased about it. Mercy watched Tom Freeman glare at Frank from his place among the men lined up by the green, as if it was his fault. She wasn't the only one to have seen it. One of his friends placed a restraining hand on his shoulder until Frank, laughing, had gently pushed Jane aside.

By now Blanche had finished with the flags. She'd trotted out what was left of the Waterbeck inheritance, a gold brooch in the shape of a swooping eagle, an ostentatious display of noblesse oblige at odds with her down-to-earth nature but in line with what her husband, and the villagers, expected of her, and it flashed at her shoulder in the sun. The job of distribution done, she handed Sally over to the care of Mercy's mother, Carrie, and took her place next to Sir Henry at the head of the welcoming committee. The assembly stood frozen for a moment until Blanche gave her husband the subtlest of nudges. These days he needed to be chivvied into doing anything — and who could blame him? — but he responded to the prompt and stepped forward to offer Frank his hand.

And then, mercifully, the bus, the one towards Penrith and the station, towards Edinburgh and Teddy, appeared in the west and Mercy, grateful, stepped away from the crowd and held out a hand to stop it.

'Excellent stuff, Holland,' Sir Henry was saying, obedient as a child reciting a lesson. 'Good man. Good to have you back.'

She couldn't help looking round. There was a smile lurking beneath the expression of puzzlement on Frank's face, and he took off his cloth cap as if he thought he ought to salute. 'I'm right glad to be home.' Before the Great War he'd have shown more deference, but today it was clear he had less time for Sir Henry even than before, and the spoils of war included the courage to show it. He turned his back on the lord of the manor, on Lady Waterbeck, on the hordes of small children, on his mother and his friends, shaking them off like a cart horse shaking off flies.

'And where are you off to, Mercy Appleby, all dressed off like a lady? Aren't you stopping to welcome an old friend home?'

Frank was the other reason Mercy wouldn't stay. 'Welcome home,' she said, her breath tight in her chest. She should have known she wouldn't lose him that easily. 'I'm so glad you're back.' It was true. The place would be better with him around. He'd always managed to lift the atmosphere, always made her smile. She liked him. There was no reason not to be glad.

'There's to be a big do, they tell me.'

'Yes.' There would be the parade and a brief service of thanksgiving in the church where those who'd lost faith paid lip service to God alongside those who hadn't. In the afternoon, there would be a party for the children and the proceedings would conclude with a dance in the grounds of Waterbeck Hall that would go on late into the night. Blanche would change her outfit at least three times and there would be more food than anyone had dreamed of in the dark days of wartime. There was just one thing missing.

'You'll be there?'

'No. I'm going to Edinburgh.'

Frank's eyes crinkled into a smile. He was, or had been, Teddy's best mate. 'The old man will still be there tomorrow.'

And the next day, and the next. 'I'll be working tomorrow.'

'Edinburgh and back is a long day for you.'

It was a couple of hours each way on the train from Penrith, plus a tram at the other end, a trip she did without fail every week, making an effort to dress up so Teddy knew he was still important to her. 'He's my husband.' Her heart fluttered with optimism. Days – even hours – in Teddy's company were still precious.

'Tell him I'm asking for him,' he said, with the lightest of laughs, and then, as the bus rattled closer, he came too close. 'If he'd died,' he breathed, 'would you have been the one to greet me with a kiss?'

She pushed him away. 'Don't be daft. Look, that's my bus.'

'Tell him I'll go up and see him,' he called, as Blanche stepped forward to claim him and draw him back into the bosom of the village.

'I will.' She put a hand for the bus and scrambled up the steep metal steps, taking a seat so she could still see the goings-on even though she was safely away.

'Not staying for the party, Miss?' The conductor, an older man, clearly not sure of her status and intrigued by what was afoot in the village, hammered out the ticket and handed it over in return for her pennies.

'I have to catch a train.'

She shifted round to watch the scene unfolding behind her as they drew away. Someone must have alerted Frank to the plan the vicar and Sir Henry had hatched between them over a glass or two of port and that her father had shared with the rest of the village over a pint too many in the pub, and he seemed to be falling in with it readily enough. The men had formed themselves into a group and were marching in pairs back towards St Mary's just as they'd marched away together over five years before, Guy Waterbeck at their head. The last glimpse she had of them was the vicar's white surplice billowing in the breeze as he brought up the rear.

Once they were out of sight, and the bus was bone-shaking its iron-tyred way along the road that skirted the Waterbeck estate, she folded her hands on her lap, daydreaming like a teenager. Teddy was two years older than she, so heart-stoppingly handsome that even when she was a child she hadn't been able to keep her eyes from him. Her older sister, Hope, who'd married a surly mine manager and moved to Workington, had said his good looks had turned Mercy's head, but that had been envy. It was Teddy's sensitive soul and touching innocence that had captured her heart.

Her mother had wanted her to marry Frank, and if it hadn't been for Teddy, she might have done. Then she'd have been with him at the centre of this jamboree, not fleeing it like a beaten enemy. In her mind's eye, she imagined the parade marching smartly down towards the church. There had been a discussion, her father had said, about whether they would leave a gap in their ranks to remember Teddy, and she was glad she wasn't there to see what they'd decided. Whatever they chose would only have reinforced his absence.

She didn't begrudge the villagers their party, though there was a niggling feeling of outrage on Teddy's behalf, as though they had no faith in his recovery. But he'd come back and Frank's return was nothing to the celebration they'd have when Teddy did too, and Waterbeck would finally be healed.

She felt in her pocket for one of the handkerchiefs she'd embroidered for him when they were newlyweds and had sent out to him in parcels wrapped in brown paper and string. When Sally'd arrived, within a year of the wedding, there had been no time to sit stitching by the fire in the evenings, even if the war hadn't meant that men's work had become, of necessity, women's. She yawned. At least her mam had Sal for the afternoon. Blanche had promised to help take extra care of her too, and would ply the little girl with candy her sister sent from New York.

A few hundred yards down the road, the bus juddered to a halt, and a soldier swung his kitbag over his shoulder and stepped on board. Mercy spared him a surreptitious glance. Men in uniform were no longer a common sight almost two years after the guns had fallen silent on the Western Front and something about his open countenance reminded her of Teddy. He merited a second look, and a third, but she stole them from behind her handkerchief. It wouldn't do for a married woman to look so obviously at a stranger. His blond hair was a little too long for a regular soldier, his sensuous lips curving into what looked like a permanent, knowing smile. There was a softness to his blue eyes and the crinkling around his mouth suggested he laughed often.

The bus was busy and, having dropped his kitbag on the rack at the front of the bus, he took the seat next to her. For two minutes, they jolted along the road past fields full of inquisitive-looking cows. In the distance, a bank of cloud was building stealthily above the Pennines.

'It's a lovely day, ma'am,' the young man ventured, touching his cap.

He must be younger than Teddy. How did he seem so untouched by what he must have seen? 'Indeed, it is.'

'Are you heading to the town?'

Not too many people had reason to come through Waterbeck and when they did so she, buried among the accounts in the estate office, often never found out about them until they'd gone and her mother could fill her in on the village gossip. But she was in a cheerful mood and her father wasn't there to lecture her about respectability. She placed both hands on the rail of the seat in front of her so that her wedding ring was obvious rather than just visible, the charm that would protect her from any ill intentions. 'I'm going to Edinburgh. To visit my husband.'

'Just to visit, eh?' He cocked his head to one side.

Did he think Teddy was in prison? She felt herself going pink with annoyance. 'He's in the hospital at Craiglockhart.'

'Ah.' He nodded. Everyone knew what that meant. 'Chap had a bad war, eh?'

Teddy's war had been among the worst, or else he'd been among those who found it hardest to deal with. Mercy still didn't know which. Never assertive, nowadays he cowered in the corners of his tiny room in the hospital, starting at a crash of thunder or the banging of a door, while the doctors and the psychiatrists tried this therapy and that in an attempt to heal his mind. On every visit they told her his state was temporary, that he'd be out in no time, but more than two years had ticked by since Teddy had been the first of the men to come back to Blighty and there was no sign of any improvement. 'Yes. But he'll be home soon.'

The stranger's expression softened. 'That was a funny old to-do going on back in your village.'

It was rare that she felt the urge to confide in anyone, least of all a man she'd never met before, but the likeness this soldier bore to Teddy appealed to her. His attraction wasn't physical, but emotional. Whatever Teddy had seen in his nightmares, this man had surely seen, too, but unlike others, she sensed he wouldn't mind talking about it. 'Yes. We sent a dozen men to the front and the last of them came home today.' Frank, who'd waltzed through the war as he waltzed through life. There was a certain injustice around that.

'And that's a reason for a party, eh?' His mouth twisted a little.

'They seem to think so.'

'Don't you?'

She wanted to look closely at this man, to divine how much he understood. 'It was an idea the men cooked up in the pub, I think. Because we're such a lucky village. One lost arm, one lost eye.' And Teddy, his injuries life-changing but invisible. Such a lucky village. 'Everybody survived, so they thought we should have a party. And a parade.'

'A parade!' he said, and laughed, his distaste at the thought mirrored in his face. 'You'd think we'd all seen enough marching, wouldn't you?'

'It's what they wanted. They all marched off together and they wanted to march back together. That way, they feel it's all over.'

'Then that seems reasonable enough.'

'Yes. But, of course, they didn't all come back together. That's why I don't want to stay. No-one thinks it matters that Teddy can't be there.'

'Teddy's your husband, eh?'

She nodded. 'Yes. He's one of them, too, and I won't let him think they've forgotten him. And you?' She pulled herself together in an attempt to deflect from any more talk of the goings on. 'Do you have family round here?'

She couldn't place his accent. He wasn't a northerner, that was for sure, but nor did he have the drawling vowels of the London nurses who'd been deployed to the county's auxiliary hospitals during the darkest days of the War. A covey of them had descended on the Hall when Sir Henry had offered it as a convalescent home, giggling and marvelling at the strange sights and sounds of the countryside and being stared at for their alien ways in return.

'No. I'm a regular,' he said with an easy laugh. 'Royal Artillery. On leave. I'm a Manchester lad, but I've a sweetheart in Keswick.' He winked at her. 'The war's long behind us now and compared to what we've been through, the army is Easy Street. Proper food, a regular wage. I thought I might as well stay in as come out. It's better than working in the mills or the mines, and I don't have to throw one of you lovely young ladies out of a man's job to earn my shilling.'

Mercy's blush deepened. She was a married woman on her way to see her husband, and this charming young man with a sweetheart of his own was teasing her like an old uncle at a wedding. Nevertheless, she was won over. 'I think we did a grand job of keeping the home fires burning.'

'Were you a nurse?' he asked. 'Bessie was. It's how we met. Or did you work in munitions? Delivery driver? Insurance clerk?'

'None of those. I took over my father's job and managed the local estate.'

'A remarkable achievement.' He dimpled that smile at her again, as if he could possibly know what an achievement it was. 'I'm sure you surprised everyone with how well you did. But now you can leave that and go back to home and hearth, eh?'

Mercy's mother had looked after Sally while the menfolk had been away at the war, but though her father was back, he was no longer in any state to undertake the work required. It had taken a month after his return before they'd realised nothing was normal and the man who used to get up with the dawn and be in his office by six now wanted nothing more than to drink to drown the memories. 'Yes.'

The bus was on the outskirts of Penrith now, bumping along the Ullswater Road and pulling in outside the railway station. He stood aside for her as they got off, heaving his kitbag onto his shoulder and following her down to the station forecourt. 'This is where we part. You go north, I go south, but something tells me we'll meet again.'

In the distance, a train whistle sounded. Mercy looked at the station clock. 'That will be my train. I must go and get my ticket.'

'I never introduced myself. Lt William Edmundston. At your service.' He held out a hand.

'Mercy Appleby.' She extended her hand, fingers together the way she'd seen Blanche do when she was trying to keep a civil appearance with someone of whom she disapproved. 'Mrs.'

'Goodbye, Mrs Mercy Appleby. And I don't blame you for wanting to dodge the homecoming party. Why celebrate teaching our young men to kill?' To her surprise, he raised her fingers to his lips. 'It's been a pleasure to make your acquaintance, Ma'am.' He turned his back on her and headed into the station.

She kept her back to him because she sensed he was the type to take liberties and would wave at her, or even wink, as he left, but she was smiling. Doubtless, someone on the bus would already have noted the conversation and marked her behaviour down as scandalous, and the news would get back to the village. Her step lightened as she hurried to the platform. She cared neither for gossip nor for Frank's over-obvious interest in her. There was only one man, would only ever be one man, for her.

She was no Jane Freeman, loose and flighty in her manner and bound, so everyone said, to come to a bad end.

CHAPTER TWO

FRANK

Frank Holland, onetime farm labourer, latterly a corporal in the Cumberland and Westmorland Regiment and now, thank God, a survivor and a man with opportunities to better himself, stepped away from the evening's festivities for a quick fag and a moment of silence. He'd always known coming home would be difficult.

The way they'd looked at him when he got off that bus. What did that say about them all? Had they forgotten so quickly what it was they were celebrating?

He shrugged. What the hell? It made a pleasant enough change to be the centre of things in this village. Curling his hand around a full glass tankard, he retreated across the courtyard until he stood with his back against the wall of the stable block, commanding a view of the front of Waterbeck Hall. He'd begun to see the only difference between classes was chance. He could just about handle the attention and the congratulations, but back in the ballroom the band was beginning to strike up and even for someone as hard-headed as he it was too soon to celebrate. God knew where Lady Waterbeck — or Blanche, as she was in his head now — had dragged the musicians up from but their reedy wailing triggered the echo of a siren or a shell whining above him, in a way he didn't like. The war would always be with him, imprinted on his mind and his memory, but a resourceful man had options. He could live his life waiting for the nightmares to ambush him or he could go out and take it all on, apply the experiences he'd endured, and turn them into profit. Most people he knew fell too easily in with the first, easy option but smart, entrepreneurial Frank hadn't hesitated to choose the second.

It wasn't late — maybe nine-ish, he couldn't be sure — but time had moved swiftly enough for the stealthily mounting clouds behind Blencathra to snuff out the last of the evening haze. He drew heavily on his cigarette and looked back from his sanctuary in the growing shadows at the imposing limestone edifice of the Hall, three floors of magnificence for the benefit of just three Waterbecks, and shook his head at the extravagance, though not without admiration. The main reception rooms were at the back of the building, making the most of the southwards views to the Lakeland fells, and the curtains had been drawn early behind the tall windows of the rooms on either side of the front door, giving much of the building a blank, closed-off appearance.

Tonight, though, the ancient oak doors stood wide as the Waterbecks welcomed their guests and a hundred candles augmented the dim glow of the electric lamps. Light overspilled the building and flowed down the steps, and on the far side of the marble-floored reception hall, the bright figures of partygoers flashed across his view as they whirled around the ballroom past the dour portraits of Sir Henry's ancestors.

Frank took a few moments to look from the outside in, to smoke another cigarette, to understand that he didn't know how he felt, and to listen to the laughter and chatter drifting across the courtyard. The sound disturbed the occupants of the stables and the restless whinny of a carthorse drifted out across the yard along with the pungent scent of horse dung.

War gave you opportunities, he thought as he blessed fresh air and warmth, honest mud a man wouldn't drown in and clothes he could take off and change for fresh ones whenever he chose. You'd be foolish not to take them. Four years in the trenches had taught him more than anyone was surely ever capable of processing, but as his experiences crystallised, one thing continued to intrigue and amuse him. His comrades — his brothers in arms now, those he would have died in a ditch for not so long before and would do so again if the need arose — seemed to a man to have chosen to go back to the security of the old ways. He shook his head. His days of letting other people choose the path his life would take were over.

Reviewing his opportunities for avoiding the rest of the party, he strolled around the perimeter of the courtyard and across to where the estate manager's house stood, at right angles to the main part of Waterbeck Hall. From the attached office, connected to the servants' quarters of the main building by a recently constructed single-storey annexe, George Smart ran the Waterbecks' agricultural affairs. How much work George actually did was a matter for debate, as he plodded through short days in the office on the strength of long nights in the pub, or so Frank's mother had told him. These days it was Mercy who picked up the slack, corrected her father's many drunken errors and kept the estate's business in some kind of fettle while her mother, Carrie, ran the household and looked after Sally. Some people seemed surprised by how effective and efficient Mercy was, but from the days they'd been playmates at the village school, Frank had always had the highest regard for the girl who lived up by the estate office.

Oak Tree House, the estate manager's home, was a handsome one, though something of a mongrel, its walls a mottled mix of pale limestone like the Hall and local brown sandstone like the village. Its seven sash windows, four upstairs and three down, were lightless but for the dim glow of a nightlight on the upper storey. That must be where Sal was sleeping, a tiny scrap of a child whose face, he'd seen at a first glimpse, wore the imprint of her luckless father's charm, an echo of his brown eyes and guileless smile in Mercy's strong and characterful face.

Mother and daughter had moved back in with Mercy's parents after Teddy landed in the hospital, his mam had told him. It was easier for work for Mercy. She had childcare on hand, she'd said, and the poor girl didn't have to live alone. Which was fair enough, but it had dealt a major blow to Frank's hopes of catching a quiet word with her now and again.

When he looked more closely, he spotted a sliver of light between the shutters in the ground floor office. That must be where Mercy was hiding, avoiding him as she always avoided a difficult situation; but when he strolled over and put his eye to the narrow crack, he saw that the office was empty.

It was no surprise. She must have known he'd come looking for her after she'd eluded him on the village green and she was sharp enough to take avoiding action. His mind set on confrontation, he headed back across the courtyard intending to rejoin the party and track her down among the guests in the brightly lit hall and its increasingly shadowy lawns, but something on the far side of the courtyard alerted him and he stopped for a second, sensing a human presence in the avenue that led between the Hall on the right and the walled kitchen garden to the left.

If Mercy wasn't in the Hall and she wasn't at her house, she must be here in the garden. He took a step in that direction, ready to challenge her over why she was so keen to avoid him, but he'd barely reached the entrance to the green lane and the tangle of young rhododendrons that had escaped from the shrubbery before he caught the whiff of someone else's cigarette, the blink of a lit fag.

That was another peacetime luxury. If your light gave away your presence, it wouldn't kill you. Frank stepped towards the scent and the gleam, intrigued. Whoever was in the lane it wasn't Mercy. She didn't smoke. 'Hello?'

'Oh. Holland.' A shadow freed itself from the grip of a deeper shadow and took the apologetic form of Guy Waterbeck, the only surviving son of Sir Henry and Lady Waterbeck and heir to whatever the changing times would leave him. Not that long ago, Frank had been obliged to call him Sir, but those days, too, were gone.

'Ah, it's you, me marra.' Frank puffed contentedly on his cigarette and chose to treat his superior as a mate. Guy had always seemed uncomfortable in uniform and barely looked at ease in the dinner jacket he was wearing for the occasion, so it was easy to overlook the astonishing courage he'd displayed under fire. God knew where it had come from — the spartan conditions of his English public school, in all probability. Whatever the source, it was another thing that had changed — the weak, vapid country-squire-in-waiting had turned out to be a leader.

It counted for nothing now. Guy, who must have learned a few things himself, shrugged off the familiarity, but he didn't reciprocate. 'Thank God it's only you. I thought you were Kitty.'

'Kitty?' Frank's interest deepened. He'd been away from Waterbeck longer than he'd thought. It was beginning to dawn on him how much he had to catch up on.

'Oh, just a girl.' Guy twitched the ash from the end of his cigarette. His face remained in shadow, but he'd already given away a nervous secret. 'I didn't invite her, but I think Mother's keener than I am. That's why she's here. It should be all about us, about the village.' He shook the cigarette again. 'One mustn't complain about squiring a good-looking girl, but a chap needs time out sometimes, Holland. Eh?'

Frank lashed out with a boot as something — a large mouse, perhaps, or a small rat — scuttled from the yard into the hedge. 'One does.' It was hard not to mock even though Guy was one of the better officers culled too young from his class, and had played no small part in bringing them all home safely. At times like this, you began to wonder if some were born lucky. 'Settling back into it, are you, pal?'

He thought Guy twitched a little. To him, no doubt, in peacetime Frank would always be the man who'd driven the horses behind the plough. 'Will any of us ever?'

'Of course we will. There's plenty of time to settle in. The war's over. It's done. We'll all move on to better things. I'll start by finding me a wife.' He thought again of Mercy, and his brows darkened.

'Mother tells me we'll be in great demand,' Guy said, the hint of a laugh in his voice. 'Being the last of the eligible gentlemen of our generation.' The laugh found full, sarcastic expression as he finished speaking. The best, the bravest and most eligible had perished.

'A bonny country lass'll make a change from the jolies mademoiselles of Amiens. Though I imagine your ma will be setting her sights a little higher.'

'I'll say.' Guy laughed again, a thin sound, bereft of humour. 'Not that she put it like that, and not that she knows anything about the jolies mademoiselles, but underneath all that etiquette she's a woman of the world.'

'And is this Kitty the one she thinks you should set your sights on?' Frank chanced his luck.

'She's certainly one of the front runners in the filly stakes.' Guy fidgeted with his snow-white bow tie.

A chuckle formed in Frank's belly. He was testing the boundaries of the new order and finding, to his surprise, that Guy was responding. 'Is she good-looking? Well connected? Rich?'

'She's local gentry,' Guy said, shaking his head. 'Eminently suitable. One or two distant connections to the aristocracy, and she has an independent income.'

'But?'

'Mrs Watson-Cooke. She's a widow.'

Frank understood. After all, weren't so many young women widows these days, or as good as? 'Lost him in the war, did she?'

'Early on.'

Silence settled on them, as if Guy had taken his confidences as far as he dared, but Frank read between the lines. A man like Guy Waterbeck wouldn't want to be second best, chasing a woman in mourning for someone else. No matter how eligible this woman might be, he would have his pride.

'And you aren't ready to settle down,' he prompted, not because he needed to know, but from sheer devilment.

'It's difficult to love after everything we saw.'

Frank disagreed, though he kept his thoughts to himself as the clouds broke and what was left of the sunshine illuminated them. In the bright optimism of life after war, you could reshape anything to the way you wanted it, even loss, even love.

On the steps of the hall a scarlet skirt whisked across the slash of light and Blanche's slender figure appeared, silhouetted in the doorway. 'Oh God, that's Mother. I'm really not in the mood.' Guy paused. 'They don't understand, you know. Any of them. That's one thing you'll learn now you're back.'

By mutual consent they broke apart, Guy taking off down the sunken lane towards the formal garden as the sun went in again and wrapped him once more in shadow. Frank sensed he was standing still, pressed into the thick growth of the rhododendrons and waiting for Blanche to walk past the end of the narrow lane.

She didn't. 'Frank. I'm looking for Guy. Have you seen him?'

And I'm looking for Mercy. Have you seen her? But instead of offering to exchange information, Frank remained true to his comrade, merely jerking a thumb in the opposite direction to distract her attention away from the lane and towards the front of the house. 'Only in passing. He went that way, I think.'

'Oh… I suppose I'll find him later.' She'd dressed up for the occasion and whisked across the yard towards the estate office in a flash of diamonds and a stripe of velvet, daringly cut a few inches below the knee. Blanche turned a shapely ankle, he thought, for a woman in her late forties.

The band wheezed into silence and a smatter of applause. From the ballroom, there was laughter and a ragged toast. 'Here's to our boys!' More laughter. 'May they live long and prosper!'

This was a new world. His perception simultaneously sharpened and blunted by a cocktail of alcohol and freedom, Frank grasped the nettle that was Mercy Appleby. One man's misery was another man's opportunity. Every one of the village men, who'd signed up and served together, had seen Teddy crying like a girl in the trenches, curled up in a cramping, cursing ball of humanity even in one of those rare moments of sweet silence, and they knew he'd never come home – not properly. People who hadn't been there might persuade themselves otherwise and Mercy, who'd chosen Teddy over him, his best mate, might persist in the misguided idea that she'd stay faithful to him until he came back to their cottage in Waterbeck, but she couldn't delude herself for ever. Eventually, she'd become tired of a husband who couldn't give her what a young woman in her twenties would want.

But he'd never let the lad down, Frank promised himself, already justifying whatever he planned to do; not when Teddy needed him. He'd look after his mate's wife and his child, too, as best he could, but life moved on. Surely Mercy must soon realise she was without him for the rest of her life? The women might tut and whisper, but none of his or Teddy's mates would think the less of Mercy if she looked elsewhere. Before the war, divorce would have been a scandal and even now it might raise an eyebrow or two among the more traditional, but it was a matter of pure practicality in this changing world. No-one should expect her to remain trapped in her no man's land of a marriage, neither widow nor wife.

He tapped a foot on the ground. Ever since he'd understood that village men always married village women, he'd been sure he'd marry Mercy and somehow had never realised Teddy had had exactly the same idea. That was the only time in his life he hadn't moved quickly enough, had missed the opportunity. He hadn't even realised he had competition until the eve of the War, when the ring was on eighteen-year-old Mercy's finger and Teddy, a simple labourer with no ambitions, had carried off the prize.

That had taught him not to take things for granted. His life's plan now lacked a wife. 'But the game's changed now, Mercy, hasn't it?' he said under his breath. Visiting Teddy when she knew his return was planned could only have been an excuse for avoiding him. He'd caught a glimpse of her descending from the return bus as he'd waited for his mother to get ready for the party, but she'd been nowhere to be seen at the meal and now the dancing had started and she was still absent. That could only mean she was aware of her predicament and knew he was on the way out of it. She was avoiding facing up to the reality, for now.

But he could wait. Years, if need be.

'Were you talking to someone?' The click of heels sounded behind him. Blanche was back, her quest for her son unsatisfied.

'Myself.' Frank rolled the end of his cigarette between his fingers. Sometimes your own company was all you could trust.

She stopped beside him and the light spilling out from the house glittered on the gemstones at her neck and earlobes. 'Oh.' A pause. 'Tell me, Frank…'

'What?'

Another pause, this time a slightly abashed one. 'I thought you'd be inside. Didn't you want a party for your homecoming?'

He stifled a grin. Naturally, he hadn't been consulted. People like him never were, only expected to be grateful for what they were given. 'Well, the do wasn't really for me, was it?'

'Not exactly, no. It was meant to be for everyone. To show how grateful we are for how lucky we've been. There must be other places in the country that have all their men back, but I haven't heard of any. There certainly aren't any locally. Sir Henry and the vicar thought it would be a nice gesture. But now I wonder if it was a little premature.'

The war had ended more than eighteen months before, long enough for communities to think about carving names on memorials and beginning to live again. What changed you forever needn't change you for the worse and for Frank the Great War was consigned to the past. 'It's never too early to be grateful.'

'You know what I mean. Half the men aren't in the ballroom for the dancing. Even Guy has sloped off and he would never abandon his social obligations.'

He dropped the cigarette end on the floor, extracted a crumpled packet of Woodbines from his pocket and offered it to her. It was almost thirty years since Blanche Hardacre had breezed like a summer storm into the village and marriage to Sir Henry Waterbeck. Her mother had once worked in a saloon bar, so they said, and her father had worked his way out of poverty to earn millions in coal and steel and transport. Even after three decades of rural life, she was refreshingly and uncaringly different to the slow society in which she'd buried herself. She spoke her mind, and he liked that. It meant he could do the same and not suffer for it. 'Mind if I say something?'

'I'd be glad of your candour.' She tilted her chin towards him, as if she was unsure what to expect but ready for anything.

He struck a match and lifted it to light the cigarette for her, then touched it to the tip of another for himself. 'It's all different now.' They were hardened, cared less for what others thought, and owed themselves a little self-love. At least, he did. On reflection, it was a mistake to judge all the others by his own experiences.

'I know that,' she said, missing the point. 'But we've done our best, Sir Henry and I, to make sure that everyone who came back would find the village waiting for them exactly the way it was before. Even those who were wounded… they've all got their jobs back.'

'Except Teddy Appleby,' he said before he could stop himself.

'Mercy says he'll come home, and his job will be there when he does. I don't want you to think we won't look after you. You'll have your job back, too. Of course. Please tell me you weren't worried about that.'

'I'm grateful for the offer, but I've something else lined up.' In the future, the only furrow he'd plough would be his own.

'Another job?' In the fading light, her expression showed perplexity.

'Yes. Wilson's in Penrith have taken me on as a mechanic. I start at the turn of the month.'

'Well, I didn't know you knew about motor cars, Frank. Goodness. How exciting.' And he read the subtext: who would they get, in this world, robbed of so many men, to fill his place on the estate? Who would walk the fields sowing seed and building stocks at harvest?

'I learned a lot in the war,' he said to her with a laugh, 'and some of it was worth knowing. Tractors and things. You should be looking at getting one to make life easier around here.'

'Well, indeed.' She puffed a couple of times on her cigarette and a shrug of resignation told him she recognised him as an entrepreneur. 'About the party. I guess we've all been a little over-enthusiastic, perhaps. I know it's been eighteen months, but I should have thought. Even Sir Henry still has nightmares.'

God knew what Sir Henry had nightmares about when he hadn't even been there. If he'd heard stories, they couldn't have touched on the truth. Frank chose not to voice his scepticism. 'The lads will need a lot of time to think about things.' Or to learn how not to think.

'Then I shan't chivvy them too much. Except Guy, of course. However he feels about it, he has to come in and do his duty.'

'If I see him, I'll send him in.'

'Thank you so much.' She turned and headed back to the Hall.

For a moment longer, Frank waited in the gathering darkness, then strolled away from the sound of the merrymaking, craving silence. The band had lurched into a drunken, fast-paced rendition of some tune so modern it hadn't made it to the dance halls of Suffolk, where he'd worked out his time in the army garage learning about cars and tanks and motorcycles, skills for a new and optimistic world.

Ahead, the shape of the narrow lonning, a sunken tunnel of dark green shadows between the walled kitchen garden and the Hall's extensive lawns, brought back a flashing reminder of the trenches but he strode through it to prove his strength, past the gate which led to Blanche's private garden and through which Guy must have disappeared. Even in these days of change, he didn't dare follow and instead took the path along the to the end of the hedge where it veered left towards the fields and the woods of the Waterbeck estate. The sun had all but gone, the sky black in the east and midnight velvet blue in the west. Stars shone through like tiny shrapnel holes, way above him. Night fragrances of roses and stocks billowed out from the formal garden, secure behind thick banks of yew, hundreds of years in the making.

Both an optimist and a pragmatist, Frank rolled the next cigarette, unlit, between his fingers and contemplated a future in which he was prosperous. In time he was sure the practicalities of bringing up a child alone, and the knowledge of the wealth that would surely be his, would prove too much for Mercy and then, for certain, Mrs Teddy Appleby would agree to become Mrs Frank Holland. It would require patience to overcome her stubborn loyalty, but if the reward was the soft warmth of his only love in his bed, he would wait. He smiled.

Even here, though the sound of the band had stopped and the laughter from the Hall had faded into almost nothing, the silence wasn't absolute. If he listened, he fancied he could hear the flapping of leathery wings as bats dipped in and out among the trees. And a much more human noise — a woman succumbing to a deep-throated, carnal giggle from somewhere on the other side of the hedge, a man's animal growl to match it as the two came together. The woman stifled a squeal, and the man failed to silence his guttural roar, and the only words Frank Holland heard were the man's climaxing prayer.

'Oh, Mercy. Mercy!'

CHAPTER THREE

MERCY

'I'm starting to think this party wasn't a very good idea.'

Mercy looked up. It hadn't taken long for Blanche to run her to earth. She'd half-expected it, so keen had Blanche been to make Frank's welcome home a success.

'It's just bad timing,' Blanche went on, closing the office door behind her and standing with her back to it. 'I guess some of them will never get over it, but most of them are going to have to. They might as well start now.'

Mercy pushed her chair back and closed the dusty ledger that listed the manpower required for the upcoming harvest and the amount of money available to pay for it. The Waterbecks had fared better than many estate owners, largely because when Blanche had been sent to England from Philadelphia to marry a duke, she'd confounded her father's instructions and fallen in love with a country squire. The fortune she'd been sent to bargain with had found its resting place in the Waterbeck estate and proved more than ample to fund Sir Henry's limited undertakings and obligations without too much collateral damage. Since Milton Hardacre's investments in transport and metal had been war-proof, cash flow wasn't the problem for them it was for other, larger estates. Waterbeck Hall was large and impressive in its context — twelve bedrooms for the family and guests, each with its own bathroom with running water, and the whole house equipped with electric light from the day it was available in the county — but it was no grand stately home. With no great property to maintain, no entourage to feed and clothe, no royalty to impress, no face to keep up, and now, with a country needing to be fed, they were in a healthy enough position.

Waterbeck was, indeed, a lucky village. The problem with the finances wasn't the quantity but the quality, the constant errors in her father's book-keeping.

Pushing the book away, Mercy sighed. Did they expect too much of their returning soldiers? 'It's hard.' Teddy's broken life tugged at her heart as surely as Sally, out on a walk, tugged at her hand. One day soon, he'd be released into her care. Changed for ever, maybe, but home.

'I'm aware of that.' Blanche hesitated inside the door, as if the office weren't part of her domain and she couldn't have bought the village out ten times over without noticing. It was her philosophy to show respect to everyone. 'But the men keep drifting off from the party. Every time I chase one of them back in another one's gone. I hounded Guy into doing his duty, but all he seems able to manage to do is stand in the corner.' She tossed her bobbed head and frowned, as if the glimpse she caught of herself in the mirror disappointed her with its threads of grey. 'I thought you'd join us.'

'I meant to.' But there was dancing. She'd last danced in Teddy's arms at their wedding, on a summer evening just like this. He was elegantly light-footed, his hold strong and safe, and waltzing with him had been like living in a dream. 'I don't want to leave Sal alone in the house. Though I went up a moment ago and she's sound asleep. I was going to sit with her.' Blanche's obvious disappointment pricked her conscience. 'I could come for a moment, I suppose.' But not dance. Another day, another homecoming, and she would have been more enthusiastic, but the famine of separation gnawed inside her. And Frank was a difficulty she wasn't in the mood to navigate.

Blanche was too self-disciplined to fidget and too honest to dissemble. 'It was thoughtless of us to hold this whole rodeo, given that poor Teddy—'

Mercy bit her lip and thought of the time Blanche had gone with her to visit. They'd found him sitting mute on the narrow hospital bed, his eyes as wide as a frightened child's, waiting in fear for a sudden sound that might herald the end of the world. He either hadn't known or was refusing to admit what had brought him there; the only reality had been his nightmares. 'I probably shouldn't have gone to see him today. It's a long day and always puts me out of sorts, and if I'm honest, I don't know that it helps him. But I didn't want to leave him on his own, to feel left out.' Sal and I love you so much, she'd whispered to him, and that was the only time he'd managed a smile. 'You're right. I should show willing. I'll go now.'

'Oh, honey.' Blanche's voice softened. 'No, I meant it. I didn't expect you to come along. Go and sit with Sally, if it's best for you. It's just that I didn't expect you to work instead.'

'It needs to be done.' Getting up, Mercy replaced the ledger on the shelf and brushed a smudge of dust from the olive serge of her skirt. Her natural positivity reasserted itself. 'I should show my face. I'll go and see how things are.'

'Your father is fine,' Blanche said, guessing what was in Mercy's mind.

Silence, while Mercy shifted all the ledgers into line. Even before the war, George Smart had had a weakness for drink, brought on (so her mother said) by the loss of their three infant sons. He'd been too old to fight, but he'd volunteered as a stretcher bearer and the war had put its mark on him just as surely as on the millions who'd died and the millions more who'd come home scarred, in body and in mind. Correcting his many arithmetical mistakes was barely the start of it. She shifted the ledger again.

'Sally will be fine. We don't have to join the party. We could get a drink and take it into the garden.' Blanche shook her head. 'I'm finding this more of a trial than I thought I would, if I'm honest. Dear Lord, that young woman Guy's courting can be hard work sometimes.'

'Mrs Watson-Cooke is very outspoken.' Mercy struggled not to smile. Blanche's impatience with the otherwise-ideal Kitty was both obvious and entertaining.

'Guy said we shouldn't invite her because today is for the village, but she turned up in full rig saying she'd heard there was a party and her invitation must have been overlooked. I had to pretend I was expecting her.' Blanche looked at Mercy with an anxious, appealing gaze. 'So very tiring. I think she just hates the idea of missing out.' Waterbeck was a long way from Philadelphia, further than Mercy could comprehend, and despite all the years Blanche had been embedded in the Cumbrian countryside, she hadn't made any close friends; nor, occupied with her four children, had she seemed to need them. 'That's settled. We'll go and sit in the garden. It makes me think of home.'

Mercy shot a quick look out to the leaping shadows of the courtyard. It would give her a chance to avoid Frank for a while longer. 'Well, then,' she said, bracing herself, 'let's get on.'

They walked down the corridor from the office, Blanche's spangled pumps tapping alongside Mercy's sensible black T-bar shoes on the slate flags as they slipped through the corridor, linking the main house and the estate office. In the hallway, a pair of village girls were giggling with a couple of the young men, flirtations that would surely drift into marriage in months. The chatter from the ballroom had risen and the soft light of a hundred candles, which Blanche preferred on such occasions to the electric lamps, lit the Victorian crystal chandeliers. Brightness rebounded from the mirrors and the polished marble floors, picked up by the cheap sparkles of mass-produced jewellery around the throats of the village's women.

On the edge of the ballroom Blanche paused, scanning the room as if remembering her responsibilities as hostess. Beside her, Mercy gazed beyond the girls circulating with food and drink, and her eyes rested for a moment on Kitty Watson-Cooke, who stood alone by the tall windows that opened out onto the terrace. Her blonde hair was cut in a severe bob, the neck of her violet silk gown plunged daringly both fore and aft, and she flaunted a full set of amethysts to match. Her face bore a fixed frown of politeness as she too swivelled to survey the room, an empty champagne glass held between manicured fingers. And beyond her, behind a hideous aspidistra on a carved wooden stand, Mercy's mother and father were having a row.

Thank God, thought Mercy as she wriggled her way through the crowd to the rescue. It looked a quiet, repressed row. For the moment. But when she got there, she saw that her mother was almost crying and her father was incoherent with a cocktail of anger and drink.

She didn't stop to find out what trivial comment had started it. In reality, it would be about her father's drinking and her mother's embarrassment. They'd had the beginnings of it the night before over supper, and George had promised to stay sober. His failure and her mother's distress, like Teddy's doleful incarceration, were painful markers of how the war had torn her family apart. 'Dad. You'd best come home.'

'But I'm having a good time.'

'Too good a time,' interrupted Carrie in a fierce hiss of pain rather than anger.

'Hush, Mam. Leave this to me.' Turning her back on her mother's torment, Mercy concentrated on its cause. 'Were you in the pub with the men this afternoon?'

'Few drinks after church,' he mumbled.

'Fine.' She put her hand under his elbow and he was already too far gone to resist. 'And then a couple more later, I imagine.'

'S'Henry. Rude to refuse.'

And then the party. She managed to steer him around the edge of the ballroom without attracting anyone else's notice.

Thank God everyone else was too keen on making the most of the best food and drink Blanche's money could provide. 'Okay. But I think you need to get home.'

'Rude to leave.' He tried to snatch his arm away and failed, too lacking in co-ordination even to do that much.

'Just come with me a minute.'

'Master in my own house,' he protested, as he suffered himself to be towed out of the room, through the hallway and out through the open front door. Behind them, the laughter faded, the cool evening air swirled around their feet, the light receded, and the darkness enclosed them. In the shadows, there was a whisk of white fabric and a woman's giggle.

Mercy ignored them. If some village girl wanted to court some village man in the darkness, what business of it of hers? Hopefully, they'd be too preoccupied with each other to pay any attention to George's plight. 'Careful on the steps, Dad.'

'C'n manage.' And he did, with her help, across the courtyard, into the kitchen of Oak Tree House. There, he found some level of control, rallying to the attack. 'Your mam's no right to talk to me like she did.'

'She was upset. You promised. You said you wouldn't drink so much and you wouldn't humiliate her.'

'Woman should do as I tell her. Vows. We made—' He tripped, stumbled and would have fallen but for Mercy's steadying arm.

'Dad.' With relief, she manoeuvred him to his armchair, and he dropped like a dead man into its russet leather embrace. 'I'll get you a cup of tea.'

'All those boys we couldn't save. I tried. It was useless.' A fat tear rolled noiselessly down his cheek. 'A wee dram, lad. That'll help.'

'I'm not a lad. I'm Mercy.' She turned away to fetch the kettle which had been hissing on its metal cradle on the range, spilling the scalding water into the teapot. 'I'll pop up and see Sal, and this'll be mashed and ready by the time I come back.' Leaving him, she ran up the stone staircase, pausing at the threshold of her bedroom. In the darkness, she could make out Sally's sleeping form and the rise and fall of her body, but the sound of her breathing was drowned by the laughter from the Hall.

Oh Sal, she thought. We love you so much, all of us. And then, remembering George, she headed back down to the kitchen. He'd already slumped into unconsciousness, chin on his chest, legs stretched out on the stone flags.

With a sigh, she replaced the kettle at the edge of the range so it would still be hot if they needed it later. 'Dad?'

No answer but a shuddering, irregular snore. She dropped to her knees, unlaced his boots and slipped them off, resting them neatly at one side of the fire. Then she turned and headed back to the ballroom.

* * *

'Disaster averted?' asked Blanche, obviously on the lookout, as she hovered behind a pillar. 'Thank heavens. Your father is a good man, Mercy, but drink is a weakness. To excess, at least. Having said that, I've only had one glass all night and you look as if you need some, too.'

Mercy scanned the room for her mother and spotted her standing by one of the long tables laden with sandwiches, laughing with a friend. Carrie was exceptionally good at putting on a brave face. She needed to be. But all seemed well, and yes, the trials of the day might be easier if they were washed down with something indulgent. 'Just a glass.'

Blanche spun on the heel of her glass-spangled slipper and held out a hand to one of the maids. 'Lottie! Could we trouble you for some punch?'

'Yes, ma'am.' The girl diverted from her route between kitchen and ballroom, proffering a tray with a choice of drinks. Bubbles raced up through flutes of pale champagne alongside tall crystal glasses of sugar-pink punch, rich with summer fruit.

'Thank you.' Blanche took a glass of punch and passed another to Mercy. 'I thought Jane was in charge tonight. She doesn't appear to be here.'

'I don't know where she's gone, your ladyship. She was in the kitchen an hour back, but I haven't seen her since.'

In a moment, Blanche would suggest going to look for her. Just then Mercy cared nothing about the whereabouts of Jane Freeman and everything about getting out of the ballroom before someone, seeking entertainment, asked after her father so they could snigger about it when they saw him next. Or, if she were honest, before Frank appeared and turned his casual charm on her, before he asked her to dance and she refused because he wasn't the man she wanted to dance with. 'Does it matter? Everyone looks as if they're having a wonderful time. That's all that counts.'

'No, you have a point. It's a party, after all. No-one else cares who's serving as long as they get their victuals. Though I'll speak to Jane about it later.' Blanche turned away from the ballroom. 'Let's get away from here. And for God's sake, make sure Kitty doesn't see us. She'll want to come.'

Successfully avoiding Kitty, who had drifted away from the window and become mired in dutiful conversation with the vicar, they slipped out through the French doors and onto the terrace. Making her way through a knot of guests with no more than a polite word and without breaking stride, Blanche led the way along the back of the house, through the courtyard behind the kitchen and thus, in a roundabout way, to the sunken lane. Someone had set lanterns along the road and in the garden, but those leading to the gate had guttered out or never been lit and the gate itself, which should have been left open, was closed. Another figure stood smoking in the darkness, in watchful stillness.

'Tom,' said Blanche, in her bright, hostess voice, 'you should be joining in the party.'

'Thought I'd take a break.' A pause. 'M'lady.'

'I do hope you've been enjoying it.'

Tom Freeman, husband to the flighty — and mysteriously absent — Jane, merely nodded in response. One of Waterbeck's less lucky sons, he held an empty glass in his right hand, a cigarette smoking between his fingers, but the left sleeve of his Sunday jacket was pinned down at his side, where his arm had been when he left for the front in 1915.

'Come along, Mercy.' Blanche strode on, down the leafy lane with its shifting shadows and through the garden gate. Mercy lingered a moment longer to smile at Tom. His noted temper always made her a little wary of him, but today he seemed calm enough, though a little distracted. He might treat Blanche with respect verging on the frigid, but he managed a nod for Mercy.

The lanterns were lit in the lane, at least, shivering among the thick summer foliage in the trees as she hurried to catch up with her friend, but no-one had taken advantage of them to spend time in the garden. An unknown animal rustled in the hedge as they passed.

'Tell me about Teddy,' Blanche said, taking a seat on the bench at the top of the artificial hill that had been one of the early fruits of her fortune. In the west, the last scarlet flash of the dying sun dipped below the horizon. The outlines of the mighty trees that some ancient Waterbeck had planted in the parkland faded into silence and the shadows tightened around them. Only the meagre half face of the waning moon lightened the darkness. 'You must be tired after such a long day.'

He was the light of her life and the song in her heart. 'It's worth it.' There were those marriage vows, though whoever had turned that crafty phrase in sickness and in health could surely have had no idea of the bitter twist the war would wreak. 'It's the waiting. Every week it's the same. The doctors tell me he'll get better. It's just a matter of time. But it's past two years now, and no sign.' She raised her glass and the punch, sweet as young love, slid over her tongue.

'Then try other doctors.'

'They're the experts in their field.' And yet. 'He's still the boy I grew up with,' she burst out. 'He's still the man I fell in love with.' And the soldier she'd married. Distant laughter rippled across the garden towards them. 'He barely speaks. And when he does, he tells of dreadful things. But I want him home, with me.'

'He, too, has resigned his part in the casual comedy,' said Blanche suddenly. 'He, too, has been changed in his turn, transformed utterly.' She wasn't often this whimsical, but it was late and the punch was potent. 'It's a poem by William Butler Yeats. I thought of it just now, as we passed Tom. We have all been changed utterly by this terrible war.'

'Yes. But we've all come through it.' At least Mercy still had Teddy, and Tom still had his wife Jane despite the loss of his arm, and Blanche herself still had Guy, the last of her children, to cling to. But it wasn't always easy to be thankful. She took a long sip of the punch and thought of her parents, reaping a grim harvest from her father's desire to do good.

'Jane! Where the hell are you?' The harsh shout came from the entrance to the garden, where Tom Freeman's silence must have cracked under the weight of cider and frustration.

'Lordy.' Blanche set her glass down and directed a fretful glance towards the lonning. 'What's going on?'

'Tom's had too much to drink. Poor Jane. She can't get a moment's peace from him.' Jumping up, Mercy hurried along the narrow path between the shadows of the hedges towards the gate. If it wasn't one man, it would be another. Men had always drunk to excess, but the brutality of the trenches had added a new dimension, and since his return, Tom failed to hide his suffering. Who wants a one-armed husband? Mercy had once heard him shouting in the bitterness of his drink as she'd headed up from the village one Saturday night.

'I really do regret this party,' said Blanche as they walked. 'I had my misgivings when Henry suggested it, but he was so pleased with himself and there seemed no harm. Though, I guess tomorrow there will be sore heads and then we can all forget about it, but we have to get tonight over and done with first.'

'Tom.' As they emerged from the gate, Mercy turned towards him, her restraining hand no more than an outline in the darkness. 'Is there a problem?'

'I want my wife!' Tom bestrode the narrow lane outside the gate, but he was too respectful to go further. 'She don't want an old cripple like me, but she's still my wife! She promised she'd love me until death parted us and so she will! If she doesn't want to, I'll make her!'

'I say, Freeman.' Guy, appearing behind him, had lost his officer's authority, offloaded, it seemed, as easily as his uniform. He snatched at one of the lanterns and held it up, no more than an anxious onlooker. 'Calm down, old chap.'

'Tom, marra.' Now it was Frank Holland, materialising from the shadows. He laid a hand on Tom's useless shoulder and the other man turned towards him, ignoring Guy, his good fist clenched around a cigarette that had burned down to its end. 'Calm down, pal. Calm down.' The three of them stood together, their faces bright in the yellow circle of light that enclosed them — Tom anguished, Frank steely calm, Guy strangely flustered.

'She's been avoiding me all evening. I know what she's like. She likes a bit of a handsome laddo. Always did. And now I'm no use to her. She thinks she can find something better. I swear if she's been doing what I think she's been doing, I'll break her neck!' He swung his arm half-heartedly at Frank. 'And what about you? Back from the war with your fancy suit and your fancy new job and all the girls wanting a ride in your new motor car—'

'I don't have a motor car,' said Frank, his tone more affable than Mercy thought possible under the circumstances. 'Yet.'

'The first thing you did when you got back was kiss my wife!'

'Your wife kissed me,' Frank said, 'and you can rest easy. She's not who I've got my eye on, and if she was, I wouldn't lay a finger on her.' In the half-light he flicked a machine-gun-rapid smile at Mercy and passed on. 'You're my mate and we went to hell together. Never forget that.' He locked his gaze back on Tom's.

'Lordy!' said Blanche again. She stepped forward, as if she wanted to impose authority where Guy had failed, but there was no space in their pool of lamplight for her and so she stayed outside it, in the darkness. In the vacuum she left, Mercy moved forward to intervene. 'Tom. I'm sure there's nothing to worry about. I expect Jane's busy. She's working tonight.'

'Don't talk like that, Freeman.' Belatedly, Guy made another attempt to bring some control to the situation.

'It's okay.' Even under the tricks of the harsh lamplight, Frank's face held compassion. 'You know you can trust me, Tom. I'm your pal. Come with me, man. I'll look after you.'

In a moment of silence, the throaty roar of a motorcycle ripped the still night as it tore along the road from Keswick to Penrith and Frank lifted his head as if to listen. Then he looked at Mercy again, an appeal for help.

She responded. How could she do anything else? 'I'll go and find Jane and tell her you're worried.' Jane would need a word of warning, too, if she'd been flirting. Normally there'd be no harm in it, but with Tom in this mood, it was different. 'Why don't you go back to the Hall?'

'Someone said they saw the little tart going in to the garden!'

'We were just in the garden now, Tom, and I'd swear it was just the two of us.'

'What are you hiding? Why are you helping her?' Breaking free from Frank's restraining hand, Tom pushed past the two women and broke along the broad, hedged path.

'It's dark,' Guy whispered, clearly unnerved. He lifted the lantern, and it swung wildly in his quivering hands. The shadows lunged forwards and leapt back with each movement 'I can't go in there!'

'No. It'll be all right.' But Frank, too, hung back.

Mercy, for whom the darkness held no demons, acted. 'Tom!' She took off after him. If Tom came across his Jane with another man, which he might well, no matter how innocent the explanation, there would be trouble. 'Come back!'

Behind her, Blanche's low-heeled shoes pounded the grass. Around the corner in the dark. Back to the artificial knoll where they had so recently sat. Past the two abandoned glasses of punch set on the grass behind a guttering lantern, around the next bend, the shadows trembling as the lamps danced in Tom's furious wake.

At the end of the dark path, he came to a sudden halt and let out a long, low, howling moan. In the crazy light, a slumped form stretched out below the hedge, a swathe of black cotton spread like a void upon the earth. Jane Freeman lay on the grass, her glassy eyes staring up at the rising moon.

Her heart beating so loudly that everyone must be able to hear it, Mercy pressed her hands to her eyes and turned away to where the other men's footsteps shuddered up the path behind them. When she opened them again, a triptych of faces showed haggard in the lamplight, every one of them familiar companions with violent death.

CHAPTER FOUR

MERCY

Waterbeck was too small to have a policeman of its own, so PC Davy Robinson had bicycled the three miles from Penrith. A minute afterward, a car coughed its way up the drive and disgorged an inspector. From the marginal disarray of his clothing and the unpaired socks in different shades of grey, Mercy, deputed by Blanche to meet the two police officers and guide them away from the guests, deduced the inspector had been on his way to bed, if not already tucked up, when the call had come.

'Inspector Livingstone?' She guided the two men up the steps, keeping a wary eye out for any strays from the party as they clattered across the hall. I'm Mercy Appleby. I work in the estate office. Lady Waterbeck has asked me to take you through to the office.'

'Mrs Appleby.' Livingstone was a thick-set, coarse featured Scot with thin lips and an unreadable expression, though his face was startlingly strange, the white of a wall eye reflecting the candlelight from the Hall. 'You discovered the body. Is that right?'

Speaking it aloud rammed home the reality of what had seemed like a strange dream. 'Yes. This way.' In the background, the band, like most people unaware of the developing drama, switched into the strains of Dardanella. A lone baritone voice rose above the noise to join in. The vicar's, Mercy realised with astonishment.

'Is this the police?' A high-pitched, refined voice preceded the flash of amethysts. 'Good.' In a whisper of silk and a waft of floral scent, Kitty shouldered her way past Mercy. 'At last. I'm so glad someone is here to take charge.'

Livingstone turned to look at her. Now he was in the light, Mercy could see his face and found his thoughts unreadable. 'Yes, Ma'am. And you are?'

'Kitty Watson-Cooke. Mrs,' she informed him. 'I live in Brampton. I'm a friend of the family. This is a very bad business, I know, but it would be good if you could be discreet.'

Kitty was clearly set on taking charge, but Mercy wasn't having that. 'Lady Waterbeck asked me to take you through to Sir Henry's study. This way.'

'You're having a party,' observed the inspector, pausing for a moment to look through the open double doors.

Lord, spare us from them as states the obvious, Teddy used to say. Amid the shock, Mercy found a smile, though it was shadowed by irritation as Kitty's heels tapped behind them on the green marble floor like a soprano melody above the bass drum of the policemen's boots. 'It's a homecoming party.'

As they passed the supper room, she thought the constable looked longingly towards the buffet table with its sandwiches and pies and bowls of fruit and jelly, but she hustled them on through a maze of long corridors, round a corner and out of sight. Sir Henry's study was at the back of the house, with a daytime view across the lawns and down to the pond, which this evening would have been a vantage point for the goings-on across the torch-lit terrace and lawns. Tonight, someone had drawn the heavy curtains so no-one on the outside would be alarmed by what was going on within.

'Inspector.' Blanche had been standing behind her husband as he sat shrunken in the wing-backed chair by the unlit fire. Sir Henry was shaking his head, slowly and almost in wonder. Dressed, like Guy, in white tie and tails, his thick silver hair gleaming and his face pale grey, he was a study in silent film, expressive and monochrome against the dark wood panelling. 'It's good you could come quickly. I realise this is irregular, but

I didn't think it was sensible to tell everyone what's happened. Kitty, darling. I'm so glad you're here. May I rely on you to go back and play the hostess while we sort out this little difficulty?'

'Oh, but I can help. My uncle is Sir Arthur Henderson, the Chief Constable, you know, and I—'

'Thank you so much, Kitty. I knew I could rely on you.' Blanche steered her out of the room and closed the door. Many square yards of Turkey carpet and heavy curtains, so dark a green that they were almost black, deadened the sound of their voices and isolated them from the world outside.

'Now, Sir Henry.' Motioning to the constable to stand by the door, Livingstone took charge, placing himself in the middle of the room and dominating it. 'I'm told a woman has died.'

There was a decanter of brandy and glasses on the sideboard. Recognising Sir Henry's silence as either confusion or resignation, Mercy crossed the room and poured two glasses. The first she handed to Blanche and the second to Sir Henry.

'Her name is Jane Freeman,' said Blanche, as so often, speaking for her husband. 'She worked in the kitchen here.'

'You and Mrs Appleby found her, I believe.' Livingstone moved to sit behind Sir Henry's desk, and no-one pulled him up on his impertinence.

'Yes. And her husband. He went into the garden to look for her, and Mrs Appleby and I followed him. My son, Guy, and another man, Frank Holland, were also there.'

Livingstone looked around him, as if he expected to see the three of them lined up somewhere like prisoners in the dock. 'Where are they now?'

Mercy found her breath tight in her chest. 'I thought it would be sensible to keep them away from the rest of our guests just now. I put them in Lady Waterbeck's drawing room.'

'Obviously, you'll need to talk to them.' Blanche was addressing the inspector as if he were her bank manager. 'I don't want fear and alarm raised tonight, thank you very much, so I prefer to keep this discreet. I accept we can't keep it quiet beyond this evening. After all, it's murder.'

'So people keep saying.' Livingstone nodded at PC Robinson, who got out his notebook. 'What makes you think it's that?'

'A good point.' The acid in Blanche's tone betrayed her irritation. 'Obviously, you're the professional investigator. I shall leave it to you to draw your conclusions.'

Still standing by the sideboard and at last with a moment to think, Mercy finally understood, with a sudden shock, the implications of what had happened. Jane was dead and it must, surely, be someone she knew who'd killed her. Drink, anger, even accident. What and who? Tom? One of the other village men? Guy, even?

'I'll see the body now, then, if I may. She's still where you found her?'

'Yes. And then we must move her,' Mercy said, springing into the discussion. The moment of shock had passed and practicality reasserted itself. Out in the countryside, nature moved swiftly to capitalise on death. As the sun came up, the early birds would close in and the crows that cruised the fields for worms and scavenged the springtime hedges for other birds' eggs would move in for Jane's wide-open blue eyes. She shuddered. 'We can put her in the mortuary.'

'You have a mortuary?' There was incredulity in Livingstone's voice.

'Yes. We had to have one during the war. The house was an auxiliary hospital and a convalescent home and when the poor boys died, we needed somewhere for the bodies until we could bury them. When the army moved out, we just shut it up.' No-one had had the enthusiasm to remove the cold marble slab on which the dead had been laid in that chill, windowless room and so no-one had taken responsibility for it.

'It'll have been handy in the Spanish flu, too. I daresay. I imagine this village lost a few folk.'

Mercy saw Blanche's fingers tighten around the crystal glass in her hand, a vein pulsing in her slender throat. The Great War had been cruel and the flu pandemic that had ridden on its coat tails, overshadowing the beginning of the peace, had been crueller still, snatching away so many of the young and the vigorous, the survivors on whom the future should have been built. Waterbeck, so grateful to have escaped the worst of the war, had suffered disproportionately under the peace.

'Indeed.' Blanche's voice was chilly with suppressed grief. From the mantelpiece over the fire, her image gazed down at them, immortalised in a silver frame with her four children, laughing on the lawns of the Hall. 'Including three of my children.' Flora, Annie and Edward, beautiful and privileged, lay in the churchyard among those who'd lived longer and harder lives and those whose lives had barely begun.

'My commiserations.' He turned away. 'I'll leave Constable Robinson to take your statements, and those of the men who were there when she was found. Mrs Appleby, perhaps you'd be so good as to show me the body.'

'Of course.' Mercy led him out of the room and along the corridor, not the way she and Blanche had taken to the garden, but along the corridor. On the way, they passed Blanche's private drawing room, its door standing open. Mercy took a moment to glance in. Tom Freeman sat on the edge of a chair by the empty fireplace, his face a mask, while Guy was sunk into an armchair like a younger version of his father, the day's copy of *The Times* clenched in his right hand. Standing near the window, Frank, always alert, threw her a quick, questioning look from the sofa. I'll explain later, she mouthed to him.

'Inspector Livingstone, wasn't it?' Kitty pounced from her position on the other side of the fireplace and out into the corridor. 'What's happening now? Are you going to view the body? Perhaps I can—'

'Oh, for God's sake, Kitty.' Guy raised his head from the newspaper. 'Leave the man alone to do his job.'

'Thank you, Ma'am. Mrs Appleby is helping me.'

'It's really important to follow the correct procedures.' Painted lips twisted into a stubborn line, Kitty glowered at them. 'Freddie — my late husband — was very interested in procedure. And I'm sure I mentioned my uncle is Chief Constable.'

'I'm aware of the procedures, thank you.'

'This way, Inspector.' Thank God Kitty had backed away. Mercy led the way out through the back of the house. At the door, the inspector produced a torch, and they followed its thin beam along the lane. Only a yard or so of hedge separated them from the partygoers and sheltered them from a gale of drunken laughter. Listening to it, Mercy thought of her father. In his cups, he lost his reason, became angry at the futility of a wasted life, sometimes shouting, crashing the crockery against the wall when she or her mother tried to calm him; she knew it was frustration that drove him, like the incomprehensible anger of a toddler who can't handle the world. The raucous shouts from the garden showed he wasn't the only one to take refuge in drink.

They moved swiftly over the damp grass, Mercy a step ahead as the beam of the torch swung across the grass. Shadows whooped and swirled in the dark lane as crazily as the revellers on the other side of the hedge, where the singing had begun. 'The squire had a daughter…' wafted through the scented night air.

'This way, Constable.' Behind them, the song continued:

She lived in her satins and silks at the hall
But she married a man who had no balls at all.
No balls at all, no balls at all
She married a man who had no balls at all.

Guffaws followed, faded away, and the company back at the hall launched into another song, a little less crude. The gate to the private garden creaked like old bones as Mercy opened it and the cold reached up through the soles of her boots. Some of the lamps had guttered out but a few still spangled the hedgerows. A loose strand of rambling rose dropped down at their passing and its drunken shadow leapt and dived in the beam of the torch. The punch glasses were still there.

'Tom Freeman was looking for his wife,' Mercy said, filling in the silence as they trod the damp paths. She shivered. Radgie Tom, the local kids, called him, the braver ones to his face though always from a safe distance, but everyone knew he loved Jane, to distraction. 'He came in here and we followed. This is where we found her.'

They stopped. Jane still lay beneath the hedge, her black servant's dress and white apron damp in the dew. Already it had begun, a large moth settling on her still face. Unable to bear it, Mercy reached down and touched the creature away. Beside her, the inspector shifted uneasily, as if he were about to warn her off, but he said nothing. In the yellow light of the torch, Jane's tongue lolled, grotesque and swollen, from the side of her mouth and a collar of half-formed bruises circled her slender, once-white throat.

'You may leave me here, Mrs Appleby. PC Robinson will take your statement up at the house.'

She turned to follow the broken path of lantern light back to the Hall, but at the first twist in the way, she looked back. He'd dropped to his knees beside Jane on the wet grass and was staring at her in the yellow circle of torchlight.

Back in the house, the door to Blanche's drawing room was closed. Before she returned to the study, she paused a moment on the edge of the ballroom to take a final look at her friends and fellow villagers as they danced towards the last hour of the party. Drink and darkness had created an opportunity and now, after the war, handsome Tom had become angry Tom. He was the perfect suspect. It would surprise no-one, be they sympathetic or judgemental, if Jane had been with a man in the shadow of that hedge. But surely there wasn't a single villager who'd think succumbing to the need for a little tenderness was something she deserved to die for.

CHAPTER FIVE

MERCY

The grandfather clock at the foot of the staircase had struck two reproachful morning chimes before any semblance of calm returned to Waterbeck Hall. Once Jane's body had been discreetly laid out under a sheet in the mortuary ready for a pathologist to give his official blessing to the obvious course of events, and the inspector had disappeared back to where he came from, leaving his constable with Jane's body, Mercy made her way back to the Hall. In the middle of the abandoned ballroom, she found Blanche and Kitty trapped in a standoff about what to do.

'She's safe,' Mercy told them. A ridiculous thing to say. There was nothing anyone could do for Jane to make her safe now.

'Well, that's something at least,' Blanche said, briskly. 'You've missed all the fun here. Tears and hysterics and God knows what else. I had to send Millie home before she cried herself into a state, and of course, Lottie had to go with her to make sure she was all right, so now we're two maids down on top of everything. And they've left us a rare state of chaos to clear up.'

Three maids down, if you included Jane. There were plates and glasses abandoned on tables throughout the ballroom, leftover sandwiches dropped on the parquet floor, and an overturned chair to tell everyone that Frank's homecoming party had ended on a melancholy note. Under the stern stare of Blanche's father, a formal portrait against a mountain background with a steam train crossing a trestle bridge, Mercy walked over to the French doors and pulled them closed. Moonlight nuanced the shadows in the garden and she drew the heavy velvet drapes to exclude it. The room rang with silence and in the distance, a man's heavy footsteps faded down the corridor. Sir Henry, in all likelihood, withdrawing from chaos and leaving someone else to face it.

The quiet hadn't extended to the village. When Mercy had glanced out through the windows of the hall as she made her way back from the mortuary, the glimpse of Waterbeck through the trees and across the park showed lights still lit in every cottage. The buzz of drama brought on by Blanche's announcement of what happened would carry on into the next day and beyond until whoever'd murdered Jane was taken and hanged.

'And they all went charging into the garden to see where it happened.' Kitty shook her head in frustration. It had been a long night and one side of that fierce blonde bob curled outwards instead of inwards. 'I told them, but they didn't listen. Tramping all over the place, up the lane, into the garden, and who knows what they might destroy or leave behind.'

'You can't keep people away.' Blanche picked at an earring. 'Anyway, they've all gone home.'

'They'll be back at first light, gaping like ghouls.'

'What is there to find?' asked Mercy rhetorically, and checked herself. Her relationship with Blanche might be easy and familiar, but she was less sure of her ground with Kitty, who struck her as a woman who valued social status and cherished an expectation of a certain level of respect. 'It looks plain enough what happened.'

'Yes, but Freddie always said we're so far behind the continentals in how we handle crime. There's much we can learn about investigation, rather than jumping to conclusions. He read all the Sherlock Holmes stories. They're fiction, of course, but so real. A lot of things are evidence and you may not think so.'

'I think that's for the police to determine, don't you?'

'Oh, but Lady Waterbeck, even the police aren't up to date.

Freddie and I went regularly to hear Sir Harvey Littlejohn lecturing in Edinburgh. He's very famous, you know. You can identify a man's boot from a single footmark. You can find a fingerprint that connects a villain to the scene of the crime. Then there's the cigarette end with lipstick on it,' (she touched her own scarlet lips as she spoke) 'or the dropped button. They all tell a tale.'

George sometimes brought copies of *The Times* back from the Hall when Sir Henry had finished with them. One of them had had an article on fingerprints and about how careless thieves had been caught and sentenced because of them. Blanche might be dismissive of the late Mr Watson-Cooke's theory, but Mercy was also an avid reader of Conan Doyle's mysteries and gripped by his deductive powers. No-one laughed at Sherlock Holmes. 'Is there something we should do? Should we keep people away from the garden?'

It was late, and Kitty was in a fractious mood. She crossed to the table and helped herself to a glass from a tray one of the maids must have been in the act of handing out when the news broke. 'It's probably too late, with the policemen having been all over it, and the men fetching the body, and the rest trampling over the place already. And when the news gets out, if we aren't careful, we'll have trippers coming out from Penrith.'

Blanche sighed. 'This is private land, Kitty. And we have to put our faith in the police.'

Mercy picked up an overturned tankard. The floor was sticky with beer, the air thick with the sweet, sickly scent of the lilies and the strong fragrance of red roses, already beginning to droop. 'I can make a start on this tonight.'

'Leave it until tomorrow. Maybe Kitty thinks the policeman will want to look at it.'

Kitty turned an injured look on her. 'I don't imagine there's much to learn here. I don't think the girl ever set foot in the ballroom.'

'Nevertheless. It can wait until tomorrow. When Millie has

recovered from her hysterics, she can get back to work. That's what she's paid for.'

'What happens now?' Mercy asked. 'I've left PC Robinson sitting with the body, but surely someone will come to take her away?'

'There's a procedure, isn't that right, Kitty? The pathologist comes to tell us how she died, as if we need him to, and once he's done, the hearse comes to take the poor girl to Penrith. Then there will be an inquest and then they'll be able to lay the poor girl to rest. I've told Inspector Livingstone we'll all be here to be interviewed in the morning. He has everyone's names and an outline of what happened and no-one's going to run away.'

Did they know that? 'Someone should go and sit with Jane's mam.'

'Someone is. I don't know who. One of her sisters, I expect, or all of them. And Guy, bless him, took Tom home too, though I don't think there's anything anyone can do for him. He's in an awful state.'

A large tot of Sir Henry's whisky, administered as an urgent home remedy, had merely turned Tom's anger to tears. Guy would have his work cut out. 'Is there anything else I can do?'

'I don't think there's anything else anyone can do tonight.' Swivelling on her heel, Blanche surveyed the wreckage of the ballroom.

'Should I take the policeman a cup of tea and *The Times*?'

'Yes, why not? The poor man doesn't seem capable of much, but the very least we can do is try to make him comfortable until Inspector Livingstone comes back in the morning.'

There would be more questions then. The separating of the clearly innocent from the possibly guilty. 'Please God, they catch whoever it was soon.'

'Oh, I doubt they will,' said Blanche, airily, to Kitty's disapproving sniff. 'Most of the good policemen were lost, after all, and all we have left is the men who couldn't or wouldn't fight.'

'The police do their best—'

'We all do our best, Kitty my dear, but we're entitled to expect a little more from our police than from ordinary beings.'

Normally the epitome of calm, Blanche was tetchy tonight and Mercy herself felt on edge, feeling she was watching out the corner of her eye for danger. There must be a killer close by. In their midst, even. Was it punishment for one of Jane's many indiscretions? With a flush, Mercy remembered her own encounter with the young soldier, but that had been the merest of flirtations. She forced a laugh. 'At least I have a clear conscience.'

'Oh, bless you, my dear. I wasn't suggesting anything. I know it wasn't you.' Blanche's eyes, nevertheless, darted here and there as if she, too, was looking out for danger, but there was nothing to be seen but the whisk of a white skirt that belonged to one of the maids. 'Harold will keep an eye on things around here and deal with the hearse when it arrives, and when Lottie gets back, she's offered to sit up in case she's needed. If you could pop down to the kitchen and rustle up some tea for the policeman, I'd appreciate it. I'd do it myself, but I must go up and see to Sir Henry. He seems very shocked.'

'I hope your butler is discreet.' Kitty again, disapproving.

'Harold will keep the silence of the grave. Though, of course, Lottie will talk. Perhaps you'd better keep her away from PC Robinson.' She turned away from Mercy in dismissal. 'Come along, Kitty. I suppose we'd better find someone to make you up a room. There's no question of you motoring back to Brampton tonight. Next time, give us a little more notice.'

Blanche ghosted her way through the echoing marble hall, with Kitty floating behind her. In a flash of light from the last of the candles, the violet frock and the red disappeared along the corridor. Mercy followed them only as far as Blanche's private drawing room, stepping across the threshold with unwarranted care.

She picked up the copy of *The Times* Guy had been clutching with such intense — and almost certainly false —

concentration while he'd waited with the others earlier that evening. His nervousness had been apparent at the time and had left its imprint in the creased pages of the newspaper. She unfolded it and smoothed it out under the dim and flickering light. *The Times* was concerned about Bolshevism in Persia and the results of the German election, events that seemed very far from Waterbeck. Someone had torn an article out of it — nothing unusual in itself, since once Sir Henry had finished with it Blanche was in the habit of clipping out items of interest to send to her sister, Dora, in Philadelphia. But Blanche's clippings were characteristically neat, and this one was a semi-circular patch that encompassed a quarter of the page. Curious, she inspected the remainder of the page. One side was the announcements column and the other the Court Circular. There must have been something an ardent American royalist such as Miss Hardacre would have found entertaining, but it was unlike Blanche to be so casual.

Blanche's idiosyncrasies were the least of her worries, but with luck the newspaper, missing article notwithstanding, would keep the constable amused while he waited, though she noted Sir Henry had already completed the crossword.

There had been enough puzzles that evening. This one could wait until the morning. She shook her head, paused for a moment in silent respect in front of the fireplace, and looked with sadness at the photograph of Blanche's children. Flora, the youngest, had been everyone's favourite and Mercy's closest friend despite several years difference, a mischievous spark of a child who had grown into a smart teenager, inheriting her mother's ambivalence about the system of privilege she'd been born into; she would surely have made a young woman with a burning passion to pursue.

It was bad enough that the war had stolen away the best of the country's young men. The loss of such a bright young woman was an almost intolerable cross to bear.

Turning out the parlour light behind her, Mercy descended the short flight of steps to the kitchen at the side of the house where Mrs Hepplewhite, the housekeeper, was standing with her hands braced upon the table as if to hold herself up. Helen Hepplewhite was a new arrival, a childless widow in her mid-fifties who'd lost a younger husband earlier in the war, and struggled to keep command of the cohort of maids who had continued to flutter about below stairs in defiance of wartime austerity.

'Oh, Mercy. Thank goodness it's you. For a moment I thought it must be poor Jane, her spirit come back to finish the work she left undone.'

Helen tended to the dramatic, and God knew how she'd managed to land a housekeeper's job unless it was by appealing to Blanche's charitable nature or managing to make her laugh, but Jane had a right to a restless spirit. Nevertheless, Mercy, who had always felt a little in awe of the housekeeper's predecessor, felt it best to adopt Blanche's robust approach. 'I'm sure the police will find out who did it.'

'Well, I suppose so. And in the meantime, the girls can cover Jane's duties between them.' Helen let go of the table and crossed to poke the fire in the range, sending flames leaping up the chimney and setting the kettle spitting. 'What a thing to happen. Poor Jane! She wasn't the best of girls, I know, but her heart was in the right place. Who could have done such a thing?'

Who are we to judge who are the best of people? Mercy asked herself. 'I expect we'll find out soon enough.'

'I hope the villain hangs!' Helen set about the fire again, before emerging with her face scarlet from the heat. 'Her Ladyship says the police will be all over us tomorrow with their questions. As if there won't be enough to do with the clearing up. I'd have up and started on it myself, but she said to leave it. Truth be told, I'd rather there was something to occupy me. All I can do is stand around and think about the poor girl.' She sniffed.

Mercy stifled a yawn. What a day it had been. Jane's death still seemed unreal, but she knew she'd dream about her, twitching in her death throes at the hands of an unknown killer. 'Her Ladyship wants me to take Davy some tea.'

'Useless fellow, him. We'll not catch justice with him chasing after it.' Helen slapped the tea things on the tray. Davy, noted Mercy with half a smile, didn't justify the good china. 'And Mrs Watson-Cooke arriving all unannounced, too. I don't think anyone was pleased to see her.'

'I don't mind her.'

'Aye, but you've a good opinion of everyone. You'd better take the man some cake, as well. Keep him sweet. Not that I'd fancy eating if I was sitting in a mortuary with a dead body. And if you want something yourself afterwards, just pop back.'

'Thanks, but I think I'll just head home after I've given him this.' Placing the folded newspaper beside the tea things, Mercy carried the whole collection through to the mortuary. Davy Robinson answered the door and his uniformed bulk blocked her view, something she was relieved about even though they'd laid Jane out with as much decency as they could muster and left her blackened face covered with a sheet. The next morning, Kitty had said, a doctor would come and then the motorised hearse from Penrith would take her away. 'I've brought you some tea.'

'Thanks, lass.' He took the tray and retreated behind the door. The mortuary was hidden in the block of storerooms and dusty, unused offices that linked the main part of Waterbeck Hall to the estate manager's house and normally Mercy would have gone straight through to find her way home but even if it hadn't been for PC Robinson's forbidding presence, she would have balked at creeping through the dark dusty corridors knowing Jane lay there, dead and unshriven. Despite her rigorous common sense and a fascination with the way things actually worked, she was steeped in the traditions of the countryside, as superstitious as Helen in her way. In the darkness, it was hard not to believe the dead could walk. She much preferred a detour across the courtyard through the liquid summer night.

As she made her way out of the Hall, she almost tripped over Frank, sitting on the front steps in a display of lèse-majesté no-one seemed to have noticed, let alone care about. He got to his feet as she came out and as Harold, silent as a ghost, slipped the heavy front door closed behind her. 'Eh, Mercy lass. What a day it's been.'

'I don't think I want to talk to you,' she said, though in the past his presence had usually cheered her. Frank had always been a lad with an obliging hand and an ingenious suggestion, with a steady eye to a positive outcome, and in these tough times there were few people she could trust. If he'd been a little less obvious in his intentions, she could have been glad of his company. There might yet be a moment when they could sit down together in the office or walk through the woods and she could ask him about Teddy and what exactly had happened to him to change him so much, but it wasn't now. 'It's not personal,' she hastened to add, in case she hurt his feelings. 'I don't want to talk to anyone just at the moment.'

'I understand that.' He took a step away, unusually sensitive.

She remembered, then, that this was the day he'd come home, the day when life after endless death was supposed to begin. 'I'm sorry, Frank. I hadn't thought. It's not exactly a hero's homecoming for you.'

'No,' he said with a half laugh, 'but I've never pretended to be a hero.'

'Are you all right? Is someone looking after you?'

'My mam,' he said. 'Don't worry. She'll see me right. Eggs and bacon and sausages for breakfast tomorrow. You can always rely on your mam, can't you?'

'I hope so.' Sally's trusting little gaze preyed once more on Mercy's mind and the cold chill of Jane's passing visited her, there in the moonlit courtyard. What if Mercy herself had been in the wrong place at the wrong time, walking alone in the garden? Who would have explained to the little girl what had happened to her mother? Who would have nurtured her as a mother should when she grew older? Who would have the courage to explain to Teddy?

She knew the answer to the last question. Frank, Teddy's blood brother long before they ever went to war, would have done it.

He stopped on the doorstep. 'And your dad, eh? They tell me you can't get much use out of old George these days.'

'It was the war.' She'd forgotten how easy it was to talk to Frank. Everyone else whispered behind their hands about her father's descent from reliable manager to drunkard, or referred to his troubles, but Frank saw things as they were and never shirked the consequences. 'He didn't fight, but he saw too much.'

'Aye, well. We all did. Much worse than we've seen tonight. So, you don't need to worry about me on that score. If I'm going to have nightmares, they won't be about Jane.'

They paused on the step, with nothing to say to one another that could be said at that time of night, in Jane's shadow, with no knowing what the next day could bring. 'It's good to have you back, Frank.' She pressed down the door handle and opened it. There was still firelight in the kitchen, spilling out over the slate floor, and a rumble of deep snoring, like thunder, over-rode the silence.

'Is that your da?' he asked, cocking his head to one side and listening.

'I expect so. Mam turned in a while ago. We can't always get him up to bed when he's like this. Sometimes it's easier to leave him there.'

'Why don't I come in and help? At least we can make him comfortable. We don't want anyone else kicking the bucket tonight, even by accident.'

She waved him through because it was just for a second and she didn't really care after tonight if anyone saw, if anyone talked about her. When she switched on the light, she saw her father was out cold, slumped in the chair in a cocoon of alcohol fumes, chin sunk on his chest, his breathing irregular. His boots still stood neatly under the table where she'd left them earlier that evening. He hadn't stirred in hours, and the trauma had passed him by. That could only be a good thing.

Swinging into action, Frank took a pulse, slid George out of the chair, and laid him down on the floor. If nothing else, the war had bequeathed them a cohort of men who could deal with a medical emergency.

'Shall I get a blanket?' she asked.

'Aye, that'll be grand. He'll be all right. He'll wake up in the morning with a hell of a headache, but that's all. And I don't think he'll dream tonight.'

'Thank you.' She fetched a knitted woollen blanket from the settle, and her heart warmed towards him. 'I couldn't have managed by myself.'

In the warm red light from the dying fire, he crinkled a smile at her. 'At your service, as always.' He straightened up the lapels of his jacket and backed away towards the door. 'Night, ma'am. Any time you need me, you know where I am.' A mischievous wink.

I've been winked at by too many men today, she thought as she switched off the lights. 'Who do you think did it?'

He shrugged. 'We'll find out. But don't worry about it. It wasn't you and it wasn't me. That's all we need worry about.'

Without another word, without another look, he turned and left the cottage, closing the door behind him. From the kitchen window, she saw his long shadow stretching away in the moonlight until the darkness consumed it.

She swung the front door closed and turned the key in the lock, then felt her way through the darkness, up the stone stairs into the bedroom she shared with Sally. The curtains were closed, but she felt the need for light and drew them back to let in the moon. Its brightness fell on the photograph of Teddy she kept on her dressing table. One day soon he'd be home, and she'd have no need to accept help from Frank. She smiled.

A snuffling whimper from the crib signalled that Sally was awake. Suddenly overwhelmed by a need for comfort, to give it and receive it, she scooped her daughter up and held her in her arms, pressing kisses onto her soft head and rocking her gently crooning into her ear. 'It'll be all right, sweetheart. It'll be all right.'

She let the curtain fall. It wasn't you and it wasn't me, Frank had said, and she wanted to believe him, but the truth that confronted her was more difficult. The only thing she knew for certain was that she hadn't done it, and Blanche hadn't done it. Frank, Guy and Tom himself all materialising on the spot; a dozen jealous wives and half that number of tempted men; Sir Henry and her father, both changed by the war in which they hadn't had to fight. All of them might fall prey to gallons of ale and a resurfacing of bad memories.

Kitty was right. Science and logic would go a long way to finding out who killed Jane Freeman, but as she turned to lay Sally back to sleep, she knew it must be someone who walked and lived among them.

CHAPTER SIX

BLANCHE

When Blanche appeared in the dining room for breakfast, she found Inspector Gordon Livingstone standing at the sideboard in the dining room, helping himself to coffee. At least he'd had taken a little more care with his appearance than the previous night, though his suit, in an ill-advised shade of dark brown, was matched with a navy blue tie with too large a knot. When Blanche had been introduced to him the previous evening, it had taken her just three seconds to decide she neither liked nor trusted him. His presence in the dining room did nothing to ease that impression.

Still, it was prudent to be civil. 'Inspector Livingstone. Good morning, and welcome back to Waterbeck Hall. I'm sure I asked Harold to make you comfortable in my private drawing room. It's a far better place for you to conduct your investigations.' She knew immediately by the way his lips narrowed that she'd struck a false note and probably made an enemy of him. Or, worse, triggered an interest in what she was thinking and whether she might have anything to hide.

'I asked the inspector to come through.' Kitty was sitting at the end of the table nearest the window in a patch of sunlight, toying with a piece of toast. Dressed in grey and lilac, she still wore her amethysts. It had been four years since the obviously much-adored Freddie Watson-Cooke had drowned in the Flanders mud, more than long enough for his widow to shed her half-mourning colours. Blanche made a note to have a quiet word over afternoon tea with Kitty's mother, a long-time acquaintance, and see if she could discern whether grief might be a serious obstacle to Guy's courtship.

'I'm really interested in what he has to say,' Kitty pursued.

Livingstone inclined his head graciously towards her and continued pouring coffee.

'Of course,' continued Kitty, 'it will be fascinating to follow this investigation.'

Blanche took her seat at the polished mahogany table and stared at Kitty in perplexity while Harold served her with bacon and egg. Did the young woman not realise that she herself must be a potential suspect, as all of them were? She was treating this horror like a game. 'I'm quite sure the Inspector will find the culprit as soon as possible,' she said curtly.

'Indeed, I hope so, your Ladyship.' The man strayed across to the window and stood drinking his coffee so that his shadow reached out towards them.

She shook out her napkin onto her lap. 'You'll need to speak to everyone, obviously.'

'Indeed, madam. I'll take a turn around the garden first, if I may, and have a look at the scene in daylight.'

'I could come with you,' offered Kitty, 'and show you where —'

'Thank you, Mrs Watson-Cooke. I know the way.' He ambled back to the sideboard and placed the china cup and saucer on it. 'Lady Waterbeck, thank you for the use of your drawing room.' An ingratiating smile. 'I've read the interviews the constable took down last night and there are some people I'd like to speak to myself.'

Members of the household, obviously. 'The men who found her. I can arrange for them to attend the Hall.'

'Those men include Mr Guy Waterbeck, of course. Very interesting. A key witness.'

Guy, a key witness, as if he were a common criminal? Blanche suppressed her indignation, but she couldn't control the twitch of maternal fear that shook her. She could only hope Livingstone hadn't spotted it. 'I'm sure Guy will be happy to assist you.'

'Holland lives with his mother, I believe. I'll see him up here, where there's less distraction. Not Freeman. I'll see him in his own home. And if I may, I'll send for you when I'm ready.'

Send for her. Blanche gave him a scornful look. 'If you must.'

'Very good. I shall see you later.'

He swept out without waiting for a reply, his footsteps reverberating down the corridor towards the ballroom, where the maids were tackling the debris of the night before. A moment later he appeared outside the window, where he paused to fill and light his pipe before walking along the terrace and down the steps onto the lawn.

'It's terrible for your poor maid,' Kitty said, brightly, 'but I say, this is jolly exciting.'

All things considered, Jane's had been a very clean death, Blanche thought, and then disliked herself for entertaining such an idea. She lifted the coffee Harold had poured for her and sipped, waiting for its earthy warmth to give her the strength to get through the morning. She wouldn't be the only one who'd had a sleepless night and now, when she would rather have leaned on Mercy for some sound common sense, she was trapped with the insensitive, over-enthusiastic Kitty. She would like her so much more if she thought she cared for Guy, she told herself with a sigh.

'If I were a man,' Kitty observed, 'I think I would make an excellent inspector.' Her knife flashed silver in the sun as she laid it down on the plate.

Ifs and ands got you nowhere. If Blanche had been born a man, she'd be running a business empire instead of sitting in a stately home in England while her advisors ran her father's companies for her. If Mercy had been a man, her drunkard of a father would have been pensioned off, instead of still being the face of the estate for the tenant farmers and others who wouldn't take advice or instruction, or even accept information, from a woman. Instead, his daughter's competence went unrecognised as she shadowed him, correcting his mistakes, marshalling his wild suggestions about what could be done to the estate and yoking them to common sense, setting out a daily list of instructions for him to follow.

She sighed, switching off mentally as Kitty repeated her concerns about day trippers coming to the scene of Jane's death, and turned her thoughts to the inspector. Still in view in the garden, he strolled around with studied nonchalance, looking at this and that, making notes and bending occasionally to peer at something of interest. He paid close attention to the herbaceous border, currently shining with tall spears of delphiniums and clouds of pink and white stocks, and walked the margin of the sloping croquet lawn. He ferreted a stick from the hedge and poked into the reeds that fringed the ornamental pond, staring for some time at the yew hedge which separated the formal garden from the sunken lane and which in its turn formed a boundary to Blanche's personal domain. After a while, thankfully, he passed out of the main garden and she lost sight of him, but she knew he'd be pacing up and down at the spot where Jane had died.

Kitty had been watching him, too. 'I'm sure if I asked Uncle Arthur to put in a word, I'd be allowed to help.'

'I'm quite sure you wouldn't.' Blanche knew Arthur Henderson, the Chief Constable, rather better than Kitty knew. He was a stickler for protocol; or rather, for appearances. Sometimes she thought he was too much so. Reflecting on the investigation to come, she formulated a strategy. 'There is something you could do for me. Perhaps you and Guy could take the dogs for a walk.'

'I'm sure it will be much more interesting here. Perhaps one of the servants—'

'Don't forget, Kitty. We are a servant short.'

'Oh, of course.' Kitty had the grace to look embarrassed. 'Then what about Mercy?'

'Mercy runs the estate office.'

'Guy is fond of her,' remarked Kitty, without apparent jealousy.

There had been a time, a few years back, when Blanche had wondered if Guy held a candle for Mercy, but if that had been the case, any attraction had guttered out very quickly and Mercy had almost certainly been unaware of it. 'They know each other well. You know how dear she and her family are to me.' Inappropriately so, some might think, but Blanche valued friendship for itself and didn't care where she found it as long as it was real. 'She shared lessons with my daughters when they were growing up. And she has a bright and inquiring mind.' And a sympathetic ear. She'd been older than Flora and Annie but close to them and for that, if nothing else, she had earned their mother's undying gratitude and eternal loyalty.

'Oh, I see. Well, maybe I will take those silly pups out. Not for long, though. I don't want to miss anything.' Kitty excused herself and headed out, and a few moments later she appeared just as Livingstone had on the lawn. Henry's two Labradors bounded ahead, Guy trailed in her wake and when Kitty followed the inspector's steps towards the garden Blanche was intrigued to see the two seemed to have a short stand-off, she apparently urging him towards the gate and he staying put, hands in pockets, until she gave in and they drifted off towards the shrubbery on the other side of the grounds.

A key witness. The phrase stuck in her head and she wished she'd paid more attention to the look on Livingstone's face when he'd said it. There was something in his attitude she didn't like, a lurking smile on his lips as if he were mocking her and everything she stood for. Blanche, who was at heart a democrat, should have felt common ground with him, but all she sensed was hostility.

She frittered away a few extra minutes over a third cup of coffee, knowing it would give her a headache, toying with a long rope of jet beads. One did not, of course, go into mourning for a servant, but some respect was due. Eventually, when the hands of the ornate clock above the fireplace had nudged twenty to ten and Lottie had twice peeped in to see if she could clear the table, she left the maid to it and headed for the drawing room. The door was open and Livingstone stood by the window, gazing out. His back was to her.

Blanche crept in, softly, and still he stared at the garden and the fells. She took another couple of steps, caught in a game of cat and mouse and unsure which role she was playing. He'd moved her copy of Edith Wharton's latest novel, which she'd left on the arm of her favourite chair, in a way that suggested he'd laid claim to the seat. That irritated her.

She cast a quick glance around to see what other liberties he might have taken, but her eye was caught, as so often, by the portrait of Guy over the fireplace. It had been painted from sketches taken during his first leave. When she examined it closely, she could see the artist's genius, the way he'd read his subject and shaded the early hints of fear and anxiety into her son's fresh face. Guy was five years older than the portrait, now, and immeasurably more complex. She stared at it again, seeking in vain for clues about what he might have become, but found nothing.

She disliked the painting, not for its quality, which was exceptional, but because at moments like this, when she most needed serenity, it shook her with its realism. Guy posed in his father's chair, but in the background, through the very windows in front of which she stood, his three lost siblings played in the garden. If it wasn't for the fact that she'd have had to explain her reasons, she'd have had the painting moved and put something else there instead, something showy and inoffensive. As it was, she always felt compelled to stare as if she could challenge him in a way she was reluctant to do in the flesh. The world-weariness on his face troubled her. He hid it so well, so much of the time, but occasionally it cropped up and she saw it but couldn't reach out. That the artist had seen it when she had not was a mark of her failure.

The look had been in his eyes the night before, when he hadn't been able to assert his authority over Tom Freeman. Why not? What was he hiding?

She cleared her throat. 'Good morning, inspector.'

'Lady Waterbeck,' he said, turning at last with a smile that suggested he'd known where she was all along and, worse, knew what she'd been looking at. 'Take a seat. And we'll begin, if we may, with everything you know about Jane Freeman.'

CHAPTER SEVEN

FRANK

'Proper hours and holidays and all,' Frank was saying as Mercy eased open the door to the kitchen in Oak Tree House. She paused for a moment, unseen. Carrie was sitting in the rocking chair mending a tear in one of Sally's pinafores, Sally herself sitting on the rag rug gazing in awe at shadow puppets Frank was projecting through a dancing sunbeam onto the wall.

'You've come a long way,' her mam said, looking indulgently on Frank. 'The army's been good for you.'

'Aye, it has. There're always opportunities. A lad like me that never got an education… well, they show you how to make the best of it. Managed a few night classes as well. I even read books.' His fingers moved rapidly so that the dark shadow of a rabbit flickered on the wall.

'Well, you always were a lad that fell on your feet. And Lord knows, I daresay I'll envy you come harvest.' Carrie snapped the thread, pinned the needle neatly through the fabric of her apron to keep from losing it, and smoothed the pinafore into a neat square. 'Here you are, lass. We were wondering what had happened to you. I didn't think the inspector would keep you that long.'

Mercy stepped forward into the room. 'We'll miss you at harvest time, Frank.'

The show stopped instantly, as he turned and the outline of the rabbit disintegrated, to Sally's squeak of disappointment. 'I'll find you a few hours if you need me.'

Someone always needed Frank. 'It's all hands to the pump, then. You know that.' She suppressed a smile as she stood and opened the door for him. 'You'd best not loiter around here. Your man wants you up at the Hall.'

'All there with the handcuffs, is he?'

'Don't joke about it,' reproved Carrie, getting up and placing the folded pinafore on top of a pile of finished mending. 'There, Sally. That should see you through another week or so. Though you're not as hard on your clothes as either your mam or your Auntie Hope were at your age.'

'Back in a bit, Sal.' Following Frank out into the courtyard, Mercy breathed in deeply. Somewhere there was a bonfire and the clear air was clagged with smoke. 'I meant it. You don't want to keep him waiting.'

'Fierce, is he?'

She closed her eyes for a moment. Something about Gordon Livingstone terrified her, even though she knew she was innocent. There was a latent cruelty in him, she sensed, a delight in making his interviewee squirm. 'Maybe a little.'

'And you not a suspect,' he said, wryly.

'No, I was with Blanche — Lady Waterbeck — all the time. But by the end of it, I thought he was ready to lock me up and throw away the key. God help anyone who doesn't have an alibi.' Frank, she knew, was one such man. She laid a hand on his sleeve. 'You need to take care.'

He lifted an eyebrow at her. 'What was he asking?'

'What you'd expect. Where I was, what I was doing, what I saw. And he wanted to know all about Jane. Poor Jane.' She turned her head to hide the tears that were welling up, but not quickly enough; he was holding out a handkerchief. Ashamed of the unusual show of emotion, she waved away his offer and produced one of her own. 'He asked about Teddy,' she said, through a sniff. 'It's not like me to cry, but suddenly all I can think about is how terrible people are. How awful we are to each other, how much we suffer. How much I miss him. I'll get over it. I really will.'

He drew back slightly, seemingly as uncertain about her as she was about him. 'I'd best get up to see him. Keep him on side.'

'Do be careful, Frank.'

'I'm always careful. I'm a survivor.'

She watched him as he hooked his thumbs into his belt and strode off across the courtyard. Most men would have gone to the side door, but Frank took the front steps and leaned on the doorbell with the confidence of visiting royalty. She couldn't suppress a smile, but when he disappeared, the smile vanished, too. Something very dark had come to Waterbeck, and she sensed that few of them would escape unchanged.

* * *

'Tell me about yourself, Mr Holland,' invited Gordon Livingstone, and he sat back.

The bugger had taken the seat in front of the window so Frank couldn't see his face, only his silhouette against the sunlight and the mature trees of the park that sloped away southwards toward the Ullswater fells. Clever; but there were still things you could learn from the deliberately relaxed posture. An ankle rested on a knee, leaning back with both arms behind his head. Frank was happy to take his time, to talk about himself, his dull childhood, his dull war, his dull and innocent life to date. In time, it would be less dull, but for now, the more he played down his aspirations, the better it would be. 'I'm Frank Holland. Discharged from the Cumberland and Westmorland two days ago after five years of service. Corporal. Volunteered 1915. Ypres, Passchendaele, St Quentin, the Somme…'

'Yes, yes. And before then?'

So, he wasn't interested in his war record. That followed. Frank, who hoarded every piece of information on the grounds that it might one day come in useful, had heard of Livingstone from some of his army pals from Keswick way. A clever gadgie, they'd called him, all the cleverer for having avoided conscription and managed to keep some vestige of public respect at the same time, but there were different ways of being clever and Frank's own intuition warned him early that this man had him down as a major suspect, possibly as suspect number one. 'I worked on the estate. Hedging, ditching, anything heavy. But I'm good with my hands.' He laid a hand on the slender arm of the chair and looked at his own muscles with a degree of admiration. The army had kept him fit and given him nous, had taught him how to listen and how to learn. Now he was reaping the rewards; someone else would be freezing their hands to the bone, snagging turnips, come November.

'And so you were discharged and came back. Yesterday. When were you last here?'

Frank pretended to think, though the occasion was printed on his soul because it had been Mercy's birthday and he'd managed to engineer a meeting with her. That day, when she'd blushed with pleasure at the sight of him, had been the first indication that there might be hope for him. Not for long: she'd quickly wrestled it under control and never given him the slightest encouragement thereafter, but he'd seen enough. The hope persisted. 'September last year.'

'You enjoyed the army, then? After the war, obviously.'

'Aye,' said Frank, after a moment. 'It filled a gap, while I decided what to do.'

'You weren't like the others, then. They all came straight back.'

All of them had slotted into the jobs they'd left behind, except Teddy. And Tom, of course, who couldn't do the work of an agricultural labourer and was reduced to living on his wife's wages or whatever he could earn from the few jobs he was able to do. 'It's a narrow life, this. You're born to it and know no better. I've always wanted to see a bit more of the world.' And he had done. A weekend's leave in post-war Paris, a couple of longer stints in London to stay with an old comrade. London had been full of wild sights and run on lax social rules. There was nothing money couldn't buy you at any time of the day and night.

To fill in a few moments and get used to the man's questions, take the measure of him, he supplied him with details about family and upbringing, village life and labour. The man didn't bother writing any of it down.

'And now,' said Livingstone as if he were talking a child through a test, 'you're moving on. Is that right?'

'You heard that, did you?'

'I believe Lady Waterbeck mentioned it. Is it a secret?'

Frank allowed himself to show a smile. He reckoned he'd sensed admiration underneath Blanche's disappointment when he'd told her he was leaving and he suspected they understood one another at heart. 'No. Just that I hadn't told many folk. I'm starting a job come Midsummer and I'll see where I go from there.'

'Village life is too narrow for you, then.'

'Do you need to ask?'

'I'm asking the questions.' There was no malice in the tone as Gordon Livingstone leaned forward to make a close inspection of his teacup. As he shifted out of the sun, the distractingly wide white of his left eye seemed focussed upon Frank like the stare of a malevolent god. 'Did you know Mrs Freeman well?'

It was a fair enough question and one he'd been expecting, but nevertheless, it was potentially incriminating. One of the many things Frank had learned was that justice didn't always work out the way he thought it should and that it was too often the well-meaning innocents who found themselves staring dazedly at the wrong end of society, morality and the law.

His mates had told him something else about Livingstone — that he was a proud, defensive man who hated to lose face and for whom any conviction was better than none. Frank shifted in his seat. There would be a supreme irony in meeting his death on the gallows in Durham Jail after all the cunning and the luck it had taken to avoid it in the mud of France and Flanders, and though he had a keen enough appreciation of irony, he wasn't yet ready to fall victim to it. 'Jane Freeman? Not what you'd call well.'

'You grew up in the village together, I believe.'

'Aye, as bairns, but my mam and dad didn't have a lot to do with the Leslies. She was a Leslie before she married. We left school at twelve, the two of us. She went into service at the Hall and I went to work on the land. I didn't see much of her after that.'

'This is a small village. You must have met each other around. Village dances and so on.'

It would be prudent to treat this as an informal chat. In any case, Frank nursed a real sense of moral authority over the policeman who wouldn't fight. He could have got out of it himself, if he'd tried hard enough, could have pleaded a far better case to be indispensable in the parish of Waterbeck than some had done. But he hadn't. Make yourself a hero to those at home and a survivor to your mates and come back alive. That was how you did it. 'Aye, those. But there wasn't a lot of socialising. Jane wasn't one for the inn and that's where I'd go after a hard day's work.'

'At village dances. I believe Mrs Freeman was...' Livingstone pulled out a packet of cigarettes and offered them to Frank. As he turned, there was no concealing the expression on his face, and it was friendly. 'Popular with the gentlemen. Is that right?'

Extracting a Woodbine with finger and thumb, Frank narrowed his eyes as he pretended to struggle with what the man was driving at. 'Jane was always a bonny lass, like her sisters.' He thought of her, a tiny, fragile woman-child with that mass of blonde curls she so readily shook free from the cap she was obliged to wear for work, the blue eyes that sparkled with mischief and fun.

'An obliging lass?' Livingstone struck a match, touched it to the tip of his own cigarette before offering it to Frank. 'I'm not saying there's anything wrong in that. Not before she was married. You understand me?'

'Not obliging to me,' said Frank, sitting back and drawing deeply on his cigarette. Despite the sombre circumstances and the shadow of the noose that undoubtedly hung over him, a deep chuckle rose within him. Who'd ever have thought he'd be sitting smoking in her ladyship's private drawing room? All it needed now was a glass of his lordship's brandy.

'Is that because you never asked, or because she turned you down?'

Frank pulled himself up. The cigarette was a trick, lulling him into a false sense of security. This man was his enemy. 'I won't lie to you. I don't think she'd have turned me down if I'd asked her for a bit of something. Saying no wasn't in her nature.'

'So you never… propositioned Mrs Freeman? Either before or after her marriage?'

Frank puffed on, steadily, considering ways he might answer the question without the stain of a lie on his conscience. 'I never did.'

'We're both men, Mr Holland. I'd lay a shilling to a penny. The bonny Mrs Freeman set a lot of pulses racing in the village.'

'Aye, and so she did.' There was no point in arguing with that. 'Jane was free with her favours before she married. But when she made up her mind, she loved her man.'

'Yes, the unfortunate Mr Freeman. What did Jane make of a husband with one arm?'

'Losing an arm doesn't make a man a bad husband.'

'I'm told it made him a drinker and a violent man.'

'He was always a drinker, but when he came back from the war, he was angry. Frustrated. He'd get kaylied most nights.' Whatever anyone else thought, Tom would feel less like a man. 'You can't blame him. War changes folk in strange ways.' The song they'd been singing at the previous night's party echoed in his ear. Funny then, not so funny now. She married a man who had no balls at all. Suddenly he was angry too. 'You won't know that. You had to be there.' He dared to challenge this arrogant shyster.

Livingstone looked at him stonily. 'No doubt you're a brave and clever man, Holland. You are a survivor, and something of a hero. You're correct. I didn't serve.' He lifted a finger to his wall eye. 'I was passed medically unfit, but don't allow yourself to underestimate me. For your information, I have kept every white feather given to me by patriotic ladies during the war, and I display them in a vase on my mantelpiece. I served my country in the best way I was able and I'm proud of that. Now, shall we get on? You are implying Mrs Freeman had liaisons with other men after her marriage.'

'It's common knowledge.' Drawing long on the cigarette, Frank debated about what to tell and decided, in the end, on the truth. 'I've been away, so you'll need to find some other body to spread the muck about what and who, and when. But I'll tell you one thing free of charge. She was with a lad last night.'

'Is that right?'

'Aye.' The cigarette had burned down now. Frank leaned forward and stubbed it out in the heavy gold ashtray on a table inlaid with a rich swirling wood he couldn't identify. Through the open window came the bleating of a sheep, grieving for a lost lamb. How much should he tell this man? 'I heard them.'

'Oh?'

The carriage clock on the mantelpiece chimed the half hour, and dust motes danced in elegant downward spirals through a sunbeam. 'A man and a woman. The woman laughing. Not a sound you'd mistake, if you take my meaning. Like an animal.'

'And this was when?' Livingstone sat forward. His fingers tightened around his pen. 'And where?'

'I don't know the exact time. Maybe a shade before ten, somewhere between sunset and full dark. After I'd spoken to Lady Waterbeck. I went along the lonning beside the garden for a breath of fresh air. Some open space. Silence.' He relaxed, mimicking the inspector's action by resting his right ankle on his left knee as if he were settling back in his own cottage kitchen. 'That's when I heard them. Through the hedge, right by where they found her.'

'Are you sure it was Jane?'

'No. But it was the right place and not long before she died.'

'Were you jealous?'

Frank went cold. This man wanted to hang him. The stranger's voice breathing out Mercy's name at the climax of sexual ecstasy caught him in the solar plexus in the morning just as it had done in the night. If it had been Mercy Appleby with anyone but her husband he would have been jealous as sin and who knew what he might have done? 'No. Why would I be jealous if someone wants to take Jane Freeman behind a hedge? I'm a man who does things properly. And in any case, my heart belongs to another.'

Livingstone tilted his head again, raised that questioning eyebrow.

'I fell in love with a sweet little French lass,' said Frank, unperturbed. The cigarette had burned down now, and he leaned forward to stub it out in the ashtray. 'Faithful to the death, I am. Maybe one day I'll go back and find her. When I'm more than a ragged old Tommy, she took pity on. Maybe one day I'll marry her and bring her home. But Jane Freeman? No. Not when I know the temper her husband has on him.'

Silence ticked between them. The curl of a smile on the policeman's face suggested there was something about the answer he liked. Frank remembered watching Guy playing chess with a fellow officer in the trenches, sitting staring at the board. The other chess player's expression had been identical to Livingstone's in its cool self-satisfaction. It had been obvious even to Frank, who'd never lifted a chess piece in his life, that Guy was trapped, his every move resulting in loss, his only choice which piece to sacrifice. At the time it had appealed to his dark sense of humour, a metaphor for their entrenched position, but now it was a different game, with Livingstone as the player and himself and his friends and neighbours as the pieces.

'Since he came back from the war,' the inspector said with a sigh, 'Tom Freeman has had two convictions for common assault and somehow got cleared of assaulting the ticket officer on Penrith station when reasonably challenged for having the wrong ticket. We know he's a man not afraid to be violent in public. Do you know if he was ever violent to his wife?'

'I haven't been here to know.' But he wouldn't be surprised. Jane could try any man's patience.

'Thank you, Mr Holland. You may go. But I'll have many more questions to ask you later.'

'Let's hope you get the right man.' Frank pushed back his chair and stood up, stretching a little. It was almost a shame to leave. It would be a long time before he was back in Blanche's parlour smoking a cigarette. As he left, he found himself humming, again, one of the old songs. Oh Mademoiselle from Armentieres, Parlez-vous… you didn't have to know her long to know the reason men go wrong, Hinky-pinky parlez-vous.

CHAPTER EIGHT

FRANK

The song, and the touch of amusement that had accompanied it, died away as Frank left the cool elegance of the Hall and, stepping outside, became once more a piece of jetsam washed up by the tides of war. He loitered by the wide stone steps for the duration of another cigarette while he tried to work out precisely what the inspector was trying to get him to admit to. An affair with Jane? Her murder? Knowledge of her killer? Being targeted by the thoughts and judgement of a single individual was new to him; he was used to taking his chance among thousands of others.

When the cigarette had burned down to its tip, he discarded it in one of the tubs of vermilion geraniums that flanked the steps and set off to march the boundaries of the village, to reacquaint himself with the places with which he was once so familiar. If anything had changed, he wanted to know. Loitering down the drive, he took off through the woods before he met the main road, skirting the village itself and ambling across the open parkland where crows flocked in the ancient trees and yellow-eyed sheep cursed him with their cold, distrustful stares.

Fittingly, under the circumstances, the day after his homecoming wasn't as brave as the one before though the sun, shimmering underneath a shawl of thin cloud, was warm enough for him to shed his jacket as he strode beyond the boundaries of the park and up the hill towards the edge of the parish. As he walked, he marked off everything old and familiar with a curious satisfaction, pacing the fields where as a younger man he'd tumbled behind the wall, just as he'd told the inspector he never had done, with some girl who'd blown through with the gypsies on the way to Appleby Horse Fair. At the time, making love had seemed fresh and immediate, but now he understood that all they'd been doing was manufacturing memories to look back on as they grew old and bitter.

In the woods at the northern edge of the Waterbeck Estate where he and Teddy used to go to trap rabbits someone had made a campfire, cutting back the thin, springy turf to make the hearth and replacing it over the ashes to bury the remains, though they'd left the broken brown shells of hens' eggs crushed on top of it as a reminder of their picnic. Leaving them behind without a thought, he continued upwards where the grass grew thinner, the birdsong more urgent and the path rougher until he reached the highest point on the estate and paused to look down on the village, cramped in the curve of the beck. The squat red tower of the church where Jane would be buried proved one focus for his view and the timeless frontage of Waterbeck Hall, a little way to the east, offered the other. Even from that distance, he could pick out the unusual buzz of activity in the courtyard and grounds, the figures heading to the formal garden and combing the hedges. His mother's cottage stood on the Penrith road a few hundred yards on the other side of the entrance to the Hall, close enough yet isolated from its neighbours. Behind, low-lying fields of ripening corn along the beck billowed in the wind and in the distance a trail of steam marked the passage of the northbound express along the London to Glasgow railway line.

As a younger man, he'd come to the brow of this hill, stare southwards and dream of leaving home, but dreams had a habit of turning on you. His plans for adventure hadn't gone the way he'd intended.

'But I'm not finished dreaming yet,' he said aloud. His energy and aspirations were too big for Waterbeck and servitude with the family, no matter how generous and paternalistic Blanche might be. A job in the garage was only the first step. Later, not too much later maybe, he'd have his own garage, a chain of them, and a big house in a bigger town. Maybe one day he'd be invited to visit at the Hall. Sir Henry would always see him as a Johnny-come-lately who'd over-reached himself but Blanche, who was more open-minded and had proper respect for new money, would appreciate his talents and seek his opinion on what kind of machinery they should buy for the estate. And Mercy, who was always at his side in these harmless fantasies, would tilt her little finger in the manner born as they drank tea and ate cake. Then they'd leave together with a butler handing them their hats and coats, to be driven away by the chauffeur, in their Rolls Royce, to their own mansion in the country.

He laughed at himself as he strode down the track that led from the crest of the hill to the village. There would be some gossip to be had down in the Dog and Blanket in Waterbeck all right, though most of it would be the product of empty heads and idle minds and not worth listening to. But it paid to be solicitous, to remind them all of his presence and his energy and his positivity and these days, in these particular circumstances, he wanted his neighbours to think well of him when it was their turn to be questioned by Inspector Gordon Livingstone.

He was still thinking of how to begin resettling himself in the village, at least for the year or so he reckoned it would take him to move on, when he reached the road. A gap in the trees to his left offered him a clear view of the driveway to Waterbeck Hall and there was Mercy, heading down the driveway with a shopping basket over her arm, Sally skipping beside her, clinging to her hand.

Abandoning his train of thought, he scrambled over the stile and ran the last few yards to the edge of the village, then ambled quietly back up towards the Hall to cut her off before she could reach the knot of villagers who would be chewing over the recent events. Taking a moment to run his hand through his hair and flick away the grass seed from his trousers, he dangled his jacket over a shoulder by one finger, hoping to capture the casual insouciance he'd observed in Parisian men-about-town. As she rounded the corner of the drive onto the main road, he feigned surprise.

'Mercy. Well, well. Fancy meeting you here.'

He was pleased to see she still understood when he was teasing her: her lips twitched into a smile. 'Frank. It's good to see your face around the village again. Have you been up at the Hall?'

'Aye. Getting the third degree from that fellow that thinks a policeman's a match for an old soldier.'

'He was a little bit scary, wasn't he? Not that he'll scare you.'

Livingstone had terrified Frank, but he wasn't about to let on, even to Mercy. 'I've met worse.' He smiled at her, thinking of the tear that had flashed in her eye up at the Hall. If she hadn't been married to his best mate, he'd have succumbed to his sentimental side and gathered her up in his arms to comfort her, but he'd sensed her fragility. She wasn't sure how to deal with him and he didn't dare put a foot wrong. It was a long game, he reminded himself. Move on. 'How's your da this morning?' he asked. 'A bit crook, eh?'

'Surprisingly, he isn't too bad.' She paused on the grass verge, swinging Sally's hand until the little girl, distracted, tweaked her fingers free. 'He slept very late and woke up complaining of the headache to end them all, but he felt up to going in to the office so I thought I'd go down to the shop and use up the week's sugar ration. We all need a treat.'

He looked down at Sally, who'd dropped down to her haunches on the verge and was poking around in the damp ditch. As if sensing his gaze, she turned her face upwards and handed him an untidy sprig of scarlet. 'Flower.'

He grinned, dropped down to her level. 'That's soldier's buttons.'

'Take,' she instructed.

'Sal,' said Mercy from above, sounding amused, 'that's very sweet, but Frank doesn't need flowers.'

'A lad gives a lass flowers,' he whispered to Sally, accepting the blossoms nevertheless, and reaching behind him to snap off a stem of his own, 'and here's something from me to you. Do you know what this is?'

'Flower!' she pronounced triumphantly.

'Those are buttercups. Now you take these and look after them, eh? As a present from me to you.' He stood up, brushed a trace of dust from his knees and was warmed by Mercy's smile, though he knew it was more for Sally than for him.

'Thank you for being kind to her,' she whispered. 'She gives everyone flowers.'

'A good thing to do.' He fidgeted, twisting the sprig of soldier's buttons between his fingers. 'About your da. Has your man from the town talked to him about yesterday yet?'

'No, but his whereabouts are hardly in question, are they? He was out cold in the kitchen all night. He can't have slept well on the floor, but he'll have endured worse.' She sighed.

This woman's sighs and sadness would make a fool of him yet. 'It's hard,' said Frank, gently.

'He always had a weakness for the drink, I know, but he kept it under control until the war. Now he's seen too much. Too many people died. There were too many he couldn't save. That was the first thing he said this morning when we told him about Jane, as if death is all he can think about, as if everything is somehow his fault. But I know he did his best.'

'He did better than many.' Still clutching the wild flowers between his fingers, Frank stuck his free thumb in his belt, enjoying the fantasy of standing in the sun with his secret sweetheart, pretending she cared about him as much as he did for her. 'I'll talk to him, tell him he can hold his head up high. Unlike some.'

'You mean Inspector Livingstone?'

'If I was a shirker like him, I wouldn't be parading about letting folk think I was better than them. I'd have kept my face hidden out of respect for the lads who died.'

'Oh, but his eye… it wasn't his fault he couldn't fight.'

Mercy was always sympathetic, but in this case, he reckoned her sympathy was misplaced. 'Aye, right. There was a fella in the regiment with a wall eye and he was a crack shot.'

'You old soldiers are so unforgiving.' She smiled at him and his heart flipped over slowly, deliciously. 'He's doing a job. Someone has to do it.'

'Is that what you think? The way I see it, his job is to hang one of us.'

'Well,' she said, defensively Frank thought, 'one of us killed Jane.'

'And you think that lad deserves to hang?'

She tightened her grip on the basket, and her bottom lip jutted out in defiance. 'Did Jane deserve to die?'

'Does the one have to mean t'other?' Even her annoyance charmed him. He struggled not to smile. 'Seems to me folk do mad things more now than they ever did before, and they're keen to hide them.'

'Frank,' she said, turning to face him foursquare, the first time she'd looked him straight in the face since he'd come back. 'What are you saying? Did you lie to the inspector?'

He took a moment to savour the look, the heavy wing of dark hair that slid down across one side of her face and rested in a fat pleat on her shoulder, the lips formed in a delicate O of shock, even the appalled look on her face. 'Aye. Didn't you?' Because surely no-one would be mad enough to tell Livingstone the whole truth about themselves, and he trusted her to keep his secret.

82

'No, of course I didn't.' She was appalled but not, he thought, about the lie. 'Frank. Please tell me. You didn't kill Jane?'

'You know I can't have done. I was outside the garden in the lane when you found her.'

She turned away from him, snatched a nervous glance back towards the Hall as if she was expecting Livingstone to come running out brandishing handcuffs. She must know that being outside at one point didn't mean he hadn't been inside at another. 'Then what did you lie about?'

'You.' And to assure her, he rushed on with the explanation. 'I told him something I'd overheard. A lad and a lass, together, in the garden. Intimate, you might say.' His heart softened once more at the blush that warmed her cheek. 'I told him that, but I didn't tell him everything. I didn't tell him what I heard the man say.'

'And that was?' Her lips twisted as she spoke, as if she didn't want to know but couldn't stop herself asking.

'I heard him call your name.'

Her appalled expression reassured him and the doubts Livingstone had raised in his mind vanished. He'd been right to think again after that first moment of shock. The woman giving herself so ecstatically on the other side of the yew hedge had not been Mercy. Jane, then, for certain, in the arms of a lover. 'My name?'

'Yes.'

'You think I'm the sort of woman who'd—' Her face went a delicious, deep scarlet, but with fury, not embarrassment. 'Really? You think that of me?'

'Did you never have a tumble with Teddy when you were courting?' he mocked her, irritated by the high moral stance she was taking and knowing she was judging him for lying when he'd only lied to spare her embarrassment, maybe worse. 'Did you never shout out something you shouldn't? Did you never take the name of God in vain when you—?'

'Stop it!' She gestured frantically down to Sally and then lifted a finger to her lips, though the little girl was still far too absorbed in plucking the petals from one of the buttercups to pay any attention, even if the conversation had meant anything to her. 'If I did — I'm not saying I did — but if I did, we were going to be married. And I am married to him, and of course I would never consider doing anything like that with any other man. How dare you even suggest it?'

He was regretting it already. 'I'm sorry. I'm not thinking straight. The man's already wondering if I killed Jane. I'll bet my job on it. Just because I was near.'

'He'll think it even more if he finds out you're a liar.' She turned sharply away, obviously having had enough of the debate.

'I didn't lie about that.'

'Does it matter?' Reaching down for Sally's hand, she lifted her to her feet. 'Come along, petal. Let's get your sweetie.' She took three steps towards the village. 'You mustn't lie,' she said over her shoulder. 'Do you want him to think the worst of you? Do you want to hang, even?'

He went after her, still trailing his jacket over his shoulder, persisting in his effort to look casual, though with a little less of the confidence he'd affected a few moments before. Inwardly, he was furious with himself. The army had roughened him, and the kind of girls he was used to weren't as sensitive, as educated, as respectable as Mercy. It would take him longer to get used to being home than he'd expected. 'I never asked you about Teddy.'

She stopped again at the side of the road. 'What is there to say?'

'Sal will miss her dad.' He looked down at her, saw the open, honest smile that was so like her father's, looked to Mercy and saw her smiling back.

'I'll be honest.' She reached down and accepted the battered buttercup petal Sally offered her. 'She doesn't remember him. Of course, I tell her about him. I show her the picture of him and I tell her he loves her. But she was a baby when he was last here.'

'Aye, but that'll change when he's home. He will be, won't he?'

'Yes.' She stepped away from Sally, as if to spare her. 'I live for that day. I dream about him jumping off that bus just like you did.'

'But?'

'How much have folk told you? He did come home, but it didn't work. He couldn't cope. They had to take him back.' Her voice wavered. 'It was so hard to see him cry.'

He knew. He'd seen it. Was it harder to bear for him, with his long-time friend sobbing in the darkness, or for Mercy, wiping away the tears of the man who should be the one looking after her now? There were those who thought Teddy had always been soft in the head because his father had been, but it was the horrors he'd seen in France and couldn't talk about, the constant drumming of the guns inside his head, that had landed him in hospital. 'Maybe tomorrow I'll go up to Edinburgh and see him.'

'That's very sweet of you.' She tossed the stem aside. 'But I don't think you should.'

'Why not?'

'He's not good with strangers.'

'I'm not a stranger.' Outrage bubbled within him. Teddy had been brought up with him, taken in by Frank's mother when his own, recently widowed, had fallen in with another man and gone off to bring up a stepfamily in Yorkshire. Two years younger and much more pugnacious, Frank had begun by looking up to him and gone on to look after him. 'As near as damn. He's my brother.'

'That doesn't matter. Everyone's strange to him now. Even me. Even Sally. Visitors unsettle him, and he gets few enough of them, being so far away. I'm the only one who visits him now. I go every week.' She hesitated. 'I'm so scared. The longer he's away, the harder it'll be for him to come back.'

'He'll want to see me. I'll go. I've time before my job starts. He'll need to know I've not forgotten him. It'll help.'

'I really don't think you should.'

'And I really think I will.'

'Have it your own way.' She shrugged. 'Thank you for caring. But it's more complicated than you think. If you must go, don't do it without speaking to me. I might try to come with you. Maybe that would help if you insist on seeing him.'

'We'll go on Saturday. I've never been up to Edinburgh. If nowt else it's a day out.' A day out with Mercy, her company, and her conversation.

She nodded, reluctantly. 'I'll see if Mam will look after Sally for me. But Frank.'

'What?'

'I can't tell you how bad an idea this is.'

They'd reached the edge of the village by then, and his route to his cottage lay to the right. He turned back rather than be seen so obviously craving her company and swung along the narrow lane and past the open gates up to the Hall, thinking about Teddy, who was a stranger to everybody, himself included, and about whether he would hang for throttling the life out of some girl who gave herself away too easily, or survive and continue in his pursuit of one who did not.

CHAPTER NINE

TOM

The cottage was dark — too dark. Jane's mother had already been round to sniff out the gossip and to trump Tom's grief with her own, though she pretended it was to see that he was all right. She'd drawn the curtains and lectured him on proper respect when he'd complained about the dimness. With his head still thick from grief and all the ale he'd sunk early in the previous evening, before he'd found himself staring down at Jane, dead at Lady Blanche Waterbeck's feet, he'd lost patience and thrown his mother-in-law out. 'You're no family of mine any more,' he'd shouted at her, and ordered her out of the house. As she'd gone, flouncing and cursing just like Jane would do when she was in a mood for a fight, he'd noticed her eyes, as blue as her daughter's, were rimmed with red, just as his must be.

Jane, his beloved, sweet, infuriating butterfly, would destroy him in death as she'd begun to do in life. He didn't dare look at his ravaged face for fear of the guilt he'd see in it, so he'd covered her tiny looking glass with a dishcloth to spare himself.

'Mr Freeman?' A knock at the door, an unfamiliar voice, followed by a brief pause and, when Tom declined to answer, a broad figure in the doorway. 'Inspector Gordon Livingstone. From the police in Keswick. I need a word with you, sir. About Jane.'

Folk called the working man the salt of the earth and Tom had begun to think of himself, with a grim irony, as the bloodied, crusted mud of it. He wasn't used to being called sir. 'Aye, that's me. But there's nothing I can tell you about what happened to Jane, except it wasn't me who did for her.'

Livingstone drew the curtains, and the sun came spearing in. 'Let's have some light on the proceedings, shall we? It's awful dark in here.'

With a shot of surprise, Tom realised he liked the man's style. 'Better shut those sharpish. My ma-in-law'll kill me if I don't show proper respect. That's if she doesn't kill me anyway for not looking after her lass.'

'I expect I'll be speaking to your mother-in-law later. I'll explain.'

Explain what? Tom suppressed a wry grin. As if he didn't know why the policeman wanted light. It was to note every expression on his face, judge every involuntary move he made in his grief, and scour his soul for traces of a guilty conscience. 'Aye, right. You'd better sit.'

He stayed where he was, waiting for the man to come and sit opposite him in the only other available seat, the rocking chair he'd made for Jane as a wedding present. Her sewing still lay on the arm, strands of green and pink and red trailing down onto the threadbare rug. He'd never paid it any attention before, had no idea what she was making. When they'd sat there of an evening, she'd concentrated on her work in silence, occasionally looking up to stare into the heart of the fire. They'd exchanged few words, but he always suspected she was thinking about the latest man who could offer her what she couldn't get from him.

The visitor looked at the sewing with interest before lifting it, folding it neatly and setting it down on the workbox on the stone floor. His gaze continued around him to take in all that was left of her — the wedding photograph on the dark walnut sideboard, the misshapen blue felt hat she'd abandoned casually on the table. Tom leaned his head back against the snow-white antimacassar and crushed a sob remorselessly down. She'd gone and there was nothing anyone could do to bring her back.

'I won't keep you long, but I have an obligation to do my duty. Let me begin by offering you my condolences on the loss of your wife.'

Tom touched his empty, folded sleeve with his good hand. If he'd somehow managed to come back whole like the others had, even if he'd come back a gibbering idiot like Teddy Appleby, he'd have had a chance of keeping Jane. A chance. He didn't delude himself too much, knowing she'd almost certainly been lost to him long before she'd tempted life once too often in a secluded garden. 'Ask me what you like. There's not much I can tell you.'

'I wanted to ask you how well you got on with Jane.'

The baldness of the question surprised him. 'She was my wife. How do you think we got on?'

A laugh, underpinned by a Scotsman's humour. 'Aye, well. Plenty of married couples fight their way from the altar to the grave.'

'Not us. I've loved that girl longer than—' Longer than she deserved. 'Than I remember.'

Livingstone's eyes flicked to the other photograph of her, the studio one taken in Penrith. The photographer had tried to make her sit with a stern look on her face and a finger in a Bible, in the Victorian style, but she'd succumbed to a fit of the giggles. Tom had preferred the resulting photograph to the more formal version the photographer had produced. He'd taken it with him to the war, tucked in his breast pocket so anyone who found his body would know how much he'd loved. With her fingers up to her mouth and the look of a naughty imp caught out in some mischief, Jane might have raised some pity for him in an enemy.

'Jane was a beautiful woman,' the policeman said, still staring at it.

A stab of envy caught at Tom's soul, even though Jane was beyond temptation. Marrying someone so desirable had proved a curse in the end, rather than the blessing he'd hoped for. There wasn't a man who didn't look at her with interest, even if that interest wasn't serious, and Tom had long ago lost faith in man's innocence. 'Aye. That she was. And many a chap ready to tell her that, too.'

'You were jealous,' remarked Livingstone, 'weren't you?'

He could try to pretend, but what was the point? Everyone knew. He was born a fighter, but he saved his strength for the important battles and there was no point wasting credibility on lies in which he'd be too easily caught. 'You'd have been, if you'd been married to her.'

'I daresay.'

'Any man would have been. Christ himself would have.' He ignored the way his visitor lifted an eyebrow at this blasphemy. 'When I married Jane, I was the best man I could be. She could have had her pick of the village, beyond it, found a rich farmer from over Eden way or up by the sea. She chose me. I was the proudest man in the world the day I walked her down the aisle.' He shot a savage glance at the picture on the mantelpiece, himself and Jane on the steps of St Mary's in the village. He was holding her hand and waving his left arm at the photographer. 'Now look at me. Why would she want a man like me? I'm no use to anyone.'

His voice came back to him, bouncing back off the walls and the window and the hearth, and Livingstone kept a moment's silence as he looked at him. More conscious of his disability than he'd ever been before, Tom stared back at him, suddenly loathing this coward who'd shirked the war and now came to lecture them about right and wrong.

'What did you do,' asked the inspector, 'before the war?'

The life Tom had once cursed now seemed like a golden age — a hard one, in which they'd worked from dawn until dusk but, nevertheless, one in which they had been innocents. 'I worked on the estate. It was tough going, but there was no-one could do it better. Fourteen hours in the summer, longer if there was moonlight. There was always something. Stock to feed, sowing, harvest, hedging and ditching in the winter.'

'I see you were a wrestler,' Livingstone noted, nodding towards a trophy on the mantelpiece next to the wedding photograph. 'Is that right?'

'Aye, that's right. Local all-comers champion, three years running, 1910-12. I'm in my prime now, or should be.' At the local show the previous year, the champion had been a man he could once have snapped in two, if he'd chosen to.

'You're heroes to a man.' The lurking smile on the inspector's lips failed to convince Tom of his sincerity. 'I take my hat off to you. If only I could have played a more active part.'

Looking at him, Tom recognised the type. There had been men like Livingstone in the army. Most of them had been behind the lines, sending others to their deaths and sometimes diverting a little bit of this or that, blankets or bandages or chocolate, from the front line to wherever their own interests lay. If Gordon Livingstone had been passed fit for service, he could imagine him ending up one of those, then going home and flaunting his service medals in the faces of the bereaved. Tom said nothing, letting his silence speak for his contempt.

'So how do you earn your living now?' asked Livingstone, as if it were casual chat. 'Army pension. Anything else?'

'A bit of work here and there if I can do it. My wife's pay.' Life had been difficult enough, even with Lady Waterbeck's insistence on paying Jane a wage above what she would have expected elsewhere. Charity stuck in Tom's craw, and being dependent on his wife hurt him even more, but his pride wasn't so strong he'd die in a ditch for it. He'd have to beg the estate to let him stay on in the cottage, find some more work to do, if there was any more a man could do with one arm than deliver the milk. Otherwise, it was the poorhouse for him. He clenched his good hand in anger. 'She was worth more to me alive than dead. Think on that when you're looking for who killed her. I've nothing to keep me going now.'

'Oh, I don't know about that. You look mighty strong to me.'

'You think I'm strong enough to kill my wife with just one arm, do you?' Tom's temper was rising. 'You think the bitch couldn't fight back? You think she wouldn't try to claw the eyes out of my face if I'd tried to give her what she deserved?'

'I didn't suggest that,' the man said, and his tone had chilled from friendliness to hostility. 'But I'm interested that you think she deserved it.'

Tom pulled himself up. Grief and exhaustion were only the strongest of the emotions that assailed him, but he clung to some measure of common sense. These people could hang you if they wanted, and he wasn't ready to die. 'She swore she'd be mine until death parted us and she wasn't.' The truth about him and Jane was bitter and brutal, a tale of love gone sour.

'Do you know that for sure?'

'Aye, I do. She admitted it. More than once. And I didn't kill her then, Inspector, though I might have wanted to. But it's not about what you feel. It's what you do. And I didn't do it.'

The clock ticked. Out in the village a cock crew. A pair of children bolted a hoop past the front of the cottage with a rattle and a shout. 'Radgie Tom killed his missus!' A flash of colour across the windows, a giggle, and they were gone.

Tom met the inspector's gaze and held it while he thought of the times his anger had the better of him and how he'd regretted it afterwards. The last time he'd sent Jane sprawling across the kitchen with a blow from his good arm, she'd reacted with submissive sweetness, only to go ghosting off between work and home the next day, no doubt for an assignation with some other man. If he knew who it was, he'd have killed him for sure. 'She was no better than she should have been,' he said, his rage taking second place, for once, to self-preservation, 'but it wasn't me who killed her.'

'You were on the spot, angry and shouting that you'd break her neck. And you could well have done it. And believe me when I tell you. If you did, you'll hang.'

Cold sweat shivered up Tom's spine, fear of a different death. 'Aye, and I'd deserve to. But I didn't.'

'Who did you think did?'

'One of these men who couldn't keep their filthy hands off her.' One of his comrades. One of his mates. One of the men he would have died for.

The clock ticked on. The children came back again, bolder, closer to the front door, louder, and their words echoed in his head long after they'd sped past. *Radgie Tom killed his missus.* It was flighty Jane they should have been singing about, who'd made eyes at everyone from Guy Waterbeck to any passing stranger tramping through the village in an attempt to escape the city and find the great outdoors.

'All right,' said Livingstone, once the silence had thickened so much as to become suffocating. 'I'll give you the benefit of the doubt. I'll assume for now that you didn't do it. But in return, you can tell me about the other men she was carrying on with, and which one might have killed her.'

CHAPTER TEN

MERCY

On the edge of Waterbeck, before she could place herself under the scrutiny of her fellow villagers who would surely already be manoeuvring themselves into position to quiz her over the goings-on up at the Hall, Mercy stopped and watched Frank strolling casually back home. A sudden urge came over her, to call him back, but she resisted it even though their parting had been unsatisfactory.

'But that's my fault,' she said to Sally, knowing the secret was safe with her two-year-old. 'I shouldn't have been so blunt about your dad.' But Teddy and Frank had been close, and she and Frank had been close, and so he had a right to know how the land lay.

'I'm still in love with your daddy,' she reminded herself out loud, immediately feeling foolish at needing to do so when the ache of his absence was always with her, a long low moan of loss in her heart.

Now Frank was back, and his very survival accentuated what she'd lost. She wanted to be friends with him for Teddy's sake, and if she'd got used to his teasing persistence while Teddy was at her side, it was different when he was absent. He'd have to learn that.

Worse was the uncomfortable feeling that he knew her too well. She was no Jane Freeman, unable to resist a man who teased her with a compliment and a kiss, but nor was she a fearful Victorian who made sure her man turned out the lamp before he came to bed and shut her eyes tight when he claimed his marital rights. Loving a man was a joyous physical experience and there had been more than one time with Teddy, before the marriage vows, when passion had overridden discretion and the thrill of his touch had swept away restraint. But that had been with the man she'd married. Even if she could ever be tempted, she wasn't the type of girl to get carried away with someone she shouldn't.

Wistfully, she trailed at Sally's slow pace across the green towards the post office. Teddy was afraid now, even of the gentlest touch, and his eyes were empty when he looked at her. Her heart and body still yearned for him, but there was no hope of comfort in his timid embrace. Maybe Frank had guessed that, and maybe that was why he'd thought so harshly of her, judging her by the standards of others, but, as long as Teddy lived, there would never be a man who would tempt her.

It would be a lonely life for her until he came back.

A bell jangled deep in the depths of the shop as she opened the door and stepped in. The two women inside, one on either side of the counter in a conspiratorial pose, looked up as she passed from the brightness of the green to the dimness of the interior.

'No better than she deserved,' said one of them, Beth Blunt, apparently concluding the conversation, 'and that's about all, as you can say. My ma always said some man or other would kill her. Well, here's Mercy. I bet you've got all the chat, haven't you, love?'

The shop smelt of furniture polish and onions. Mercy slid her way past the bins of flour and oats and a shelf of Pears soap and set her basket on the counter. She hadn't had any real reason for coming to the village other than a half-hearted hope of bumping into Frank and reassuring herself that he was all right, and she'd accomplished that. Now she was here, she'd have to deliver on the day's gossip. 'I don't know if there's much I can tell you.'

She edged to the counter and inspected the glass jars of sweets on the shelves behind it. Her mother liked lemon drops. Teddy adored humbugs. Sal, staring up at the jars with round-eyed awe, could be pleased with something as simple as a square of milk chocolate.

'Well, we all know who did it. I'm surprised poor Tom never lifted a hand to her before.' Behind the counter, Vera Mounsey rang up the total for her customer with a sanctimonious rattling of keys on the cash register. 'I'd have done, if she was my wife. A good clattering might have taught her to leave other women's men alone. Then we'd all have been a bit happier. But he'd no call to go as far as he did.'

Jane, for all her weaknesses, had had strength. Mercy suspected that her husband had indeed raised a hand to her, more than once, but the girl had gone about her work at the Hall with the cheeriest of dispositions and no complaint, only the shadow of a bruise under the sleeves of her blouse ever giving any hint of his fury. 'I felt sorry for her.'

'You can afford to. Your man's not going to beat you, is he? He'll never know if you've been up to owt.'

'Meaning?'

Vera fixed her with a knowing look. 'We all know Frank's a bit of a lad. And we all know he's got his eye on you.'

So, Frank's attentions the previous day had been obvious. It didn't matter how well behaved she was. If there was a hint of licentiousness, Vera would find it and everyone would know. Mercy fought rising irritation and lost. 'Frank can have his eye on whoever he chooses. It's nowt to do with me.'

'Well, don't be so snooty, lass. I don't imagine anyone would blame you if you were tempted. A handsome lad he is, and all.' Beth allowed herself a strangely childish giggle.

'And I daresay not the only fellow has his eye on you.' Without elaborating, Vera slammed the cash register shut and turned back to Mercy with open interest, a smile that was an invitation to confide. She was fifty but looked older, hands chafed from hard work, back bent from heaving pallets and cartons of goods around the shop. In the light from the window, her red hair looked harsh in its tight plait, and her high cheekbones seemed sharp and unforgiving. 'You found Jane, didn't you?'

'What did she look like?' Beth, whose husband was a solid, silent dairyman too old even to be interested in his wife, had less of an axe to grind with Jane, but there was a scurrilous interest to her, nevertheless. 'Peaceful? I never seen a dead person. Even my old da passed away in the night and Ma had him in the grave almost before I knew it. But I was only a wee lass, then.'

'It was horrible.' Mercy placed her basket on the counter. 'I need a couple of pounds of flour, Vera. Mam's baking and we're short.'

'Strangled, Millie said. What does a strangled body look like?' Beth placed her purchases neatly in the basket and lingered, eyes aglitter.

'It was dark. I couldn't really see. And I don't want to talk about it in front of Sally.' Mercy closed her eyes for a moment. In the torchlight of the night before, Jane's body had been all too clear to her, her face black with clotted blood like a guiser on Halloween, but it had told them nothing other than the means of her death. Kitty was probably right; there must surely be something else they might have seen, some clue that would give away the killer. Whoever he was, he must have been hiding nearby. 'And I'd like a quarter of lemon drops. And another of humbugs. And a bar of the Dairy Milk.'

'Throwing the coupons at it today, eh?' The shop must have been quiet because Vera had already bagged up some flour behind the counter. She slammed a couple of brown paper parcels on the counter and slapped a bar of purple-wrapped chocolate beside them, then turned her back, reaching up to the rows of sweetie jars behind the counter. 'Sounds like someone needs cheering up.'

'For my money, it was Tom that done it, for sure. Big strong man, even with one arm, and a temper on him. I'm surprised he hasn't had a swing at someone before,' pursued Beth, going over old ground for the benefit of a new listener. 'That man from Keswick's interviewing him right now.'

'I think that's routine.' Mercy looked down at Sally, running her eyes over the row of sweet temptation, striped sugar canes, pink strawberry bonbons, shiny black liquorice, all playing their part in a rainbow of pleasure. When she'd sent parcels out to Teddy at the front, she'd always included as many sweets as she could manage alongside the socks and the tobacco. 'He's talking to everyone who was near the garden. Even Lady Waterbeck. But Mrs Watson-Cooke says it's nothing to worry about.'

'Oh, her. She knows everything, doesn't she, or thinks she does. Went to university and everything, though I don't know what use it'll be to her. She's not one of those poor souls that needs a job now they've lost their men. Inherited his money and got some of her own. Life's not fair, is it?'

'She's sweet on young Guy, so they say,' sighed Beth, who couldn't resist a sentimental take on anything.

'So they say, but I never hear of him spending a lot of time with her, so maybe he ain't as keen as she is. Taking his time, no doubt, until someone better turns up.'

'Come to that. Where was he when poor Jane was killed?'

'Ha!' Vera tumbled the lemon drops into the scales and then tipped them into a paper bag, twisting the ends of it over and dropping it on the counter before turning her attention to the humbugs. 'Not him. Why would he need to? It could have been anyone. I was in the ballroom when it happened and what was outside but dark? Anybody could get up to anything,' she said, with relish, 'and I dare say there was some as did.'

'It wasn't my man, at least. I kept him in my sight all the time. We were talking to the Horners, the time she must have died.' Beth sniffed. 'Charlie Horner's another one that looked too long. I expect the police will be talking to him and all.'

'We'll find out in the end, I daresay.' Vera screwed the lid on the jar of humbugs and returned it to the shelf. Even she seemed to be losing interest in the increasingly long list of people the police were talking to. 'I'll put it on your account, Mercy.' She stamped the ration books, then reached under the counter for the collection of stray treats she kept there and fished out a broken fragment of cinder toffee, which she handed down to Sally. 'There you go, lass. A wee treat for you.'

'Thank you.' Grateful for the reprieve, Mercy smiled at her as Beth, unsatisfied, withdrew. Beth might have a malicious tongue on her, but gossip was village currency and, as the shopkeeper Vera dealt in it. It was expected of her.

'Going to visit Teddy, are you?' asked Vera, busying herself with the jars. Humbugs, everyone knew, were Teddy's favourite.

'Not today. I went up to Edinburgh yesterday.'

'Poor lad. At least he's well out of it.'

That was a matter of opinion. 'We'd rather have him home.'

'Aye, but we all know what happened last time. You're a good girl, Mercy, sticking by him like that. There's many as wouldn't, and who'd blame them?'

'He's my husband.' More than that; he was her lover and her friend, the missing part of her heart. 'What else am I supposed to do?'

'There's a lass from over Penrith that's asking for a divorce, her man not being what he was.'

'Teddy's just fine. Or he will be.'

'Aye, but.' Vera's smile was tinged with malice. 'It's easier for him in that hospital than coming home to face the rest of us. Wouldn't want him being a risk to his little lass. Him being either not right in the head or not right in the heart, if you get my meaning.'

Mercy got the meaning well enough. It wasn't the first time someone had implied that Teddy's illness was a moral weakness rather than the fruits of war. 'Teddy's no coward, Vera, and I won't have you say it.'

'Not right in the head, then?'

Not anymore. Irked, Mercy nevertheless knew better than to pick a fight with Vera. 'Teddy's my husband. I love him. I won't abandon him.'

'In sickness and in health. Aye. Of course. And you still think he'll come home?'

'Yes.' Mercy placed the paper bag of humbugs in the basket, along with everything else. 'I'd better get back. Dad's in the office today, but they're short-handed up at the Hall and there's plenty to do.'

'It's not right you have to run round after him like a maid.' Vera was in a cantankerous mood today, nipping at everyone. Not a good word to say. 'Them up at the Hall must be soft the way they keep your da on.'

'He does his job just fine.'

'No-one can do their job that well when they ship the amount of drink he does.' Vera sniffed, as if she was someone who was never known to take a drink or two herself. 'He should be ashamed of himself, letting you go walking round the estate in breeches like a lad.'

'Do you think I should go round the farms in a party dress, Vera?' If she'd been irritated at the injustice of Vera's comments about Teddy, this time Mercy's rising anger was because they were too close to the mark.

'You shouldn't be going round the farms at all. Your da should be doing his job and you should be at home with your husband and your wee lass.'

Yes, in a perfect world. 'I'd best get on.'

'Aye. Oh.' Vera raised a hand to brush back the hair from her forehead. 'My memory's so terrible. There's always summat. A postcard for you. Here. Saves our lad, delivering it up at the Hall. And as I said, Frank's not the only man as seems sweet on you.'

The postman would be up at the Hall anyway, because Blanche was in constant correspondence with her family in

America. Clear as day, Vera wanted to telegraph that she'd read the postcard, but there was no way Mercy was going to give her the satisfaction. 'I'll see you later, Vera.'

She waited until they'd reached the edge of the green to read it. It bore a tinted image of Carlisle Castle with a horse and cart parading below its walls. Addressed simply to Mrs Mercy Appleby, Waterbeck, in unfamiliar writing, it carried a message a single line long. I know we'll meet again.

She stared at it. It was unsigned, but she knew it came from the soldier she'd met on the bus. She'd thought he'd said he was heading south. She read the card again and flushed at its audacity. What was it implying? 'The cheek of it!' she said aloud.

'Picture!' said Sally, reaching up, but when Mercy handed it down, she gave it a disgusted look, as if it wasn't pretty or bright enough, and dropped it on the floor.

It was bad enough having Frank back, buzzing at the edge of her conscience like a mosquito on a summer night. Mercy didn't need the attentions of a stranger to boot, and certainly not if she was going to become the talk of the village because of it. She wished, now, she'd given Vera a piece of her mind. Picking up the postcard, she tore it in half and thrust it into her pocket.

CHAPTER ELEVEN

TOM

Sometimes you needed more than sunlight. You needed solitude. When Livingstone had gone, Tom twitched the curtains closed again, less to show respect for his dead wife than to spare himself from seeing the judgement of his peers. Then he slipped out through the back door of the cottage and into the garden. The gate opened onto rolling fields and a secure route into the sanctuary of the woods around Waterbeck Hall. At least, there, he'd be able to breathe without one of the local witches casting her evil eye on him for what had happened to Jane.

There were figures working in the second field along. He wasn't a sociable man, or not in the way he had been before that shell with his name on it had landed too close. Humiliation did that to you, turned you inwards. He paused to assess them. Working on the gate, by the look of it, and one of them was Harry Mounsey, who was a mate but talked too much. The other, Jesse Turnbull, was a severe fifty-year-old who served as the churchwarden and by God, his eyes could drill a hole through a man who liked a drink or turned his back on the church. He'd be poor company for anyone suspected of killing his wife. For a moment Tom toyed with his pride and considered taking them on, but the risk of landing his fist on the churchwarden's sanctimonious face was too great. Instead, he watched them lifting the gate off its hinges and busying themselves with a mallet and a pole before he turned off from the path.

If you walked far enough along the field edge, following the strip of lush green that flagged the presence of a tiny beck even in the height of summer, you came to the wall that marked the inner boundary of the Waterbeck Estate. For a moment he thought of scrambling over a recently tumbled section of stone and disappearing among the glossy rhododendrons that occupied this part of the grounds, but although there were signs that someone else had clambered over the fallen wall Tom's respect for the gentry, underlain though it might be with resentment, held him back. The way his luck was going, if he tried to hide there, then he'd run into the gamekeeper and there'd be more explaining to do.

These are who I went to fight for, he thought, but it had turned out a bad bargain. No-one was standing up for him now and everything was the way it had been before. 'The poor work for the rich,' he remembered Frank saying with a lazy laugh one Sunday when the guns were quiet, 'and that's why the poor will always be poor and the rich will always be rich.'

They gave you nowt in return for your service but a few shillings a week and their pity. He slunk along the path. It would run out eventually and he'd either have to turn back to his cottage and risk curious callers peddling false sympathy or keep on walking. The challenge of the road, where there would be no escape from a chance encounter, was too much for him, so he clambered over the stile onto the part of the estate that surrounded the village. There, the Waterbecks traditionally turned a blind eye to the villagers who cut through it to spare themselves the huge loop of the road and avoid the part where the beck burst its banks in heavy rain. He might run into someone on that path, but the folk from the Hall, more distant from his life than his immediate neighbours, were less likely to shoulder their way into his grief.

The gentry were untouchable. He sighed. If anyone were to point the finger at Guy Waterbeck, the family and their friends would close ranks and bring every lever to bear to save him from the noose. Lady Waterbeck would write to all her influential American friends and even Sir Henry might get off his old, privileged arse and go down to London to call in a few old favours to save his son. If they would do that for weak-chinned, rich Guy they should do it for him, who'd given up so much.

The thought formed as he strolled along, allowing the dappled sunlight and the sounds of the woods to melt the tension from his shoulders. In the trees above him a red squirrel chattered and a second later a beech nut came down to the path with force, as if it had thrown it at him. As he ploughed along without looking where he was going, he succumbed to a curious and paradoxical optimism. There was something else Frank had said, often enough. 'Times are changing.' They might not be changing quickly, certainly not quickly enough. But the Waterbecks should take his word without question, just as they would for one of themselves, shouldn't they?

Was it impossible that they should use their influence to save his neck?

'Tom!'

He'd been paying so little attention that he hadn't even noticed Mercy Appleby and her little lass heading along the path. It was narrow and the undergrowth thick on either side, so she'd nowhere to go to avoid him. He collided with her as she stood in the path, holding her arms out in front of her to stop him from knocking her over, but to no avail. The two of them bounced and rocked in an attempt to keep balance and eventually it was she, reaching out with her free hand, who stopped the two of them from falling.

'Ah, sorry!' Even as he realised who she was, she slotted into his unformed plan like an angel from the heaven he'd stopped believing in.

Tom liked Mercy, though he didn't know her well. Living up in the estate office kept her at a distance from the village and she'd hung around with the Waterbeck children when she'd left the village school, acquiring la-di-da manners and a cosiness with the gentry on the way, but she wasn't a bad sort. Jane had liked her, too, though she'd mocked her for what she saw as her primness. In the early days of the war Teddy had never stopped going on about her many virtues — her common sense, her sympathetic nature, her desire to do good for everyone else, never mind the crude hints at a passionate streak hidden behind her morally upright facade. Sometimes, when he'd listened to his mate praising a woman so obviously both adoring and adored, Tom had wondered if he might have been better off with someone like Mercy, steady, reliable and dull, but life hadn't turned out like that and instead he'd had the misfortune to fall in love with Jane.

Love, that bastard, tricking you and torturing you and leading you, in the end, to places you'd never wanted to go.

'Sorry,' he said again, sizing her up but making no move to stand aside and let her past. He wanted — no, needed — to talk to someone.

She twirled the basket, then delved inside and brought out a paper bag. 'Have a lemon drop.'

He dipped his fingers in, waiting for the questions, but they never came. Instead, she smiled encouragingly at him, her dark hair gleaming in the June light and a faint pink flush upon her cheek. Beside her, Sally's brown eyes gazed up at him from a sticky face; a broken yellow petal clung to her hair.

'I thought I'd take the short cut back from the village,' she said, as if she needed to justify herself. 'It's such a lovely day.'

'Lovely,' he agreed.

'And here you are, charging along like an army's after you. Trying to get away from it all?'

He nodded.

'I don't blame you. It's so awful, Tom. I never had the chance yesterday to tell you how sorry we all are. Poor you. Poor Jane.

We'll all miss her so much. But not as much as you will.'

Mercy's sympathy only fuelled his anger at the system. 'They'll not even let me have her back in her own home. I want to give her a decent burial.'

'I know you do. But they have to do a post mortem. A pathologist came from Carlisle this morning. They've taken her away now until the funeral. That's the procedure, Mrs Watson-Cooke says. She knows about these things.'

'There'll be an inquest, they say. We'll all have to go up there and go through all that again. I can't bear it.'

'Yes. I know. Awful. I'm so sorry.'

He drew a long breath. Mercy had a reputation in the village for being thoughtful and wise, even though she was so young, and something always made him want to confide in her, though he never did. If he had done, he might have been able to salvage something from his marriage and Jane might still be alive. 'That inspector thinks I did it.'

'Really?' Her brown eyes were anxious. He couldn't know whether she thought he was guilty, but he was sure she agreed with him about what Livingstone thought. 'I don't know about that. He's trying to find out who did kill her. Kitty — Mrs Watson-Cooke — was telling me about it this morning. He's talking to everyone. We all want the right man caught, don't we? So he has to ask difficult questions.'

All of Livingstone's questions had pointed the same way — towards Tom's guilt. Which men had Jane been with? How angry had Tom been about it? Had he confronted them? Had he confronted her? What had he thought of doing to her if he'd caught her last night? How often had he hit her?

The answers to those questions had been hard enough, and he was afraid the man had seen through his half-hearted version of the truth. I'm a good man turned bad, Tom said to himself. He slipped the lemon drop into his mouth and turned it over on his tongue, sweetness giving way to acid. He'd mistreated

Jane, but there was a reason. Would anyone understand that? 'I need someone to put in a word for me.'

'With the inspector?' She backed away a step, as if she didn't believe him either. 'I don't know that he'd listen to me.'

'No, nor the likes of me, neither. No-one listens to poor folk with no education. But he might listen to his lordship. Or her ladyship. If they'd speak up for me. But I couldn't ask them myself.'

'Oh, Tom,' she said, still wide-eyed. 'I don't know if there's anything I can do. Justice has to take its course.'

Justice never favoured the likes of him. 'I loved her. You know that.'

'Of course, I do. And she loved you, too. You had your difficulties—'

'You don't know what they are.'

'Your arm, of course. That wasn't your fault.'

His arm was the least of his problems. He didn't have the words to tell Mercy the extent of his humiliation, so great that even Jane had been too sensitive to gossip about him to her friends in the village. He'd rather have died under the guns than lived on as he did. A man degraded, but he had to tell someone. Mercy Appleby understood how a man could suffer, even if Teddy's pain and humiliation was different. And he had to tell someone. 'I loved her. I did so. But I couldn't give her what she wanted. You understand?'

She shook her head, her expression still blank. He could feel himself blushing like a girl and he hated himself for it, but he ploughed on, committed. 'I'm not the man I was when I married her.' And then, because he couldn't find the words to express himself, he whistled the tune that had everyone laughing the night before, everyone but him. She married a man who had no balls at all.

At last Mercy understood. Her free hand flew up to her lips at the indelicacy of it. 'Tom. Oh dear. Poor you.'

'I'm a man who can't even make love to his wife!' he shouted, and the thick foliage of the woods and the underlying rhododendrons soaked up his bitterness and his fury. At his feet, Sally whimpered. 'What chance did I have of keeping her? I was jealous. Folk only see the bad in me, but I need you to help me live.'

Sally's whimper was turning to a rising wail. 'Shhh, sweetheart! It's all right.' Mercy, distracted, swooped to soothe her treasure, scooping the little girl up. 'I don't know what to suggest. Perhaps if you talked to Lady Waterbeck? She might be able to suggest something.'

Would Mercy go away and tell the Waterbecks his shameful secret? Would she tell the inspector? And would this confession make it more or less likely they'd decide he'd killed his Jane? 'I shouldn't have said owt.' Humiliated, he brushed past her, forcing her to step aside from the path.

'No. Tom, come back. We won't abandon you. Talk to Sir Henry.'

That was bloody impossible and, even if it wasn't, the old man was as useless as Tom himself, though in a different way. 'Aye. Right.'

'Well, maybe not him. But Lady Waterbeck—'

'You know she'll not listen. None of them will.'

'I can talk to her if you want, but I think it's better if you do it yourself. I think she'll listen. I think she'll help.'

'I've still got my pride.' He pushed past her.

'Tom!'

He strode on, but he kept listening until the crackling of twigs behind him indicated Mercy had given up on him and she and Sally had turned off up to the Hall. In the emptiness he stood for a moment with his forehead pressed against the rough trunk of a tree, his optimism blown away even as grievance blossomed in his heart. Why ever had he told her? Because he needed to tell someone, he supposed. There was surely no shame in asking for help when he'd been prepared to lay down his life for everything the Waterbecks held dear in this green corner of England.

The newspapers and the officers had called them all heroes, and he'd begun to believe it. Then he'd come home and found that no-one really understood how much the men had been prepared to sacrifice.

Turning, he followed Mercy's route up to the Hall, where a smart two-seater motor car was parked outside, with the neat blonde woman Guy Waterbeck seemed to be keeping at arms' length standing beside it. Guy was nowhere in sight and Kitty Watson-Cooke was in conversation with Blanche, who was seated astride a tall chestnut horse.

It was his opportunity, but his courage deserted him, draining away as he lurked in the trees like a fugitive. Five minutes passed before Blanche tossed the young woman a casual wave. 'Tell Guy and Sir Henry I'll be back in time for tea,' she called, and set the horse to a trot down the drive. The trot turned to a canter, and she disappeared from sight.

Tom's heart failed him. He knew his place and everyone else knew it, too. He turned and headed back down the hill.

CHAPTER TWELVE

MERCY

'Flower!' Turning back from the herbaceous border at the back of Waterbeck Hall, Sally offered her mother a beaming smile and a fat buttercup, yanked up with barely half an inch of stalk.

'That's a buttercup,' Mercy said to her, accepting the mutilated bloom. 'Like the one Frank gave you. Remember?' She thought of Tom as she'd last seen him, turning away from Blanche like a coward, not a man who must have looked death in the face, not just that one time in the garden but on countless occasions in France and Flanders, in mud and dust, in rain and sun. 'Say buttercup.'

'Flower.'

Blanche, surely, would have helped him. If he was guilty, he'd be found out, but if he wasn't, then surely, she'd want to help him prove his innocence.

Someone was guilty. That was the problem. 'Come on, Sal. Let's get back.'

When Sally had slipped her fat toddler's hand into Mercy's, mother and daughter made their way back around the side of Waterbeck Hall towards the estate office. Gordon Livingstone's car was parked in the courtyard and he was standing on the doorstep of the manager's house with his hand lifted to the knocker.

'Inspector.' Mercy hurried over towards him, slowed by Sally beside her. Something about the man made her want to justify her every movement. 'We were just in the garden. Lady

Waterbeck lets me take Sally in there to play.'

'Your daughter?' he asked, looking down at Sally while she, with a child's innocent fearlessness, looked straight up with Teddy's generous brown eyes.

'Yes. I was just bringing her home for a treat. Because—'

'Sometimes we all need a treat.' He moved away from the doorstep to stand next to the car. Under the unnerving stare from that convenient wall eye she thought, inconsequentially, of Frank and his newly acquired talent for fixing motor vehicles. In other circumstances she could envisage him leaning on the bonnet and engaging the man — any man, or woman for that matter — in easy conversation about its horsepower and the sweetness of its engine and the best way to keep it running well, but these were different days. A low cloud of suspicion hung over them all.

'I'm looking for your father,' he said in that rich but slightly mocking drawl. 'I was told he'd be in the office, but there's no sign of him and no-one's answering the door. Do you have any idea where he is?'

A glance in through the window confirmed that it was after five, time for Sally's supper, never mind a sweetie. The last twenty-four hours had thrown her routine and no doubt they'd all pay for it before too long. Sally was a sweet-natured child, but she needed the familiar. 'He may be out on the estate somewhere.'

'I was looking for him this morning, too. To no avail.'

'He must have been out and about.' The front door was never locked, but she dug in her pocket for a key nonetheless, to give her an excuse not to meet his eye, fidgeting with it, fitting it into the lock, pretending to turn it. He'd probably see right through the tactic, she realised even as she jiggled the key in the lock, and all that would happen would be that she'd alert him to her furtiveness and he'd think she had something to hide. She didn't, unless you counted the sense of great weariness that came with fear, but someone around her did. Someone she knew was a murderer and even Frank had admitted to lying.

'I understand.' He moved too close to her, so that her hands grew damp with perspiration and she became flustered. 'Since I'm here, I can inform you that the inquest into Mrs Freeman's death will be held tomorrow afternoon at the George Hotel in Penrith. Of course, you'll be required to attend.'

'Tomorrow?' Mercy put the key back in her pocket but didn't open the door. 'So soon?'

'Yes. A mere formality. We'll be asking the witnesses to the discovery of the body to describe what happened. The cause of death is straightforward and I daresay the outcome will be equally so. Unless any new intelligence comes up before, then it'll be murder, of course. Person or persons unknown.'

'And then what?' Mercy kept fidgeting with the lock.

'We continue the investigation until we bring the criminal to justice.'

'Horse!' cried Sally, enraptured.

Livingstone stepped back, just as the muffled clip clop of a horse's hooves on the soft ground heralded the arrival of Blanche, astride a tall chestnut stallion, emerging from the lane. A sweat on the horse's flanks and a pink flush on Blanche's cheeks told a tale of a carefree gallop over the fields, but the crinkling of her brows suggested the ride hadn't solved all her problems. She brought the horse to a halt a couple of yards away and sat looking down on them.

'Well, ain't it just like Grand Central Station around here? I didn't realise you were still here, Inspector. If you're looking for me, you nearly missed me. I took to the open country for a dose of sanity and fresh air.'

When Blanche was on edge, it always showed. She became crisp and acerbic, and her speech lost the patina of British refinement it had acquired over a quarter of a century. Her native accent was evident now, and so was her dislike of the man in front of her. She jerked the horse's head back and clicked her tongue at it.

'I was explaining to Mrs Appleby about the inquest. I spoke to your husband earlier today.'

'He mentioned it.' She nudged the horse with her knee and it danced sideways, as if infected by her impatience. 'Well, if that's all…'

'There's one more thing. I have a question for the two of you.' He backed away a little so that he could see them both at the same time and, Mercy noticed with a trace of amusement, to put himself out of range of the horse's hooves.

Seeming to spot his nervousness, Blanche turned the horse through a quarter of a circle, presenting them with her profile and further underlining her impatience by staring at the distance. 'If we can answer it, we will.'

'Last night Mrs Appleby kindly brought PC Robinson tea and the newspaper as he sat with the body. He noticed there was half a sheet torn from it. I wondered if either of you ladies could tell me what that sheet was, and why it was taken away?'

A jackdaw fluttered down from the roof of the hall with a loud chack-chack, and the horse, which seemed in as skittish a mood as Blanche herself, bucked a little and rolled its thick lips upwards over long yellow teeth. Livingstone took a further step backwards.

'Well, I sure don't know. Mercy, do you?'

'No, I'm afraid I don't.'

'I guess it could have been anybody. We aren't proprietorial about newspapers here, Mr Livingstone. When Sir Henry's read them and I've had a quick look, it's a free for all. We're really very democratic here. I encourage the servants to read.'

'You didn't cut the article out?'

'I don't remember. Today has been such a carry on, as the villagers would say, and I often take articles out to send them to my sister. Today? Yesterday? I really don't remember.'

'The newspaper was *The Times* and I believe the missing page was the Court Circular and the personal column. Of course, it may not be important.'

'Dora has a fondness for royalty. I've had so many other things on my mind.' Blanche nudged the horse, and it shuffled sideways again; each time they repeated the action, she put a little more distance between herself and the inspector. 'You'll have to excuse me. Kaiser is getting a little impatient right now. I should take him back and stable him up. It wouldn't do to hold him back, would it?'

'I'll see you at the inquest tomorrow, Lady Waterbeck.'

Blanche said something under her breath that sounded suspiciously like 'I can't wait', then dug her heels into Kaiser's flanks and trotted smartly across the courtyard towards the stables.

Mercy hid her sigh. Sally's hot, sticky fingers tightened around her hand. 'Is that all you wanted, Mr Livingstone?' There was teatime and bedtime and stories to deal with before she could settle down to her own thoughts.

'Thank you, Mrs Appleby. Yes.' He turned back and cranked the Ford to life.

Mercy watched it spluttering its way out of the courtyard. An inquest. That meant lawyers and with that, the whole circus would take on an even more formal twist. Men like Tom, lacking education and without the native cunning that would get Frank out of many a tricky situation, were at the mercy of formal language and processes that seemed designed to keep them in their place.

Still trailing Sally by the hand, she made her slow way across past the front of the hall and round to the stable yard. Blanche had dismounted and handed Kaiser over to the attention of one of the grooms, an elderly man with the insufferably smug expression of someone who'd been in full view of half a dozen independent witnesses at the time of Jane's death. 'Put him back in his box. I think he's had a decent ride out today. And he's like the rest of us. He's not getting any younger.' She turned towards the house and a smile bloomed on her face. 'Sally. How are you, sweetness?'

Livingstone must have put the fear of God into Sally's timid heart. She clung to Mercy's legs and peered out around her skirt, even though she was used to Blanche. 'She's a little shy today.'

'Well, don't we all want to hide behind someone?' asked Blanche rhetorically. 'Look, here's Kitty.' She lowered her voice. 'No doubt she'll bend our ear about procedure and what the late Freddie would have said.'

'Well, everything's happening now, isn't it?' Kitty called, clicking her way across the cobbled yard in heels too high to be comfortable. A mixture of mud and muck flicked up into the air and spattered her stockings and the hem of her pale summer frock. 'I don't expect there will be a lot of new information at the inquest, but it's a sign things are moving.'

You could never be sure with Kitty whether she knew what she was talking about or was parroting what her late lawyer husband had said. 'Is it?' Mercy asked.

'Oh, yes. And the sooner they find whoever killed this poor woman, the better.' Kitty tossed her blonde head and wrinkled her eyes in the bright sunlight. 'I saw her husband as I was on my way up. Lurking in the trees.'

'We allow the villagers to walk on the estate. I do hope he was polite,' said Blanche with a half sigh, as if Tom's surliness was more than she could cope with.

'We didn't speak. I wonder what he was doing?'

Mercy bent to remove a piece of dirty straw that Sally had pounced on and tossed it away into the mud. 'I spoke to him. He's very distressed.'

'One way or another, that's not surprising. Distressed if he killed her, distressed if he didn't. Which is not,' went on Blanche, flapping at a fly around her head, 'to say that I don't have sympathy for the man.'

'He wanted to talk to you.' Wiping Sally's fingers with her handkerchief, Mercy replayed the scene she'd shared with Tom in the woods. 'Maybe he was scared.'

'Scared?' said Blanche, in what looked like genuine amusement? 'Of me? Well, I never. And what did he want to talk to me about?'

Exactly what had Tom wanted? He hadn't been specific. 'He needs reassurance. I think the inspector was quite hard on him.'

'He was hard on him because the first suspect is always the husband,' Blanche interrupted. 'And come to that, he was hard on us all. I'm sure some of us deserved it, but he was impatient and aggressive with me and I'm sure as hell an innocent in this. A chip on his shoulder, maybe. God knows.' She looked towards the Hall. 'Kitty. Did you want me?'

Blanche was rarely quite so impatient, so short-tempered. Surprised, Mercy seized what was probably her last chance before she was summarily dismissed. 'Tom's afraid. He doesn't know how the law works. He feels it's against him.'

'The law is inviolable, or it ought to be. We let it take its course. Tom shouldn't expect to be treated any differently to anyone else. I'm surprised he asked you to speak up for him, if that's what you're doing, and even more surprised, you agreed.' Then Blanche seemed suddenly to remember that she was the soul of philanthropy, stood up for her villagers, treated them with fairness that spilled over into generosity. 'You are a kind-hearted young woman, and I'm not surprised he appealed to you. But the law is the law.' She bent down towards a bashful Sal, still cowering. 'Goodbye, Sally, sweetheart. You must come and see me soon and we will have cake in the parlour.' She turned away. 'Kitty.'

For a moment Kitty hesitated, then she, too, turned and tottered off across the stable yard.

CHAPTER THIRTEEN

BLANCHE

'Do we have to stay here until the verdict? It's not as if we don't know what it will be.'

It was a rhetorical question, because they'd already had the discussion and come to an uneasy agreement about the virtues of being seen to be engaged in the inquest, but Blanche asked it anyway. Even Kitty hadn't stayed, but had given her evidence — a matter of five minutes' worth. Disappointingly slender, she'd seemed to think — and motored off back to Brampton.

Guy hadn't seemed remotely sorry to see her go. 'We talked about it earlier,' he reminded his mother. 'We agreed we'd stay. It shows leadership.'

Since the war, she supposed he'd earned the right to lecture them about leadership. She looked at her son as he sat in one of the deep, red leather armchairs in the room the manager at the George Hotel had arranged for them, above the bar where the rest of the witnesses had assembled while the inquest took place in the ballroom. Being gentry had its advantages. She was tired of public scrutiny. 'The sooner we get this over, the sooner we can get on and the sooner the inspector will catch the culprit.'

'You think he will?' Guy removed a cigarette case from his inside pocket and offered it to his father, who waved it aside, and to his mother, who took one. 'I don't. He doesn't seem to me to be taking much action. Anyone else would have slapped old Tom in chains within minutes, instead of sitting, asking clever questions and playing games with our heads.'

'Why so sure it was Tom?'

He shrugged. 'It always is the husband, isn't it? But our Scottish friend seems to be enjoying letting us know he's in charge, a little too much. I don't see him gathering any evidence. Kitty says he should be looking for things. Actual evidence. Not just where everyone was and when, and threatening us all with the hangman. I don't see him making a lot of progress.'

Blanche had concluded that Kitty was no more impressed by Livingstone than anyone else seemed to be. 'Let's hope he finds something, then, so we can all rest easy in our beds.' She turned to Henry, who was even more deeply sunk into his chair than Guy. 'Or so they say.'

Henry didn't answer. He rarely did. These days, they spent much of their time apart. On the increasingly few occasions when they did find themselves together he reminded her too much of the sad-looking stuffed polar bear that had occupied a corner of her father's library, positioned as if intrigued by the conversation, but with a glassy-eyed stare to attest to its lack of life.

For a fleeting moment, Blanche felt guilty about having allowed herself and Henry to drift apart. Thirty years, or nearly, was a long time to be married, though the first dozen or so had been happy enough. Her sister, Dora, had been adamant it wouldn't last and there was always satisfaction with proving know-it-all-Dora wrong. One had to count one's blessings, and there had been plenty of those. It was a blessing in itself to be still there, coexisting in what was essentially a peaceable manner, while most marriages between American heiresses and the British gentry seemed to have broken up in acrimony on the rocks of protocol and etiquette. There was a lot to be thankful for in a rural backwater, a lot to be said for not having to keep up appearances all the time. And when all was done, she still (she thought) liked him.

The smoke from Guy's cigarette drifted across in front of her face, blue in the sunlight that blazed in through the dusty windows, but Blanche set her cigarette down on the ashtray and let it smoke itself out. Instead, she lifted the delicate porcelain cup and saucer that had come with cucumber sandwiches and a jug of fresh milk, yellow with cream, and sipped at the tea she'd allowed to go cold.

Her lips twisted as she thought about blessings, and her eyes passed from the husband who had caught her eye to the young man who was the apple of it. There was no escaping Guy's paternity and nothing at all of his American Hardacre relatives about him, so that if Blanche hadn't clung to him from the moment he took his first breath she might have assumed he was Henry's bastard offspring, slipped into her bed at birth. He had his father's thin face and floppy fair hair, his disarming smile, his blue eyes, and he was cursed by his lack of drive. The whole purpose of mixing bloodstock was to improve it, but Guy had proved the truest chip off the paternal block whilst her other children had been all Hardacre, tough, active and argumentative, all of them going places fast.

And they'd gone to the grave fast enough. She contemplated Guy, as he chewed his bottom lip, and reflected on the irony that it was the washed-out Waterbeck genes that had won through in the end and it would be they that produced and dominated future generations. Her only consolation was his war record, hinting that he'd inherited some of the Hardacre spirit. He had, they said, been a fearless and well-respected leader, mentioned in dispatches for a display of gallantry so conspicuous that even his adoring mother, reading the citation, had barely recognised him from the description.

But his courage, and his inherited characteristics, didn't matter. He was her son and she would do whatever it cost to keep him safe, as she'd failed to do for his three younger siblings.

'We should go back in for the verdict.' Guy looked distinctly queasy, not at all the valiant warrior now.

'I don't think so. Someone will come and tell us when it's

done. It isn't as if we don't know what the outcome will be.' As if there could be any other verdict than murder. The only surprise would be if that inspector had, despite everyone's misgivings, been able to find out who did it and chose to spring it upon them, but even then, the verdict wouldn't be a decision for him but for the jury at the inquest. A formality, he'd said. Nevertheless, they would sit in this stuffy private room while everyone else who'd been called to give evidence and cross-questioned by the coroner waited in the bar, until they heard the confirmation that Jane's death was murder.

Whatever anyone said, however much one could point the finger at the husband as the obvious killer, Blanche knew there was no shortage of other suspects. 'Guy, I find it very hot in here.' The sun had found its way in to the room and was flooding the place with the relentlessness of hellfire. Underneath the black merino skirt and thick, funereal jacket she'd selected as appropriate for the occasion, Blanche's skin prickled with unladylike perspiration. 'Perhaps we could take a turn around the square.'

'People will stare,' he objected.

'So instead we stay in here as if we've got something to hide?' She stood up and crossed to the window. Below, in the Market Square, Penrith went about its business as usual around the Musgrave Monument at its centre. 'I'd welcome some fresh air. And your company.'

'Perhaps we can go out the back way.' Obedient as always, Guy got to his feet. 'Father? Are you coming?'

'Someone should wait here,' Henry said, with a sigh, 'in case we're needed. It might as well be me.' When Blanche had ordered tea, he'd ordered a brandy, but he hadn't touched it. Now he reached out a hand for the glass.

They went down the stairs to the main lobby, from which a back door led from the hotel into the yard. Despite her determination not to seem furtive, Blanche acknowledged

Guy's reluctance to attract any more attention. It was better to avoid the crowd of people in the lobby, and the press photographer who'd set up his equipment on the pavement outside.

She was glad when they made the open air. It wasn't so much the heat that was oppressive as the sudden thought that had come to her as they waited, the possible reason why Gordon Livingstone wasn't ready to arrest the obvious suspect. 'I find this very difficult,' she said, in a low voice, as she tucked her arm into his and they walked unnoticed out into Burrowgate and round the back of the Devonshire Arcade towards the church.

'I'm sure you do.'

Why was he so curiously unresponsive? He reminded her of a boxer her father had once taken her to see in New York, a man who wouldn't face up to his opponent but ducked and dived and swayed out of his reach, soaking up the odd punch that made contact until his opponent, eventually driven to fury, had swung a haymaker that knocked him out cold — and, they said, had left him unconscious for three days. The crowd, desperate for a spectacle, had booed this unsatisfactory victory. 'Aren't you concerned?'

'Do you think I should be?'

'I don't understand how you can be so calm,' she said, crossly as they turned around and made it to the soft shade of the churchyard.

'Kitty says there's nothing to worry about if they do their job properly.' His voice was the expression of Henry's world-weary detachment, blank and unconnected.

'But what about Jane?'

His arm quivered under hers. 'I know what you think. Of course, it upsets you. And I know you'll think me callous, but I find it hard to be overly concerned when so many other innocent people have died. I've seen them.'

He must have killed some of them, too. 'This is different. It's so close to home.'

'They're all close to home,' he said and this time, at least, he mustered a sigh.

Pausing on a path at the eastern end of the churchyard, Blanche studied him anxiously from beneath the brim of her hat. His brows were furrowed and his eyes distant. None of the men talked freely about what they'd seen or done in the war, and she was wise enough to understand that it was probably for the best. Her father had fought at Gettysburg, on the most reluctant of principles, and had emerged from it revitalised and enthusiastic much in the way Frank Holland seemed to have done, but like Frank his enthusiasm was for the new world that had emerged rather than an old one he'd fought to preserve. Being brought up by an old soldier had taught her war wasn't glorious and was best not dwelt on. I am the daughter of a warrior and the mother of a warrior; she thought in awe as she looked at her son. 'I can never understand what you've seen, darling. Don't think I'm such a fool as to think I do. But I do understand why you don't want to talk about it.'

'Then let's not.' He began walking again and she, with her arm tucked through his, had perforce to follow him. 'I don't want to seem harsh, but I barely knew the girl. She worked in the kitchen.'

Her democratic side knew she should reproach him, but it had been she, after all, who had allowed Henry, with his traditional ideas of propriety, to discourage their son from mixing too closely with the servants when he was a child. Now she saw the error of her ways, because the other three had benefitted so much from Mercy's company. It was her fault and too late to alter it. 'I want to talk to you about the homecoming dance. I was looking for you and I couldn't find you.'

'Mother.' Guy shook her arm free, almost in outrage. 'I'm twenty-six years old, an adult. I don't need to explain what I'm doing, at any time, to anyone.'

In similar circumstances, Flora would have stamped her foot and shouted. Resisting the twitch of a smile that came with memory, Blanche contented herself with being firm. But you do. The inspector asked me about it and I couldn't answer. It would be terrible if they get the wrong idea.

'I did not kill Jane.'

In profile he was white-faced and tight-lipped, a Hardacre after all. Fear fluttered within her at the thought that he had something to hide. 'I know.'

'Then let's leave it at that, then, and wait for Livingstone to make his mind up.'

'No.' She was a Hardacre, too, able to draw on just as deep a well of stubbornness as him. 'We can't. He may not seem to be doing anything, but he won't leave this unsolved.' Underneath Livingstone's polite exterior, she'd sensed a chippiness, a need to exert his power. What better way to do that than to put the fear of the hangman into as many people as possible before he pounced?

'Then let him arrest someone. He seems harmless enough to me. Kitty says he's a small-town man who won't want to hand the matter on to someone else. So, he has to come up with some answers, or I expect they'll call in the Yard.'

That wasn't what Blanche wanted to hear. A man with limitations, too proud to pass it upwards? That didn't sound like someone guaranteed to find the right answer. She thought she'd detected the smell of socialism about some of his remarks. 'You were in with him a long time. What did you tell him?'

'The truth. I told him I wasn't sure where I'd gone and when. I'd had a few drinks, so wasn't paying attention to the time. I chatted to a few people. Went off for a smoke for a while, up the path to the fields.'

'By yourself?'

'I was avoiding Kitty, if you must know, but it would have been jolly ungallant to say so. A bit later, I bumped into Holland. I couldn't remember who else I'd seen. That was all.'

The mention of smoking seemed to remind him. He felt in his pocket for yet another cigarette and offered one to his mother, who shook her head, then he turned away from her to light it. The flicker of the match, the curl of grey rising from behind his cupped hands, the fragrance of tobacco scenting the summer air. 'And did he believe you?'

'I doubt it. I don't think he likes me. But it's the truth.'

'Then can't you come up with something better than the truth?' she asked him, under her breath. 'Can't you think of something to persuade him? What if he doesn't believe you?'

'What if he doesn't?'

They were going over old ground, something that happened when there was nothing new to be said, but she couldn't let it go. He was her only surviving child. How could she bear the grief of losing him? 'If you can't bring yourself to say where you were, he might—'

'I don't need to justify myself to him.' Yes, he was all her father now.

'But you do,' she pleaded. 'If you don't, he'll find it easy to believe it's you. And the prosecutor might find it easy to persuade a jury that he's right.'

'Let them try.' He drew on the cigarette and waved it in the air with a casual negligence, but his blue eyes were ice.

And if they did try, if they succeeded... he would hang. Her blood chilled. 'Guy, darling. Think of your father. Think of me.'

'Don't you believe me?'

'Yes. Absolutely.' Out of the corner of her eye, Blanche saw a flick of navy blue as Mercy came through the gap from Middlegate and along the path that marched beside the churchyard. 'But they don't. They have to have something to believe, don't you see? They have to know where you were. Or it looks bad.'

'I can't remember where I was. To tell you the truth, I was a bit squiffy. Everything got a bit too much for me.'

She was sure he'd been as sober as a judge that night. 'Then try harder to remember.'

Mercy drew closer. Guy saw her too, tipping his hat towards her as if she were a lady born rather than an employee of the estate, albeit one who had grown to be a friend of the family. He arranged a smile on his lips, though he couldn't force it to reach his eyes. 'I'll do my best, Mother.'

'You must, Guy,' she breathed.

He turned his back on her, the rigid set of his shoulders indicating that whatever more she wanted to say, he'd had enough, and the conversation was closed. By the time Mercy reached them, he'd retrieved the old smile and was all Waterbeck again. 'Mercy. Have you come to tell us they're going to hang us all?'

'I hope they aren't going to hang any of us.' Mercy didn't seem to appreciate the joke. 'But yes. They'll probably hang someone.'

It was murder, then, even though Mercy didn't seem able to find it within herself to say the word. In Blanche's mind the image of Jane fluttered, her bright personality dulled, those dancing eyes bottomless black in the failing lamplight. 'What is it they say?' she asked, trying to bring some practical element to the conversation. 'Person or persons unknown. Why, that almost sounds like it could be a complete stranger.'

'Perhaps it was.' Mercy allowed herself a shrug.

'But there were no strangers,' said Guy, almost too quickly. 'I never saw anyone at the house who wasn't invited there. Except Kitty, of course.'

'But an unknown stranger is unknown. Isn't that the point?' Mercy flicked a look at the church, but the eastern side of its square sandstone tower lacked a clock. 'It could be someone who came to the village, came in to the party and left again.'

In which case, the culprit would never be found. Blanche shivered. Would Livingstone accept that, or would he find a man to take the blame?

'Perhaps I should get back,' Mercy said, breaking the nervous silence she'd engendered. 'It must be after four. Beth's looking after Sal for me, but I can't take too much advantage of her.'

'Join us,' Guy offered with a generous smile. 'We have room in the Rolls.'

'Thank you, but I came with my mam and dad and I'd better go back with them.'

'I'll fetch Father.' Guy stepped away towards the hotel.

'And I'll go and find Mam and Dad.' Mercy went with him.

Blanche watched them go, and her heart tightened with a mixture of anger and dread. Whatever Guy had done, whatever sins he might have committed, she would always love him, always fight for him and, whatever it cost her, she would win.

CHAPTER FOURTEEN

FRANK

Even though it was June, there was a fire in the hearth at Penrith's Gloucester Arms. The thick walls of the inn were riddled with hundreds of years of damp and never dried out, and as Frank shouldered his way into the public bar, the fumes from the burning logs choked like a hanged man.

'Eh, it's Frank. Back at last, are you?'

'Bored with them little French lasses, Frank?'

'Come by and I'll stand you a drink.'

It was inevitable that Frank would be the focus of attention. Even if it hadn't been for the goings on at Waterbeck, his return would have been news, something to talk about other than the weather or the price of fat pigs. His old mates surged round him as he entered the bar, handshakes all round, but they'd all heard the gossip, all knew what had brought him into Penrith.

'Up at the inquest, were you?'

'Lass killed up at Waterbeck Hall, they say.'

'Aye,' he said in reply, 'it's been a rough couple of days. But it's good to be back.' He gestured to the barman for half a dozen pints, but he sensed the enthusiasm of his old acquaintances was tinged with a wariness that sent a chill around his collar. He called them out on it, his challenge uncompromising. 'You're looking at me, thinking I'm a killer? You're right. I am. I killed a dozen of the Boche and never got so much as a scratch. They couldn't lay a finger on me.'

There was a moment's silence, and then the first of them laughed. 'That's my man.'

'You don't get this, Frank. No old soldier pays for a drink while I'm in the bar,' put in someone else, buying out his shame at his initial suspicion of the returning hero, and his own failure to fight alongside him.

'I did my best for the troops, too. Do I get a bevy?' joked the barmaid, as she turned away to begin pulling the pints.

'Bet you did!' came the reply, to general laughter.

Relaxing, Frank settled down at the bar and dispensed his version of what had happened in the dark of the Waterbeck estate two days before. When he'd answered all the questions three times over and the bulk of the interested customers had drifted away to their own conversations, he spent the next hour or so chewing over old exploits in the company of the few old friends and comrades he thought he could trust. Even they were wary of him at first, but when the beer loosened their tongues, they became once more his old mates.

'You're not the criminal, are you, marra?' the landlord said jovially, pulling another pint.

'No more than any of the rest of you,' he said, slapping two shillings on the bar to cover the next round and a tip for the barman, though he wouldn't be there to partake of it. 'One more for these gents, then, and I'll be on my way.'

'Aye, I know you're not the sort to kill on the sly, are you? We can all kill a man but there's not many will do it unless the King tells us to!'

There was a shout of laughter, tinged with a bitter aftertaste.

'When a man's just home, all he'd want is a pint and a good lass.' Someone else raised a tipsy tankard in Frank's general direction.

They had forgotten, in their jollity, that a good lass — depending, of course, on your definition of good — was exactly the person who'd met her end that night. He took a long drink from his glass and set it down on the counter top, pushing it away from him half-full. 'I'll be away. I've a long walk home.'

'I'd give you a ride,' said one of them, 'but some bastard pinched my motorcycle. A new one, it was. A Triumph. From outside me house, in broad daylight. If I catch him, I'll put my fingers round his throat all right.'

Frank shook his head with the rest of them over the injustice. It had been the deep roar of a Triumph he'd heard on that fateful night when they'd found Jane — a strange thing to remember, but perhaps not when he thought about how much he wanted one of his own. When he'd got himself established in his new job, he'd save up and buy one, sidecar and all, and come roaring into the village to show them all how he'd moved on, how life in the town was more the making of a man than being slave to the land. Then, in his fantasy, he would persuade Mercy to come out with him for the day, out to Windermere or the seaside for a picnic.

If he didn't hang.

He sidled out of the bar, leaving the others still laughing, and walked briskly up Castlegate, swinging round past the market and over the railway. In the distance, a plume of smoke told of a train leaving for the south. If things started to look difficult — and he was no fool and — could see exactly how the inspector could make a case for him having murdered Jane without him being able to prove otherwise he could make a dash for it. A man like him, full of optimism and native wit, could easily lose himself in London and re-emerge when and where he chose as a new, rich man.

Mellowed by the beer, he dismissed this doomsday scenario. Someone would be caught and convicted for Jane's murder, but it wouldn't be him. As he walked up Norfolk Road, past the rows of red sandstone terraces blackened by the soot from the railway, towards the beckoning summer sunset he reflected on what his future could hold, once he'd made some money.

One of those neat houses would do for a start, better than the two-bedroomed cottage he shared with his mother. After a few years working his arse off for his employers, he'd start his own business. One day he might even buy out Wilsons and change its name. Wilson and Holland had a ring to it or, even better, Holland and Wilson. He grinned as he passed the poorhouse, austere and isolated beyond the edge of the town. No-one from Waterbeck had ended up there since Blanche and her fortune had come to the village, but its shadow reached out towards them with the morning sun, a reminder of the fate of those who were neither lucky nor smart.

In the distance, a car engine growled behind him. A Ford, like the one the inspector drove. He cocked an ear in its direction. The sense of self-preservation he'd always had, and which the Great War had only honed, began to tremble but he kept walking alongside the hedges where the late hawthorn blossoms were beginning to drop and the briar roses diffused their soft fragrance over the countryside. Along the edges of the cornfields, scarlet poppies rippled in the breeze and, somewhere above him, a skylark pitted its song against the roar of the motor car.

A moment later, the car came past him and pulled up twenty yards ahead. Pretending he hadn't seen the inspector, that he was in a world of his own, Frank kept walking until he was past it, but the man wasn't for playing games. 'Hey! Holland!'

He had no choice. He stopped and turned, warily. Livingstone was alone. At least they weren't about to arrest him there and then. 'Evening, Inspector.'

The car nudged forward until the passenger door was level with Frank. 'Hop in, man. You've a long walk home.'

A couple of miles was nothing. Frank wasn't going to fall for this pretence at charity, but he had enough sense to realise it was in his best interests to play along. He swung open the door and got in, unable to keep back a cheeky remark. 'You'll have had a busy day with the inquest. Happy with how it turned out?'

'All part of the process,' the man observed blandly, resting his hands on the steering wheel and pressing his foot on the accelerator. He lifted a hand in an acknowledgement to a cyclist, a woman bobbing along the uneven road towards them. Apart from her, the road was empty.

They took the next half a mile in silence, driving towards the sinking sun and the ripple of the Lakeland fells on the horizon. By the time the church tower of Waterbeck punctured the skyline, Frank was beginning to relax, even though he wouldn't trust the man beside him as far as he could throw him.

'And so,' pursued Livingstone, slowing a little as if the journey wasn't long enough for what he intended to say, 'I'm interested in you, Mr Holland. Tell me about your war.'

'I don't talk about it.'

'You don't strike me as the shrinking type. Have you no tall tales for me about the Germans you killed? No stories about the lives you saved?'

'It was a grim time.'

'Some men benefitted from it, wouldn't you say? It broadened their horizons. They managed to reinvent themselves as heroes. They came home during their leave and managed to seem attractive to all the ladies. In my youth in the Glasgow slums, that would have been something to aspire to. Wouldn't you say?'

Frank stiffened. 'For some, aye.'

'Why did you lie to me?'

Half a dozen swallows dipped and dived ahead of them, picking off the low-flying insects that rose in a cloud from the grass. 'What about?'

The car slowed further, crawling along the bridge over the slow-flowing beck. In the distance, the sun declined behind the swelling green hills and the brown moorlands of the Waterbeck estate. 'You told me you had never had a relationship with Jane Freeman.'

'Who says I did?'

'Her husband.'

Frank laughed. 'And how would he know? Tom'll believe anything bad of the girl, and of any other man.' That was how jealousy corrupted you. He'd known Tom a long time.

'He knows because his wife told him. He challenged her after your last leave, by his account, and she admitted to it. And before your return — your triumphant return — he challenged her again and warned her off seeing you. Fortunately for you, perhaps, I forbore to mention this lie at the inquest. It wouldn't have looked good, would it?'

Did that look worse for Tom or for himself? Frank remembered how brazenly Jane had strode up to him as he alighted from the bus and how she'd planted that honey-tasting kiss upon his lips, but he kept silence.

'And so,' pursued the inspector, 'I'll ask you again, Holland. Did you have a relationship with Mrs Freeman?'

Sweet, willing Jane, encumbered by the bitterness and twisted love of Radgie Tom, occupied Frank's memory. It had been the previous summer when he'd been home on a brief leave, on an evening just like this one, with the smell of roses in the air and the twilight humming with birdsong. They'd crept to the woods and lain together until the daylight melted into darkness and the song of the nightingale had overtaken that of the lark. Tom had been at the Dog and Blanket and Jane had been so certain he'd never know. He felt no guilt, only a swelling memory of pleasure. 'Yes.'

'And you lied to me about it?'

'No. You asked me if I propositioned her and I never did.' Jane had never needed a proposition.

'Nevertheless, you misled me. We agree on that, surely. So, you'll understand I'm not going to accept your account of what happened on Monday night without question.'

'I was damned sure Tom would have killed her if he'd known.

He'd have killed me, maybe still will. The man can be mad.' They could all be mad. He'd been mad himself, to a degree, when he'd succumbed to that smile, but the sun had been out and there had been a need upon him, one that had been all the greater after he'd seen Mercy wheeling her baby down to the village in the perambulator. His unrequited desire for one woman had driven him into the arms of another. Jane had been willing, and the moment had been irresistible.

'But you didn't think he knew,' Livingstone went on, as if it were an intractable problem.

'I didn't believe he did.'

'Then perhaps you thought she might tell.'

'She'd never have told him,' he defended her — and himself — before he remembered that was exactly what she'd done. 'You should be looking at him. He's the man with reason to do it. She was never going to stop being what she was.' And he himself would be glancing over his shoulder from there on.

'I am looking at him. I'm looking at everyone, but so far you're the only one I know lied to me.'

Home was in sight now, and his mam had already lit the oil lamp in the front window. There had been times when he'd dreamed of that light, still shining, but now he couldn't face going home to explain where he'd been and why the police were driving him home. As they cruised past the cottage, Beth Blunt, walking back towards the village, stood aside for the motor car. When he looked back, she was staring in his direction. The seed of a tall tale had already been sown. 'You can drop me at the pub, if you've a mind.'

They drove on, through the village, past the green with its old stone cross, and pulled up just before the Dog and Blanket. 'Is there anything else you've misled me about?'

Frank grinned as he got out. 'I never had a French sweetheart.'

'No. I guessed as much. Your sweetheart was in this village all the time, wasn't she, and married to another man?'

'Jane was never my sweetheart,' Frank said, almost amused by how close the man had come to the real truth without understanding it. 'She was on the lookout, not me. It's what she was like. I was just a man, and she was just a woman.' He got out of the car and slammed the door shut. 'You might want to go and challenge everyone else, marra. Yes, I lied to you, but they were innocent lies. To tell the truth, until you mentioned it, I'd forgotten all about it.' He turned his back on the car and headed in to the pub with a cheery wave, but when he made it inside, there was sweat on his top lip and fear in his heart.

CHAPTER FIFTEEN

BLANCHE

It was cooler on Thursday, the day after the inquest. Blanche lay in bed unusually late, awake but reluctant to face the world and succumbing to the vague excuse of a headache so that Millie would bring her breakfast in. This was, she knew, a form of cowardice, but it was a luxury she could afford.

She was more troubled by the message that arrived alongside her cup of Earl Grey and boiled egg and toast. 'Miss Hardacre telephoned, Your Ladyship,' said Millie, setting down the tray on the bedside table and going to draw the curtains.

Blanche groaned. Her sister was due on a visit to England — thankfully brief and on her way to more exciting destinations — and Blanche, though she loved her, couldn't bear the way Dora constantly talked down to her. 'Was there a message?'

'Only that her ship docked in Southampton this morning and she's heading to London.'

'Thank you, Millie.' Blanche made a note to call her sister later, but not until she had thought of some way to prevent Dora telling her what she should do.

Eventually, when the morning hubbub had died down, and she'd heard Guy driving off in the Rolls, she sent a message down to the stables to have her horse saddled up then went out to the rose garden, where she spent time choosing three perfect long-stemmed blooms, two pink and one yellow. Carrying them carefully, she headed for the stables where one of the grooms was holding Kaiser, the unfortunately named chestnut her father had given her as a birthday gift a decade before.

At least you could trust a horse, whatever it was called. Handing the groom the roses to hold, she swung herself up into the saddle before retaking possession of them. 'Thank you. I expect I'll be back in an hour or so.' She pressed her jodhpur-clad thighs against the horse's sides. 'Come along, Kaiser.'

The name always gave her a smile, and it raised eyebrows among their weekend guests, but it didn't matter. Blanche only believed in changing things if it made a difference and Kaiser was too accustomed to his name to answer to anything else. Still holding the roses between her gloved fingers, she set off down the drive at a trot, not intending to go far. Guy had said something about Kitty motoring over for lunch and her acerbic comment about him showing a little more enthusiasm if he was serious had fallen on deaf ears. Maybe he wasn't serious. Who knew? Either way, she wasn't sure she was ready for Kitty's incessant opinions on what the late Freddie had thought or done and how her uncle was the Chief Constable, as if this tenuous relationship meant she had any more knowledge of the processes by which the police pursued an investigation than anyone else.

She allowed herself a wry smile at the mention of Arthur Henderson, the Chief Constable, too.

Fresh air always helped, and if avoiding Kitty was a benefit of getting out, then all to the good. Besides, it had been a while since she'd been down to the churchyard to talk to her children. She turned left at the bottom of the drive and headed into the village, raising her riding crop to acknowledge Beth Blunt as she passed, noting that the curtains were still drawn in Tom's cottage. Perhaps she should call in. Or perhaps he wouldn't welcome her presence and she should confine herself to offering to pay for the funeral and engineering some kind of longer-term support in a less obviously charitable way.

The dilemma still playing out in her head, she reached the

church. Swinging down from the saddle, she looped Kaiser's reins firmly around a conveniently overhanging branch and made her way through the lych gates and into the churchyard.

Her children lay, side by side, in three green graves near the church door. Henry had wanted them buried with his ancestors, closed in their own vault in the chilly crypt of St Mary's, shut away from sunlight until Kingdom Come, but Blanche had refused that honour on their behalf. All of them had loved the countryside and the outdoors, each had taken every chance to escape the schoolroom and roam free in the woods, and so all three would lie outside in the light where she would be able to creep up to them, day or night, to talk.

Death came upon you so suddenly. Her children had been merry souls, bubbling with life and fun and energy so that Guy seemed like a man three times his age by comparison, and at the end they'd disappeared like a line of candles snuffed out, one by one. On Monday there had been three laughing young people, on Sunday three newly dug graves.

'It's so unfair,' she said to them. 'I couldn't help you. I tried. I would have died for you, if I could. You know that.' In the end, all she'd been able to do was sit with them and hold their hands as they lost their fights, one after the other, in increasing order of age.

She bent down to place the flowers on their graves, yellow for Edward, pink for Flora and Annie. 'What shall I do about Guy?' she asked them. 'Lord knows I have to do something, because he won't. *The Times* personal column? Of course, that must be him. It certainly wouldn't have been your father.' And though she encouraged the servants to read the broadsheets and improve themselves, none of them would have dared take the liberty of tearing up *The Times*. 'But why? What is he hiding? And why can't he tell me?'

She stood staring down at the graves. They'd have got it out of him within the hour. Flora, in particular, would have kept on keeping on until he cracked. Oh, how she missed her younger daughter's whirlwind of positivity, her irresistible power. 'What would you have done, Florrie? Something improbable, I'll be bound. Something wicked.' But it would have worked.

She bent to tweak the flower into place as if by so doing she could hold on to the connection between them. As she straightened up, she heard a car engine coming through the village and stopping by the churchyard, and sighed. 'I expect that will be Kitty. It's my own fault for leaving Kaiser out there, I know.' But to bring him into the churchyard would have been both sacrilegious and inconvenient. 'There's no escaping her now. Though no doubt you three would have tried.'

The car door closed.

A year earlier, when Guy had first brought Kitty to the house under some pretext deliberately designed to prevent any suggestion of romance (showing her round the estate, from memory, because of an alleged interest in architecture or agriculture or nature, though Kitty had proved interested in none of those things) his younger siblings had behaved appallingly. They had constantly tried to undermine him and had teased Kitty in the most trying ways. It hadn't been malicious, just the high spirits of children testing the mettle of anyone who might be at risk of joining the family and Kitty, who had younger siblings of her own, had passed the test. Blanche smiled at the memory, even though the romance seemed to have stalled. 'I can tell you,' she said, lowering her voice, 'though I wouldn't tell anyone else. But I really am not sure about Kitty. Perfect on paper, I know, but she might not be the match for Guy. I thought she was.'

Their tête-à-tête was cut short by the woman herself crunching her way down the path. 'Blanche. Goodness, this is a terrible way of things, isn't it? But we can't allow ourselves to be carried away by events. Freddie always used to say that if we did that, we should hold ourselves culpable for any injustice.'

'Has there been an injustice, Kitty?' asked Blanche, turning away from her lost children and hoping her tone was icily polite.

'Not yet, of course, unless you count that poor woman's death, which is a terrible injustice in its own right. Not that there's anything we can do to help her now, of course, other than defend her reputation whenever we can. I'm determined to put what energy I have into helping the police clear the innocent and trap the guilty.'

'How very admirable. I'm all for justice. The way the inspector spoke to me, I was sure he was determined to charge me with murder and if not, he'd find something else. Being rich, I expect.'

'It's just his manner. You can't take a soft line with criminals.'

'I am not a criminal.'

'Well, of course. But he doesn't know that.'

'What a goddam mess we're all in,' Blanche said, disregarding the line of debate. 'I wish my father was still alive. He'd have known how to handle these people. God knows there were enough criminals in New York creeping round trying to pin something illegal on him and no-one got away with it. He knew how to keep his nose clean. I could do with some trade secrets right now to help me handle our troublesome Scot.'

'I like to give Mr Livingstone the benefit of the doubt. I don't think he's trying to pin this on anyone.' Kitty turned her wedding ring over on her finger as if she was drawing inspiration from it. 'I've been thinking about what Mercy Appleby said the other day in the yard.'

Blanche knew she'd been offhand to Mercy on the subject of Tom, and she'd lain awake for some time that night feeling guilty about it — another sign of growing strain, since guilt never normally troubled her. 'Is that so?'

'I've been thinking a lot about what she said over the last couple of days. And at the inquest. There is something so strikingly romantic about Tom Freeman, isn't there?'

In Blanche's imagination, Flora giggled and Annie, more restrained, hid a smile behind her hand. 'Well, I guess we all have different ideas of romance.'

'Not in that way.' Kitty looked offended. 'But something noble. Heroic. A man who volunteered to serve his country and came home maimed. Now he loses his wife and stands accused. It's exactly like those Nat Gould novels Guy reads.'

'He isn't accused of anything yet. Though I grant you, he's the obvious suspect.' Blanche had been thinking about it too, running through the possibilities and finding nothing to quiet her soul. 'Isn't that always the case? The straying wife, the angry husband, the handsome lover. Or did I read too many penny dreadfuls when I was a girl?' She gave Kitty a hard, almost unfriendly stare. Tom had cut a sorry figure at the inquest, trying to maintain his dignity and seeming only cowed and furtive. Quite how Kitty managed to reinvent him as a hero was both pathetic and concerning, because if she saw him that way, others might, too. And if Tom was discounted, who remained? Frank Holland, who had no motive and who, Guy said, had charmed his way out of many a foxhole, and Guy himself.

'He swears he didn't do it. I believe him. And it would be wrong, wouldn't it, so wrong, to see him hang just because he was the most likely person? Whereas, in fact, what happened is obvious to me.'

'Oh, really?'

'It's quite clear. I've asked Guy about it.'

'And was Guy forthcoming?' Blanche knew she was being rude, but Kitty was trying her patience. Interrupting her chat with her children had been unwitting and therefore excusable, but this was Kitty displaying the crassest insensitivity.

'Oh, you know he never is. And, of course, I read the report of the inquest. To me, it's quite obvious. It must have been a complete stranger.'

Blanche shook her head. No matter how much she wanted, even she couldn't bring herself to believe so convenient a solution.

'Tell me,' Kitty went on, 'what did you make of Inspector

Livingstone?'

Blanche replayed her various encounters with him. A man with a chip on his shoulder. A coward trying to earn respect among heroes of whom he was deeply envious. A weakling who'd found himself in a position of power. 'I'm afraid I didn't find him sympathetic.'

'Last night, I was thinking about what Freddie might have said about it. And I talked to my uncle about him. He's a very perceptive man. Uncle Arthur, I mean. Not the policeman.'

Mention of Arthur Henderson, heartbreakingly handsome, dangerously smooth and untouchable at heart, always put Blanche on the back foot. She said nothing.

'Uncle Arthur doesn't rate him at all. He thinks he's a very narrow-minded man. He says he's the sort who needs to prove himself. He could have fought in the war, of course. If he'd wanted to, but he's short of moral fibre. And that puts him on the defensive.'

'My view exactly.'

'Looking for a complete stranger is much harder, you see, like a needle in a haycock. It's so much easier for him if it's someone local. And that's where miscarriages of justice can occur. Because if you don't want to leave a crime unsolved, you're tempted to push for the most likely candidate. In Scotland, of course, there's the not proven verdict, so you can bring a man to trial and he might not be cleared yet won't hang. But here you're guilty or not guilty. If it's wrong, he dies. And death is so final.'

Death was unquestionably final, and it was also close. Its eternal shadows were beside them in the rows of tumbled and mossy gravestones and sparkled in the rings on a young widow's finger. 'I'm afraid I don't understand what you're saying.'

'The police have come up very early against a brick wall, haven't they? It's entirely reasonable that people might just drop out of sight at a party. If it was just one of them, then there might be some circumstantial evidence, enough to get a jury to convict.

But Tom Freeman was only one of several people who might have done it. I'm worried Livingstone doesn't want an unsolved crime and he'll push for an arrest to solve it.'

'Then he should call in Scotland Yard. Isn't that what they do?'

'Not if they can get an arrest reasonably quickly.'

'If we'd never had that party,' Blanche remarked bitterly, 'if I'd never listened to Henry and his fancy ideas about a homecoming, as if it could undo all the damage that war did to us, this might not have happened.' She turned back towards the graves. 'I don't want you to think I don't believe in justice,' she said, lowering her voice as if she was worried the inspector would be creeping about behind the yew trees and the gravestones, determined to exhume every one of their secrets. 'Of course we'll do everything we can to support Tom if they decide he must be charged. I hope it doesn't come to that, but if it does, I will hire him, the best barristers to plead his case. They'll destroy the young woman's reputation in the process, I imagine, but it can't be helped. It gets him away from the hangman and surely she would never have wanted an innocent man to hang.' And if they couldn't convict Tom, then they might move on, reluctant to expend any more effort on another failed case when the strongest contender was cleared. Maybe.

'I think Mercy was right to approach you. The system isn't going to help him. I've spoken to Uncle Arthur, but he pooh-poohs everything I have to say. I'll always be just his fluffy little niece.' She pursed her lips in irritation. 'We have to speak up for him so he won't be charged.'

'Do you not understand?' Kitty was smart enough, but sometimes she missed the blindingly obvious in a way her lawyer husband surely never would have done. 'If it was a complete stranger, he'll be long gone and they'll never find him. And if, as you say,' and as Blanche herself believed, 'he's determined to catch someone, then if we protest too much about Tom, he'll look for someone else.' Then, no doubt, Kitty would turn her crusade in favour of the next hero — Frank, possibly — until there was only one suspect left.

'I'm sure there's no evidence against anyone else. I truly believe that if he can't charge Tom, he won't charge anyone.'

Kitty had no legal training and Blanche herself had only limited knowledge of the law. Secrets and lies — and a stubborn silence — might not be evidence, but they could damage a man in court, to his death. 'Would you see Guy hang?'

'Dear Blanche. Of course they won't hang him. He's innocent and the establishment will protect him. But what interest would it have in protecting a disabled ex-soldier, even if he's perfectly innocent himself? He is the perfect scapegoat. It's not fair and I won't have it.'

She was like a spoiled child, thought Blanche. She looked down at the triptych of graves again. That was what they hadn't liked about Kitty — her ill-thought out dogmatism. 'When Inspector Livingstone interviewed Guy, he was rude and arrogant to him, even more so than he was to me. He as good as threatened him.' She bent down and snapped the full head off a dandelion. Milky sap leaked onto her fingers. 'He accused him of some kind of relationship with Jane. Of course, that's preposterous. Jane made sheep's eyes at him from time to time. She did to every man who came near. Guy never responded to it. He's far too honourable and far too sensible. But he isn't helping himself to establish his innocence. If you love Guy—'

'Of course I'm fond of him,' she interrupted. 'But I loved Freddie…'

Blanche bit back a sharper retort. 'If you even begin to care for Guy, you're going to have to understand how it is. I have lost three children. Guy is all I have left. Nothing is going to take him from me as long as I have the power to protect him. Do you understand?'

Kitty stared back at her, blue eyes cold. She, too, was a woman who mourned. 'Even justice?'

'Guy didn't do it. Justice is no threat to him. But injustice is.' And vanity and pride and silence, all of them conspiring to take away her son. As she frowned at the thought, the wind gave a playful puff and sent the dandelion seeds floating away from her fingers like the souls of her children on the way to Heaven.

CHAPTER SIXTEEN

BLANCHE

After supper, the nagging threat of Dora Hardacre calling again spurred Blanche to action. In the maelstrom of activity that had followed Frank's homecoming and Jane's death, she had entirely forgotten her sister's upcoming visit. Dora was a formidable spinster though not, Blanche suspected, a blushing virgin. She played an active part administering and increasing her share of their inheritance, and the rest of her life, which she divided evenly between her New York apartment, her country estate in Virginia and occasional travel, revolved around charitable work among the poor, both deserving and otherwise. Like Blanche, Dora keenly felt the element of chance which had led them to escape poverty and, being the older by five years, had a clearer memory of what it was not to be rich.

This year, with the Great War firmly in the past, Dora was planning to spend her summer travelling in Europe. She had no desire to squander any of her time visiting her brother-in-law's dry old family in the country and so Blanche had arranged to go out and spend the latter part of August with her in Paris. At least that gave her something to look forward to, Blanche thought, as she rose from the dinner table and left Henry and Guy to their port. 'I'm going to telephone Dora.'

'God,' said Henry, showing some liveliness at last, 'tell me you're not going to let her come up here and organise us all. The last thing we need is the old girl helping us through our traumas.'

Reminding herself of him, waiting alone in the private room at the George for the verdict while she and Guy had walked in the churchyard, Blanche surprised both herself and him by going over to her husband of thirty years and dropping a quick peck upon his papery old cheek. She was nearly fifty and Henry a decade older. Sixty shouldn't be old, but he didn't wear it well. 'I don't think she's heading this way. The ship docked in Southampton early this morning. She's spending tonight in London and takes the boat train to Paris in the morning.'

'Give her my love,' said Guy, heading to the sideboard for the port.

She should stay and join them, so they could enjoy wholesome family conversation instead of clinging to the outdated convention of the gentlemen retiring to the library for port after dinner, but it was she who'd encouraged the continuation of that tradition when she and Henry had begun to drift apart. Her own company, withdrawing to her private parlour for a glass of sherry and a book, had been preferable to his and still was, but she would nevertheless make an effort. 'I shall join you for coffee when I've spoken to her.'

'That would be jolly.' Guy cast a smile in her direction, but it was strained.

Dora was patronising, but she was sometimes a source of good advice, if you could bear the one in order to get the other. 'I shall see you then.'

There was a telephone in her drawing room, which she tended to use as a study as much for peace as anything else. Really, Blanche thought in some surprise, she had become a very solitary creature. When Livingstone had finished interviewing the staff in her domain, she'd had Millie clear away every trace of him as if by so doing she could undo the damage that had come upon them, but when she opened the desk to take out the itinerary and contact numbers which Dora had sent she couldn't rid herself of the memory of that policeman, sitting in her drawing room, trying to impose his will upon her.

Dora, inevitably, was staying at the Ritz. The call took a while to go through. First the operator, then the reception desk at the hotel, then the time it took them to track down Dora (who, they assured her, was in the dining room) and after that there would be an additional delay while her sister finished either whatever course she was eating or the conversation she was having, knowing Blanche would be picking up the bill for the call.

By the time Dora answered, Millie had been in and delivered a small glass of dry sherry. Sipping it as she gazed out over the long lawns towards the fells, Blanche was almost taken by surprise. 'Dora. How lovely to hear from you.'

'Well, Blanche.' Dora's voice was thick with an accent, one she deliberately chose to cling to. For a moment Blanche felt lost, submerged by a wave of homesickness for a place she'd been desperate to get away from. She must remember how America had constrained her and then she would laugh to see where she'd ended up, a country baronet's wife. At least there was London, a few hours away. 'I hear there're some goings-on in your neck of the woods.'

The sherry was dry and delicious on her tongue. 'Goodness, I don't know how you find out these things. You haven't even been off the ship for a day.'

'I'm dining with the Wallaces tonight, and they read the newspapers. And she loves nothing more than a gossip. It would have been good to have heard it from you first.'

'But you were on the ship.' Blanche sipped the sherry again, wondering exactly who had harvested the news story and who had embroidered it. It wasn't important enough for *The Times*, though it would certainly have been in the local papers, at which she couldn't bear to look. 'It isn't really anything to do with us. It was just one of our maids and it just happened on the estate.'

'Then why hasn't whoever did it been caught?'

'I expect it was her husband, obviously.' Who else could it

have been? That didn't stop Blanche feeling sorry for Tom — far from it, because everyone knew Jane had pushed his patience to the limits in full public view — but (she repeated it to herself, pushing her fears away) who else could it have been?

The line crackled. In the background, she heard Dora ordering a Gin Rickey. She sipped again at her sherry.

'Well, sweetie,' Dora said, reappearing on the end of the line at full clarity and full volume, 'let's have a think. Because that's why you're calling, isn't it? Let's just think about why they haven't arrested the husband.'

'I'm returning your call from this morning. But I imagine they haven't arrested him because they don't have enough evidence.'

'Or because they think it might be someone else.'

Blanche sipped the sherry once more. Her sister always had this impact on her, always made her see things with a brilliant and brutal clarity. Now she was ready to admit her fears and Dora would help her deal with them. 'I might as well tell you. That's what I'm afraid of.' Afraid barely did justice to the cold dread gathering in her heart and spilling over into her veins. 'I worry they might think it was Guy.'

A pause while Blanche listened to the buzz from the Ritz as the waiter delivered Dora's cocktail. Then her sister came back on the line yet again. 'Then he'll have to tell them it wasn't him.'

'That's the problem. He says he doesn't remember where he was; swears he didn't do it and, of course, I believe him. But he won't say what he was doing. He's so like Father. So stubborn. I don't think he realises how serious this is.'

'Sweetie, Guy may put on that slow upper-class act, but we all know he's no fool. There's no way he doesn't realise.'

The light was fading, and the windows were still open for a teasing breeze to sneak in. That must be what sent a chill through Blanche, not hearing Dora put her deepest fears into words in a way she'd been afraid to do. She was silent.

'Could he have done it?' persisted Dora. 'Let's look at it the way the police do. Is it possible?'

Of course, it was possible. Before the war, it would have been unthinkable that Guy would have hurt anyone. He'd even found it distasteful to go shooting, and he'd been quick enough to wriggle out of it at every opportunity, much to the amusement of his three younger siblings, all of them more bloodthirsty than he. That was before the world had changed and a generation of young men had changed with it. 'Yes. But I don't believe it.'

'Did the man love his wife?'

Curse Dora, sounding just like their father again, bringing a practical approach to a problem from which Blanche knew she'd never be able to disengage herself sufficiently to see it rationally. 'He adored her.'

'Then we have a problem. Because if she had a lover—'

'The villagers say she had a lot of lovers.'

'Then surely the husband would have killed the lover, not his wife. So it must have been the lover.'

'It was not Guy.'

'No? He's a man. Was she beautiful? Was there drink involved? Was she available?'

Oh God. All of these things made sense. 'Yes, but—'

'Then do you really think he wouldn't have found a woman like that sexually attractive?'

'But Guy wouldn't… he's never been a womaniser. And anyway, he's courting.' As if you could possibly describe the casual acquaintance between Guy and Kitty as courtship.

At the other end of the line, Dora produced a most unladylike snort. 'And when did that stop a man, Blanche, my dear? For someone with our background, you seem to have forgotten a lot about the way of the world. Courting? Who is he courting? Is she suitable?'

'Yes, most suitable.' For all Blanche's personal irritations with Kitty, she ticked every possible box — bright, good-looking, stimulating company, well-bred and with an annual income large enough to protect her from accusations of gold-digging.

'And this young woman who died is obviously not suitable. Does he love this woman he's courting?'

'Of course he does,' said Blanche, too quickly.

'That's a no, then. Now, I'm not saying Guy did it, but I think we need to look at it from the inspector's point of view. If Guy can't come up with an explanation of where he was, then I would say that doesn't look great for him, does it?'

'But why? I doubt if he ever even noticed Jane. She'd been in service with us for years. She was here when you came last year.'

'Oh! The pretty blonde with the wiggle and those big blue eyes? Well, if an old spinster like me noticed her, you can bet your estate every man that's ever met her has done, too. So maybe there was something going on with Guy, and maybe — just maybe, Blanche — she threatened to tell you, or Henry, or her husband.'

Now that the possibility of Guy being the killer had been presented to her in such bald terms, Blanche was better able to rationalise it away. Dora barely knew Guy and had never engaged in a conversation with Jane, so her conclusion was clearly ridiculous, yet at the same time, she was right. That was the way Gordon Livingstone, who had also never met Jane and would judge Guy on a single evasive interview and his own dislike of the gentry, would see things and so that was the problem she had to confront. It wasn't Guy's innocence she needed to think about — that was never in doubt — but how she must deal with his wrongly perceived guilt.

'Of course, he didn't do it,' she said, looking out to the shadows, 'but yes. You're quite right. Other people might not understand that.'

'Good. Now you're in the right place to do something about it.' In the background there were more voices, muffled as if Dora had turned away from the receiver or covered it with her hand, and then she came back. 'That's someone wanting to talk to me. We can speak later.'

'I'll see you in Paris in August,' said Blanche, her spirit rejuvenated.

'Bring Guy.'

'Oh, I will.'

With a click, the line went dead. Blanche replaced the receiver on its cradle, then got up, opened the French windows and stepped out onto the patio. In the east, the line of the Pennines was tinged pink in the afterglow as the sun blazed to its rest on the western horizon. The chance meeting with Kitty in the churchyard that morning had disturbed her, made her aware of the threat, but she came back fighting as she always did, and out of the dread that had temporarily overcome her, she had found strength and purpose. Three of her four children had been snatched from her, but no-one would take away the other.

What if he did it, as her sister had suggested? What if he had killed Jane and deserved to die?

She would not countenance the thought.

Nevertheless, she didn't quite have the courage to join her husband and son for coffee.

* * *

She found Henry in the library the next morning. An earlier riser than he, she'd waited a long time for him to come to breakfast. Eventually she'd given up and gone down to the stables, before taking the two Labradors for a brisk walk along the bridleway past the formal garden. That was about as much as she could manage. No matter how stout her heart, it would be a long time before she would set foot in her sanctuary again, and she thought she'd never do so after twilight. Ghosts were not ghosts, she told herself, remembering how the villagers clung to old ideas, how they would open their windows when someone died to let the spirit free, but they were memories. They were the regrets they had and the things they hadn't done.

Her lips twisted in an ironic smile. Jane would be haunting someone, no doubt.

When she came back, leaving her boots in the boot room for someone else to clean, she headed back into the house with the dogs padding behind her. The library door was open, and she stepped through it while the dogs, well-trained, flopped to the floor outside. 'Henry.'

He laid down the copy of *The Times* he'd been reading, but he said nothing.

Such passivity infuriated her. Even when he'd been young and she'd loved him, he'd never been dynamic, but disillusion had stripped him of the little energy he'd had, whereas she'd become more active, more emotional with age. You didn't submit to life. You fought it, and the tougher it was on you, the stronger you had to be. While she raged and resisted, he only listened, not in a positive way, but so that everything washed over him. He let the vicar talk to him about politics, allowed Guy to instruct him on what was happening among his friends in London, sat still while George rambled on at drunken length about the goings on at the estate. 'Henry, darling.' The darling was a sop to her conscience. She didn't love him any longer, but she had done once. 'I'm afraid we have a problem with Guy.'

He sat up at that. 'I know.'

So his silence did not, after all, mark a lack of interest or intelligence, but merely a reluctance to engage. 'He persists in being vague about where he was when Jane died. He says he doesn't really remember. He even claims he was avoiding Kitty.' That chimed uncomfortably with Dora's narrative about suitability versus love. 'I don't like Inspector Livingstone and I don't think he likes us. He has a socialist streak about him and I fear his idealism.'

'I know that, too.' He laid down the newspaper on the arm of the chair and got up, stepping away from her. Consciously or unconsciously, he crossed the room so that the long oak table was a physical barrier between them.

'If he could choose which of the men in this village was to be hanged for murder,' she went on, 'I think he would love it to be one of us.' She couldn't bring herself to say Guy's name in the context of the noose. 'He won't look at this impartially.'

'I know.' He turned his back to reinforce the distance between them even further until all she had to judge him by was the defeated sag of his shoulders. 'But what can we do? If he comes to trial, they'll surely clear him.'

'And what if the jury are socialists, too?' She touched her forehead as if checking for a fever, conscious that she was as fervent as Henry was pallid, that she was getting too carried away and that fear bred a lack of judgement. Relentlessly, she pulled herself back to how her father would have tackled it. 'Of course that's most unlikely and of course if it comes to trial, Guy is clearly innocent and the evidence can't convict him. We'll get the best defence counsel.'

'But what can we do?' he repeated.

Oh, Henry, she fumed, he's your son. Fight for him! 'You must speak to Arthur Henderson.' That was what Kitty had hinted at. The establishment will protect him, she'd said, and it would. By God it would, and she would make sure of it if Henry didn't.

There was a long pause. He kept his back to her. 'You know him better than I do, Blanche. You talk to him. He'll refuse you nothing. Remember?'

A dozen years before, charming and debonair Arthur Henderson had tempted Blanche away on a summer picnic and their relationship had swiftly descended into folly, but she hadn't been the first to stray from the marriage bed. 'There were half a dozen young women who'd refuse you nothing before I met Arthur.' It was a fight they often had, like a child's argument couched in adult restraint. You started it. I only did it because you did it. You were unfaithful first. The reason she and Henry barely spoke wasn't the affairs they'd had. Everybody had those. It was because he'd held her relationship with Arthur up against her as an example of her immorality while seeing his indiscretions as the natural order of things. She'd never bargained for marriage to a hypocrite.

'I will not beg a favour from my wife's lover.'

'Even for your son?' She and Arthur hadn't been intimate for years, not since Henry had threatened to tell the world about the affair and she'd backed away from it for the sake of decency. She still regretted it. There had to have been another way out. But there was no point in revisiting the old argument, no point in a shouting match. 'Let's not forget what this is about. This is about Guy.'

'Then ask Kitty. As she keeps telling us, she's Henderson's niece.'

Despite the seriousness of the situation, Blanche couldn't subdue a smile. 'You really think Kitty will help? That lawyer husband of hers filled her head with all sorts of fluff about social justice. She's as bad as Livingstone. She only thinks about saving Tom. Not that she knows anything about it, but she's convinced herself the system is against him and so she has to stand up for him. And no thought for the collateral damage.'

'Someone needs to tell her it's her damned young man who might go to the gallows.'

'I don't think she believes it can happen. One of us has to stand up for him. And you're his father.'

'And you're the one who knows the Chief Constable,' he mocked her, still unable to look her in the face.

She turned on her heel and stalked out of the library without another word. Henry was always too ready to leave any action to her, so she hadn't expected any other outcome, though the bitterness of his response had taken her by surprise. Her lips narrowed as she entered her drawing room and caught a glimpse of herself in the glass, the very image of that portrait of her father that hung above the fireplace in the ballroom.

So be it. If Henry wouldn't step in to save Guy, she would

manage without him. She picked up the phone, dialled and waited for the connection. 'Arthur. It's been a while since we spoke.' They played their way through the formalities, inquiries about each other's health, their spouses, their children, until he gave her the opening she was after. 'It was Guy I wanted to speak to you about.'

'Is that right?'

She never trusted the way the telephone stripped you of your ability to read people's faces. When she was with Arthur, she could read every twitch in his expressive face, interpret every lifted eyebrow, every quirk of his lips. Without that, she had to concentrate hard on picking up every inflection in his voice. 'Yes.'

'He's seeing my niece, I believe. Kitty.'

'Such a charming girl.' Blanche was wearing her pearl choker today, and she ran her forefinger around underneath the beads. 'She's been so helpful to us in our recent troubles.'

'I've been hearing about them. The chap Livingstone's onto it, isn't he?'

'Yes. To be honest, Arthur, I find him a little bit...antagonistic.'

It was the right word. He chuckled. 'He takes no nonsense from anyone, that man. I'll say that to his credit.'

The implication, if she judged it correctly, was that there was little else to be said for the inspector. 'He's very thorough. Diligent.' Where was the right word again? 'Efficient.'

Again, she'd aimed correctly. 'I'm not sure I'd call it efficient. He stands too much on his pride and won't accept outside help. That's never good. And the man makes mistakes.'

Makes mistakes. She took a deep breath. 'He seems to think that Guy may have had something to do with it.'

A pause, then a laugh. 'Good God. Guy? That young man is a credit to you and to his country. Livingstone doesn't like a man who fought and survived, you know. It undermines his moral authority.'

'I will be honest with you, Arthur. I know I can trust you.' She was playing him like a saloon bar tart, as her grandmother would have said, and her grandmother, though she had been fiercely moral and teetotal, nevertheless, knew a lot about these things. 'Some of the things he said put Guy's back up and he wouldn't answer some of his questions. I don't want the man being too smart, do you?'

'The easiest thing is always to tell the truth.'

'It's the war, Arthur. Julia will tell you how it marks these men, even those who are physically unscathed.' Arthur would know a bit about that and be sympathetic. He'd found himself a desk job in London among the brass hats and Julia, his rather younger wife, was active among charities for disabled soldiers. 'The night Jane died was difficult for a lot of the men for a lot of reasons. It's hard for them to admit their weaknesses.' She thought of Teddy Appleby and borrowed some of his tribulations. 'Sometimes Guy becomes withdrawn. He craves only silence.' She fluttered her hand dramatically, as if he could see it. 'Of course, he's far too proud to admit to suffering from what they call shell shock. He soldiers on and his spirit is as indomitable as his courage. But you can see why he might want to take time for himself.'

She stopped and waited for his reply. 'There's bravery,' he said, 'and then there's pride. The second should never trump the first.'

'He's both honourable and humble. And it must be devastating for Kitty, too,' she said, remembering another string on which she could play. 'After all she's been through.'

'Yes, a fine girl. Deserves a second shot at happiness after that lawyer fellow she married. Charming man, of course, but he did give her ideas. Someone like Guy would be much better for her. Much more stable.'

'I hope you didn't mind me calling,' said Blanche, as smoothly as possible, knowing the battle was won.

'Not at all. I'll speak to the fellow, make sure he sees it straight. There's no way someone like your Guy…well, it's laughable.'

'Thank you so much, Arthur.'

'No guarantees, though,' he warned her. 'There are never any of those.'

Arthur was always a cautious Jack, thought Blanche with amusement as she laid down the receiver, but her smile darkened as his last words lingered. No guarantees. The battle might be won, or at least as far as it could be, as far as Arthur was concerned, but he wasn't the only player. If only the inspector weren't so antagonistic. If only she didn't sense a socialist inside that badly chosen suit, barely concealed in his lack of deference. And Guy, loftily refusing to reveal the whole truth.

Was it the war? Had his survival somehow made Guy think he was invincible? Her trip to the graveyard had reminded her that no-one, in the end, would be spared, but if she could somehow ally her father's cold and ruthless business brain with Flora's endless creativity, she might save him from his own folly.

Still musing, she strayed from the parlour into the hallway. At the bottom of the staircase, a copy of *The Times* lay on the table. She picked it up and opened it, fighting its carefully ironed pages. There were no clues in this edition's personal column, nothing but a dismal list of births, marriages and deaths and appeals to St Jude.

You have to take risks, her father had always said, though he had been talking about business, not life or death. You have to do the unthinkable. She could take no chances.

What more do I dare to do, Blanche asked herself, to be sure I save my son? And the answer came to her in a moment of inspiration.

'Millie,' she called to the girl, who was hurrying from hall to boot room. 'I shall take tea in the parlour. And run down to Oak Tree House and ask Mr Smart to come and see me.'

CHAPTER SEVENTEEN

MERCY

There was a light mist lying over the south of Edinburgh and the purple slopes of the Pentlands rose above them as Mercy alighted from the tram at the stop for Craiglockhart Hospital, tucking her arm through Frank's as they approached the gateway. 'This way.'

Frank's insistence on visiting his old comrade was an error of judgment and couldn't end well. Sacrificing her precious time alone with Teddy was the only way Mercy could see to mitigate the consequences — there would be damage done, and damage only she could try to repair. 'Frank. For the last time. I don't think you should do this. There's a teashop over there. Just go in and wait until I come back.'

'And for the last time,' he said, cheerful and unmoved, 'I'm not going to let my oldest mate think I don't care about him just because he had a bad time. If the worst comes to the worst, what? He gets two visits in a week from his beautiful wife. The lad'll think it's Christmas.'

Even in his misjudgement, he managed to charm her. Despite herself, she smiled as they approached the front door of the hospital. 'I don't know if he'll appreciate it. Honestly, Frank. You don't know what he's like.'

'Honestly, Mercy,' he teased her in response. 'I do.'

'Not even your mother visits any more.' His mother had, to all intents and purposes, adopted Teddy as a boy and was as close to him as anyone, apart from herself. 'I don't bring Sally.

It upsets him too much. Imagine how bad it is, not to want to see your mother or your daughter.'

'Yes, both of 'em weeping and wailing, no doubt,' he said light-heartedly. 'I promise you I won't weep or wail.'

Hetty Holland had done more for Teddy than anyone could have asked, far more than his birth mother who hadn't seen him since she'd high-tailed it out of Waterbeck with an agricultural salesman barely six months after her husband died. She was surely entitled to weep and wail. Teddy hadn't even been crawling when his father had left, and if his mother had visited, she would have been a stranger to him. When Hetty had come to the hospital, she hadn't coped well with the state of her surrogate son. On Sally's only visit, its gloomy atmosphere had inevitably set her off, first whining, then crying with the piercing wail of the uncomprehending infant, setting Mercy's teeth on edge and driving Teddy to tears. 'If you keep calm, we might have a chance. But I wouldn't count on it.'

'Is he always all right with you?'

Another smile, this time at the thought of Teddy. Life had turned sour and their plans had foundered, but she still loved him. 'He doesn't usually say much. I sit with him and hold his hand and tell him the local news. That's enough. It keeps him in touch with the outside world and he knows we haven't forgotten him.' Or so she thought.

'We'll have plenty to tell him this time.' Frank's cheery good humour seemed to sour as they entered the building, and no wonder. Despite the wide corridors, sweeping views of the city, with its castle, and light that poured in, it was a desolate place, with only a few white-uniformed nurses scurrying around. It specialised in treating shell shock, but now there were no new casualties and many of the men had moved on. Not cured — they could never be cured — but sufficiently healed to creep out of this haven and face the world again.

She gave their names, and they waited while the duty nurse

disappeared down a corridor. A moment later she was back, striding along with a severe expression and a whirl of starched white apron. 'I'll take you along now.'

As they followed her, Mercy was conscious of Frank's nervousness. Her own skin prickled with anticipation, unease she always felt when she visited. With Teddy, you never knew what you were going to find, which of his demons — fear, anger, or silence — you would have to face.

'It's your wife, Teddy,' the nurse said brightly, as she opened a door off the corridor. 'And look. Someone else has come to see you. It's good to get another visitor, eh, especially when you're so far from home? I'll bring you some tea.'

Knowing how her husband valued the familiar, Mercy preceded Frank into the room where Teddy sat crouched in a saggy armchair, a feral shape in the dimness that existed within the curtained sanctuary. Teddy feared the darkness and hated the daylight, preferring to inhabit a half-light, bright enough to see by yet not enough to make him feel exposed.

When the door opened, he'd shrunk back a little as if he felt overwhelmed, and the nurse was quick to spot it and withdraw, even as instinct drew Mercy towards him. 'Dr Martin would like a word with you, Mrs Appleby, when you've finished.'

'Thank you. Of course.' A few visits back, the doctor had warned her they were concerned the gloom on which he insisted would damage his eyesight. How could he bear it, buried even further in a world of darkness when he'd been brought up in the open air? But she knew the answer. The world outside was a fearful place and he could bear it because the alternative was worse.

A wave of tenderness broke over her. 'Look, my lover,' she said as the door closed. 'Frank's back. And he's come all the way up from Waterbeck to see you? Isn't that grand?'

There was silence, a stillness as he rose to his feet and peered across the room. With Frank beside her, so tall and fit, shoulders back and head up so that he seemed to fill the room, it was impossible not to be aware of how much time and trauma had shrunk Teddy, how completely his farmhand's muscles had wasted away.

'Frank!' he said, and his voice quivered with some undefinable emotion, part joy, part fear, part fury. Recognition shivered in the shadows on his face and vanished in a long wail of fear and despair. 'Frank. No! No!'

'Marra.' Frank moved forward. 'It's only me. I couldn't let you—'

'Get out!' As the howl died to a whimper, Teddy flung himself from the chair and rolled behind it, kneeling his head to the floor, hands tight across his head. 'No! Go away... I can't bear it.'

'Teddy, stay calm.' Mercy ran the last few steps across the room and dropped to her knees beside him, flinging an arm around his shoulders as if that could protect him. Against her, he quivered like a child in the grip of a nightmare. 'It's all right, lambkin. He's going. He's going.' And then, in a steelier tone, she addressed Frank, who had remained fixed to the spot. 'I warned you, Frank. You'd better go.'

'I'll wait for you,' he said, in a half-whisper, and retreated. As the door banged closed behind him, Teddy flinched once. 'It's all right, my dearest. It's all right. He's gone. Come. Come and have a seat.'

By the time the nurse came back with tea and shortbread, she'd managed to coax him to the chair. 'Is everything all right, Mrs Appleby?' the nurse asked as she set the tray down. 'I heard shouting and your husband's friend—'

'Yes. It's my fault. I should have warned him Frank was coming.' Mercy pulled up another chair and sat next to him, arm around his shoulder, as close as she could. He leaned in to rest his head against her, and he smelt of sweat and fear. 'I'm sorry, sweetheart,' she whispered to him, as if he were Sally. 'But he wanted to come and see you. Because you're friends.'

'No-one wants to see me,' he said in an undertone as the nurse clicked the door closed a second time. His hand closed hard on her wrist. 'You might as well put me out on a midden for the crows to peck at. I'm not a man any more. I'm nowt but a ghost.'

She bit her lip. It wasn't that people didn't want to. It was that it was a long way to come to discover he wouldn't see them; these days she was the only one left with the strength to face his pain. When the letter had come to say he was in hospital and wouldn't be going back to fight, she'd been overjoyed at so good a piece of news among the carnage. None of them had known, then, what lay in front of them, how healing would escape him. 'You're no ghost. I love you. I'll always come and see you.'

'And I'll always be here,' he said plaintively.

For a moment or two she sat and held his hand in silence while memories flitted around the room like shadows — memories of their wedding day, of the day he'd marched away with his neighbours, of the day the war had ended, and the day Flora Waterbeck had become the first of them all to die. At that, the darkness became too much for her and she got up to twitch the curtains open, not so much as to cause him distress but enough to keep the devil of what-might-have-been at bay.

'Shall I tell you the news?' she said, when his breathing had settled.

He nodded, taking the cup of tea she handed to him and lifting it to his lips, but his eyes jumped constantly to the door as she filled him in on the doings of Waterbeck. As always, she told him about Sally, first — trivia about the new words she'd learned, the things she'd done, the buttercup, the cat in the garden. 'And I brought you some humbugs.' She opened her handbag and took out the paper bag of sweets she'd purchased on the day after Jane had died. 'And baccy.' He smoked less these days, lacking even the energy for that. She laid the red tin of Prince Albert tobacco on the table beside him. Another memory. She'd always sent it in the parcels for the trenches, alongside the toffees, the socks and the hand-stitched handkerchiefs.

'What's the matter?' he asked, as she hesitated.

He'd always been able to read her mind. Even in the half-dark, he picked up on the sober thought that skipped across her memory and must have been obvious on her face. 'Oh, nothing.'

'You were going to tell me about the party. When you came last time, you said there was one. Frank's party.' He put his head on one side and looked quizzically. 'How did that go?' It was his nerves that had gone, not his memory or, the doctors said, any element of his physical functionality other than that which had wasted away through inactivity. Sometimes Mercy wondered if there was a part of him — a part that only they had shared — that had died, too.

'It didn't go well, to be honest.' Jane's murder had made the Cumberland and Westmorland Herald, the report on the inquest taking up much of the front page, and the reporter had managed to hint very heavily that the guilty party was none other than Mr Tom Freeman, as if women who were killed were routinely done away with by their husbands or their lovers. Many of them, of course, were. Isolated in Edinburgh, Teddy couldn't have seen it, but if the case came to trial, there was every chance it would reach the national press or someone would tell him about it. With some reluctance, she chose to ease him in to bad news. 'It wasn't a good evening, as it turned out.'

'Why not?' His tone was tinged with apprehension. 'Bit of a barney, was there?'

She took his hand again and talked him through the party, smoothing away the brutality with as few and as neutral words as possible. As she spoke, she sensed him withdraw into himself, and the little positivity that had bloomed as she sat with him ebbed away. What she told him would only reinforce his fear of the outside world, confirm that the four walls of this tiny room were his only place of safety.

'Was there blood?' he asked, and winced as he spoke.

'No.'

She saw him relax, flicking his eyes closed, breathing. 'At least that was something.' He took a humbug and unfolded the paper wrapping before popping it into his mouth, chewing it slowly and solemnly. 'Everybody's going to die, Mercy. All of us. If I'd stayed there any longer I'd have died, too, Disappeared. Gone in a flash. There was a lad standing next to me one day, and it happened to him. Gone. Taken up to heaven or down to hell. I don't know which. And now Jane. God help her. A sweet little lass.'

Jane's was just one face but the outrage of her death, remote though it had been with all violence over by the time anyone had found her, had kept Mercy awake at night and would continue to do so. She had only the tiniest inkling of what it might be like for Teddy, permanently trapped in a memory in which the bodies of friend and foe shattered around him. 'Yes. But I don't think it was too dreadful.' Which was a lie, because she could barely imagine Jane's terror, but it was all she had to offer as a pathetic attempt to take the sting out of mortality, a sacrifice of respect for the dead to make life more bearable for the living.

'So, who did it?'

'No-one knows. There was an inquest but they can't say who it was.' She talked him through it – the coroner's questions, Livingstone's cryptic nods at key places – keeping it as bland and factual as she could.

'So he thinks it's Tom or Frank or Guy.' He laughed at that, but with contempt rather than humour. 'There's only one of them I can think as did it.'

'I can't imagine any of them doing it.'

His Adam's apple twitched nervously. 'I saw Tom break a man's neck with his bare hands once.'

Teddy had seen many things Mercy didn't want to know about and maybe this wasn't the worst of them. When he suffered, she suffered. 'Don't think about it.'

'I don't want to think about it. Any of it. But I keep seeing it.' He put his hands up to his face, covering his eyes as if that could block out the horror. 'It was one night. God knows what was happening. And suddenly there was this German bugger in the trench. Must have got lost. Panicked, shouting, scared. It was dark but there was a moon and then I saw his gun. This far away.' His hands hovered barely a foot apart. 'Tom saved my life. He grabbed him and the gun went off. Missed me. And then he broke his neck. Like a chicken in the yard. One twist. Oh God. But it was quick.'

'Don't think about it. Please don't.' She fought his memories as he did, not just because it gave a glimpse into a world no-one should have to endure, but because it left her with another image, she couldn't bear — that of Tom with his hands round a man's throat.

'I remember when he lost his arm.' Teddy closed his eyes. 'He just looked surprised. And his arm. His arm was gone at the elbow and the blood—'

'Hush.' She took his hand again, stroking the back of it. 'It's all right, my love. Everything will be all right.'

'So, did he kill Jane the same way?' he asked, with a sort of diffidence, as if nothing in Waterbeck mattered to him any longer.

'Tom loved Jane. Everybody knows that.'

'Aye, but you can love someone too much. He's a jealous man. And she didn't keep herself to herself in that kind of way, if you know what I mean.'

She did know. Their eyes met. 'Mercy,' he said out of the blue. 'If I come out of here and I'm not... I couldn't... or...' A long pause. 'If I don't come out.'

'You will come out. You'll come home. I'll look after you, and Sal will as she gets older, and everything will be fine.' Then the village would have real reason for a party and celebration.

'It wasn't fine the last time.'

She drew in a sharp breath. 'The last time they let you come home before you were ready. That's all. Next time, we'll be better prepared. We'll all know what to do.'

'But if I never… would you ever think about another man?'

'No. Teddy, darling. Of course not. It's always been you. It's always been only you.' Instinctively, she reached out a hand to him and, equally instinctively, he twitched away. In his eyes, she saw a new dimension to his fear — the risk that she would be snatched away.

'Couldn't hardly blame you,' he said in a lurch to self-indulgence, 'with me locked up here like a criminal when all I done was my duty. A beautiful young girl like you.' He gave her a shy lover's smile. 'It would kill me if you ever went with someone else, like Jane did.'

She had a sudden glimpse of a nightmare future if he never came home, of herself living in enforced abstinence out in a world filled with lovers and springtime, women with large families like the one she and Teddy had planned to have, older couples snatching yearning glances across a room or sharing a swift touch of hands. She would be alone with Sally, interdependent and always praying that her daughter would live as Blanche's daughters had not, an even sadder case than the millions of lonely women left unloved and unlovable by the war. 'You know I never would. My vows mean something to me.'

'I should have died. Then you'd have been free of me. I'm a burden to everyone. Especially to you. You should never have married me.'

Even as she denied it, Mercy thought fleetingly of Frank, how her life could have been if she'd chosen differently, but she was double-locked to the man to whom she was married, by obligation as well as by love. She was no blushing innocent and, even if she had been, the years that had passed in Waterbeck with its cohort of convalescent soldiers and its covey of nurses, many of them away from home for the first time with an exceptional degree of freedom, would have taught her otherwise. There was always temptation when husbands were separated from their wives, and among the soldiers who came to Waterbeck Hall to convalesce even the ones with rings on their finger and the photographs of wives and children in their breast pockets had sometimes succumbed, but she herself had never entertained a thought of infidelity.

'Of course I should have married you. I'm glad I did.' How could she not be, when Sally was the outcome? All she regretted was the way it had turned out.

'And did you really stay true?'

'Of course I did.' But the judgement in his tone irritated her, just as the villagers' judgement on Jane for the sin of wanting affection had done. 'And what about you? Away all that time? Were you never tempted?'

'What? Are you suggesting I'd go with a tart? Is that all you think of me, Mercy Appleby?' He clenched his fists in real fury.

'No!' She drew back in alarm, swaying away from him because for a second she really believed he might raise his hand to her. 'You asked me the same question, near enough. You asked me if I'd ever been tempted. And I never have.' She leaned forward to touch his rigid hand. 'You for me always, Teddy. Always.'

But the spell was broken, if it had ever existed, and the moment of companionship had gone. She chattered on for a while about Sally and the village and the various minutiae that didn't involve the death of Jane Freeman, but she sensed he was as relieved as she when the time came for her to leave.

'I'm sorry. I was angry. I'm not myself. You know that.' He got up but accompanied her only as far as the door, as if he were scared of some horror that lay out in the corridor.

Anger, frustration, the same limitations that made Sally crash her tiny fists in fury and shed a waterfall of tears over some trivial thing she couldn't understand. 'It's all right, my dearest. I understand.'

'I believe you do,' he said, holding back from the nightmare of the internal corridor through which she'd arrived but unable to resist darting a quick look down it for any signs of danger.

'I'm no use to you,' he said, hovering as the moment of parting came. 'No use to anyone. It would have been better for us all if I'd died.' And as she stepped forward to kiss him, he pulled away from her and closed the door.

Thank God another visit was over. She knew he'd lie awake that night, thinking about how everything had gone so wrong, and she would do the same, tormented by pity for him and by the guilt that came with fears and frustrations for herself. He could live for fifty years and not be healed, but he was hers and she was his, and their love would last forever.

CHAPTER EIGHTEEN

FRANK

Chastened by his experience, Frank had nonetheless regrouped, as he always did, and taken refuge in a narrow, shabby tea room wedged in a soot-blackened tenement. He'd a weakness for a chunk of home-made shortbread and this place had a neat round of it, so there was a silver lining to every cloud, though he could see Mercy's problems would need more than tea and sympathy to sort them out. Settling in the window where he could see both the tram stop and the road down from the hospital so Mercy couldn't slip past, he whiled away the time in intermittent chat with the old soldier at the next table, working their tortuous way through campaign after campaign until they came across a mutual acquaintance or two.

When the man had gone, he sat with his tea, his shortbread and his Woodbine, mulling over the waste of a day. He'd been warned about Teddy, and even if he hadn't been, he was more than familiar with the state of a man who couldn't cope with the seemingly endless pounding of the guns, but it troubled him all the same. It was worse than he'd thought. He'd been so sure he'd be able to bring Teddy some kind of comfort and it hurt him to see the man he'd grown up idolising and fought side by side with thrown into raw fear just by his presence.

That wasn't the man Mercy saw. He could tell. To her, her husband would always be a hero.

He was considering Teddy's state of health one last time,

with no great optimism, when Mercy appeared in the street, walking at pace and staring straight ahead of her. When he waved to her she didn't see him, forcing him to abandon his table with the tea half drunk and the shortbread half eaten and rush out onto the street to intercept her at the tram stop. Her face was paler than it had been even on the night Jane died, her jaw clenched, fighting both tears and anger. Something had happened in his absence. Please God, he hadn't caused Teddy any more distress. Frank was a stranger to guilt, but in that moment it tapped him on the shoulder. He hurried out to her. 'Come on, Mercy, lass. You look as if you could handle a cuppa.'

'I had tea at the hospital.' She allowed him to lead her into the teashop, settle her at the table and snap his fingers to the waitress for a fresh pot.

'This'll be much better.'

'Oh, no doubt of that.'

He waited for a second to see if she would tell him what was wrong and then, when she didn't, he cut straight to the point. 'Was he angry with you because I came?'

'Not with me, and not about you. He's angry about life, I think, about the way it's treated him.' She sat back while the young woman who'd been serving bustled in.

'Tell me he didn't hurt you?' Inside, he cursed the war more roundly than ever for its cunning assault on what they had once been. It would take a lot to drive a man as gentle as Teddy to violence to anyone, let alone towards the wife he adored, but he'd seen more timid men do worse.

She hesitated. 'No, he didn't. In a funny was it was good to see him talk about something. Most of the time he sits there and says nothing.'

And then there would be an unidentifiable something that set him off, something that reminded him of his impotence and set him lashing out in fear. Frank had seen it before, too often. 'I should have listened to you when you told me not to come.'

'How could you possibly have known?'

But he had known. That was why he'd been so wrong to persist. 'I'm one of his bad memories. I live in his nightmares. But I thought he'd have got over it.'

Mercy clenched her fingers on the table as if in prayer. 'Oh, Frank! I had such hopes! No matter what they told me, I believed he'd get better. I've been waiting for the day he comes home just like you did, and we'd all be together. Sally would have her dad back to stay and we could walk and talk and laugh.'

She reached onto her pocket for a hanky. On instinct, Frank stretched out a hand to touch hers, but he pulled it back. He couldn't. Not while she was grieving for her loss. 'What did they say?'

'He'll never come home.' She sniffed. 'The doctor spoke to me when I was leaving.' Her shoulders slumped in defeat. 'They think it's time for him to be discharged.'

'Surely that's good news?'

She lifted the elegant china tea cup, her little finger elevated just as it was in his impossible fantasies in which they took tea in the drawing room at Waterbeck Hall and its more aristocratic cousins, Greystoke or Lowther Castles or Hutton-in-the-Forest. 'He came home once before. I think I told you.'

'You mentioned it.'

'It was terrible. We were all so excited about having him back, but he was scared and nervous. Jumpy at any sound. On the very first night back, something must have startled him. A window banging, maybe, or just a nightmare. I woke up in the night and he was shouting and screaming and attacking me.' She looked down at her plate. 'When Mam and Dad came through to see what the matter was, he ran away and hid in the woods. It took us three days to find him. They won't put him through that again, and nor should they.'

'Then why are they discharging him?'

'They can't do any more for him. He'll never recover, they say. So, they're sending him to the asylum at Garlands.'

Her tears began to fall and Frank could only sit and watch while she cried for her husband, and surely also for herself. If he was a crying man, he'd be joining in. Not just because of the hurt he could see in front of him, not just because that glimpse inside the hospital had been grim enough and now Teddy would be consigned to the Victorian surroundings of the Cumberland and Westmorland Asylum at Carlisle, but for himself. Even if he'd been able to persuade Mercy, at some stage in the future, to give up on Teddy and take a chance on him, there was no way out for her. The law didn't allow divorce for a spouse who was certified insane. Whatever they or anyone else thought of it, Mercy and Teddy were truly locked together until death.

He shook his head as Mercy's tears slowed. Their lives had decades to run. There was plenty of time to find a solution. 'There's a bright side. At least in Carlisle, it'll be easier to go and visit. Maybe more people will.'

'I doubt it. It's not that hard to come and see him, even here.'

And no-one but Blanche and his mam had done so. Frank shook his head over that. It was as if Teddy was the village's shame. 'I'll visit again.'

'You can see how it unsettled him.'

'Maybe one day he'll be glad to see me. I'm still his mate.' Teddy was his closest friend and Mercy was the woman he loved, and he would give up on neither of them. Eventually, he'd work out a plan that allowed him to help them both, and himself, to a resolution.

'Oh, Frank. You're too good.' She squeezed his hand.

Not nearly good enough, he thought, wryly. 'Don't worry about anything. I'll look after you, I swear it. I'm not Teddy, but I'm me. I'm his friend and yours. If there's ever owt I can do for you, you just ask. I'll do it if I can.'

The sad smile she produced melted his heart. 'I'll take you up on it.'

'If they don't hang me,' he said, without thinking. He'd spent four years working out ways to cheat death and would do so again, if he could. But the idea of death had become a constant companion, as it was for so many others. Unlike them, he didn't fear it.

'Why would they?' she asked, suddenly alert. 'You didn't—?'

'No. But I don't know that I believe in justice any more. And because if it wasn't one of my mates who did it, it'll be another one. I've lost enough good friends.' He sat back, scratching about for a change of subject. 'Look, I've had a thought. My ma's cat has kittens and they're just about ready to leave the mother. Why don't you bring Sally down to the cottage and let her pick one?'

'That would be lovely. I'll do that. Thank you.'

The clock on the wall ticked towards three o'clock, almost time to move to the station. Frank settled the bill, giving his most charming smile to the woman behind the counter and following up with an over-generous tip, and then offered Mercy his arm as they left.

CHAPTER NINETEEN

MERCY

'Eh, Tuppence. What's the chat with Teddy?'

For once, George Smart seemed completely sober. Maybe it was the shock of Jane's death, and having to put on a good front for the constant stream of villagers and strangers who had come up to the estate office on some pretext, but were really only there to see if they could get a glimpse of where the young woman had died. It might have been the sobering experience of the inquest, where he'd had to take his turn like everyone else on the stand to listen to the stark facts about the night of Jane's death, answering questions about where he was and conceding that he couldn't be certain where he'd been or who he might have spoken to. Or it was a necessity, given his wife had unloaded Sal into his care while she baked bread and Mercy was away visiting Teddy. Whatever the reason, Mercy could tell from the twitching of his hands and the red rims of his eyes that he was itching for the tiniest sip of whisky to see him through until he could realistically have a larger one. He'd jumped when she came in, thrusting the ledger away from him before he saw who it was, and recovered his residual good humour.

She and her mother and sister had regularly discussed what they could do about his drinking and eventually given up. All three of them understood the reasons and none of them grudged him dream-free sleep, but nor could they square the circle and mitigate the damage. When they found his stash of spirits, they hid them away, but he was getting cleverer at hiding them, and Sir Henry was always ready to undermine their good work with the offer of a swift dram in the library.

Her father, Mercy, had to remind herself in this climate of suspicion, was a kind man, a loving and a good man, a man who did everything possible to improve the lives of others. These days what he could do was limited, as though he'd expended his life's energy trudging through the mud in the beats of peace between the crescendos of the guns. She bent and scooped Sal up from where she'd been sitting under the enormous desk in the office, staring in fascination at her reflection, distorted in her grandfather's glossy black boots.

'There's no change.' When she'd had a cup of tea and could understand the implications of what the doctor had told her, she'd break it to them that Teddy would be moving closer to home.

'There's a bit of chat in the village about you going off for the day with young Frank,' he said with disapproval.

She bridled. 'Frank wanted to visit. I didn't think he should go on his own. That's all. If folk can't find something kind to say, they should stay quiet. I've heard little enough charity down there these past few days.'

He closed the ledger in front of him, and a puff of dust flew up in the air. When drunk, he had a devil-may-care attitude about him, but when sober he was furtive, as if he was all too aware of his own shortcomings. 'Aye, folk are always after carrion. What are they saying about poor Jane?'

'Nothing good. They're all blaming Tom but saying she brought in on herself.'

He stood up and shoved the ledger back into the shelf where it belonged, not quite far enough in so that it sat out from the others. 'Well, God help the lass. But maybe they're right—'

'Dad. She made eyes at some of the men. That's all.'

'That's not what a wife should do.'

'She didn't deserve to die for it. Tom says he didn't do it and

I believe him.'

'Then who else was it?'

It could have been anyone at the party, anyone in the village. 'I don't know, but we need to let the police find out.'

George rolled red-rimmed eyes. 'You think they will? That fellow Livingstone is only half as clever as he looks and a quarter as clever as he thinks he is.'

'I think he's very clever.' When she'd first discussed Livingstone with Blanche, it had been clear to Mercy that the inspector's approach to each of them had been different. Presumably he'd taken yet another tack with Frank, too, and Guy, and Tom. 'He knows how to talk to people.'

'Up to a point.' George tugged impatiently at his cuff, a gesture Mercy recognised as intended to disguise a shaking hand, a yearning for the rough comfort of drink. 'He knows how to get them to say what he wants them to say. It's better to try to get them to tell the truth. Wouldn't you say?'

'Maybe.' She wondered what line of questioning Livingstone had chosen for the other possible suspects. 'What was he like when he spoke to you?'

George turned his back on the ledger. The sun sparkled on an empty glass on the top of the bookcase as he turned but, Mercy assured herself as she shifted a little closer to check, it was because it had nothing in it rather than because it had been drained. 'He was all right.'

'And you were able to tell him…' Mercy stuttered to a halt. Delicacy forbade her to state the reason she knew he was safe — because he'd been dead drunk in the kitchen. 'Of course you were able to say you were…'

'Talking to Guy. Yes.'

That startled her. 'Guy? But I thought—'

'Thought what?' George had lost some of his paternal authority when Mercy had married and a lot more of it when he'd come back from the war and found he couldn't function in his old job without her, but he seemed to remember he was still the head of the household. This time, he challenged her.

'You were in the kitchen all evening.'

'Is that what you told your policeman from Keswick?'

'He never asked me. Only about where I was and who I saw in the garden.' George turned away from her and Sally and looked at the glass with the yearning of a lover. 'I remembered. We were talking down by the stables. I went out for some fresh air. I was a bit woozy, but we talked about Frank coming back from the war and who we'd get to replace him now. He's got a new job.'

'You talked about that at a party?'

'We talked about all sorts of things. Someone's been stealing chickens from the home farm. We need to get your policeman on to that, maybe.'

Stealing chickens? She stared at him, knowing he was lying but lacking the courage to challenge him. If George had, indeed, been talking to Guy, both of them had been near to where Jane had died. She wrinkled her brows in perplexity. She'd left George in the kitchen and he'd been so drunk he was incapable of moving. More: she'd moved his boots, and they'd still been where she left them when she and Frank had returned to the house late that night. It might be strictly possible that he'd sobered up enough to put on his boots, then go out, come back and take them off and replace them, but she didn't think so. She took a deep breath. 'Dad. That's not true.'

He put his shoulders back and huffed and puffed. His face, already scarlet from the long abuse of alcohol, reddened further. 'Mercy Smart. Don't you call me a liar.'

'I'm Mercy Appleby.' She put her hands on her hips, sensed she must look exactly like her mother, and took them off again. In this situation, Carrie would be shouting already. She must stay calm. 'I'm not under your authority. And you aren't telling me the truth.'

'You're living under my roof!'

'You weren't in the garden. You can't have been, because you were here all evening. I brought you here myself when you were making a scene in the ballroom and you were still here when I came back.'

'You're my daughter,' he said, his breath coming out in a long hiss. 'I won't have you speak to me like that!'

'You're lying. To me. To the police. Don't you understand?' She clenched her fingernails into the palms of her hands. 'If you lie to the police to protect Guy—'

'He's a decent man. I don't believe he killed Jane Freeman. Why would he? Tom's far too good for the likes of her. If it wasn't her husband, it was someone else who couldn't abide not being her only lover. And anyway, she's dead. Does someone else have to die too?'

Someone did. Rightly or wrongly, the law demanded it and it might not claim the villain. 'The police will think you're protecting Guy. And you are.'

'He didn't do it!' he shouted. 'You're protecting someone yourself. Now I understand. You don't want it to be Frank Holland. Is that it? Mrs High-And-Mighty Appleby, caring more about another man than you do about your own husband!' He leaned forward, clenching his hands on the back of the carved wooden chair behind which he was standing. For a sickening moment she saw the whiteness of his knuckles, saw a latent strength he no longer had cause to use. He could strangle a woman… if he hadn't been lying dead drunk in the kitchen.

'You should know better than to talk to me like that.' She fought for calm. 'For the love of God, listen to me. You lied. I know you did.' As Frank had admitted, he had done and claimed they all had. 'Oh, God, how will this end?'

'They'll never know unless you tell them.' He shoved the chair away from him with force, so that it rattled against the table. 'I'm done with this. I'm tired of being nagged and scolded by women who ought to show me some respect.' He stepped past her in a breath of stale alcohol. 'You decide where your loyalty lies, my girl. With your father and your husband, or with some worthless lad like Holland?'

'I won't have you questioning my behaviour.'

'I'll do as I want in my own house!'

He slammed the door. Sally, who had crept under the kneehole of the desk to hide, set up a tearless wail, piercing as a siren. Scooping her up, Mercy flung the door open. 'Dad! Where are you going?'

'Up to the Hall to see Sir Henry.' His voice echoed through the dust. 'Tell your mother I'll be late back.'

She waited a moment, resting her head on Sally's soft hair, holding the child close until the wailing had stopped and her own heart had stopped beating too fast, then lingering on in a precious moment of shared calm before she turned towards the door herself. 'Come on, Sal. Let's go and see if your granny can find you some bread and honey.' It was seven o'clock, way past Sally's bedtime, but she was too tired to care. It had been a long and trying day.

She turned back through the short corridor that connected the office to Oak Tree House. No doubt Sir Henry would invite her father to join the Waterbeck family for supper and then the two of them would disappear into the library for a glass of brandy or two — an escape from his wife for Sir Henry and from the whole of the world for her father.

Sally wasn't a talker, a solemn child who clung to human company and trailed around the kitchen at her grandmother's skirts when Mercy wasn't around. When Mercy put her down on the kitchen floor, she sat solemnly on the spot, staring. Carrie had been baking, something she normally did in the mornings, but her routine had gone to pieces in the days since Jane's death, and she was removing a tray of loaves from the oven. She looked pale.

'Tomorrow you can run a loaf down to the village for Tom,' she said, placing the tray on the table. 'I daresay he'll bawl you out for offering him charity, but we've all still got to eat and I've no doubt he's grieving so much for that feckless wife of his he'll not give food a thought.' She pulled herself up. 'Not that we should speak ill of the dead, God knows. But there's a part of me thinks the silly girl had no-one to blame but herself, getting on with a man who wasn't her husband.'

'We don't know she did.' But it was a half-hearted protest. From what he'd told her in the woods, even if she'd wanted to, there was no way Jane could have had satisfaction from her Tom.

'We don't know for sure, but if it was Tom she was with, why would he want to kill her? And if it was someone else with his wife and he got that mad, he couldn't help but hurt her. I don't know that I think he deserves to swing for it. Here, Sal.' She shrugged the problem aside. 'Have some bread and honey and then we'll get you off up to bed. I'll take you up and tell you a story. How about that? There's cold meat in the larder for supper, Mercy. The Lord knows when your father will be back.' She sliced a slab of the end of yesterday's loaf and spread a piece with a veneer of butter and honey before handing it down to Sally on the floor. 'I shouldn't, but we all deserve a treat.'

'Dad's gone through to see Sir Henry.' With an effort, Mercy beamed down on Sally's sticky face and changed the subject. 'Frank says they've got kittens. He thought Sally might like one.'

'That's a good idea. I did say to your father we should replace old Tabby, but we never did anything about it. That poor little mite has no company since we lost Flora and Annie, and it'll help keep down the mice.' The Waterbeck girls had adored Sally. Everyone did. Jane, with no children of her own, had sometimes strayed from her duties if she saw the little girl playing in the garden, bringing her a biscuit or a plate of something sweet and delicate left over from lunch.

'Mam,' said Mercy, watching as Sally smeared a sticky finger on the rug. 'What's going on?'

'I don't know, love.' Carrie made a big deal of turning one of the loaves over and tapping it to see that it was ready. 'I wish I did.' A pause. 'I'm worried about your dad,' she burst out.

Weren't they all? 'I know.'

'More than usual, I mean. Not just the drinking. But everything else. God knows why he's taken Jane's death so hard...' She placed up a distracted hand to her face.

'Any death hurts him now,' said Mercy, with some sympathy. 'That's what it is.'

'Maybe there's something in that. I heard him going on to Sir Henry just the other day about your brothers, about what he must have done to be punished by losing his sons so young. Just babes they were, and so long ago. He thinks he's the only man to suffer loss. But they were my sons too, and I never even saw them laid in their graves.'

'It was the war that changed him.'

'Aye, but something else has happened. There's something about him since Jane died.' She wiped floury hands on her pinny, took it off and dropped it on the table. Her eyes were dark-rimmed after a sleepless night. 'I worry so. He drinks so much he doesn't know what he's doing and I can't help but scold, though my heart bleeds for him. Tell me honestly. Do you think he killed the lass?'

'No.' With the clear memory of George slumped in the armchair, mind and body heavy with drink, Mercy could reply without hesitation. His lies might be misplaced, but they weren't to protect himself. 'I don't know who did it, but I know it wasn't him.'

'I expect Tom will get the blame for it. That's what they're saying down in the village. But you'd think they'd know better.' Carrie managed a laugh. 'He's a rough man at the best of times, always was, but his heart's in the right place. I said that to the Inspector. They may call him Radgie Tom, I said to him, but it wasn't always that way. It was the war that made him angry.'

She shook her head. 'The war that policeman knows nothing about. We could all do with a little more compassion. It made men mad in different ways. Oh, sorry, love.'

There was a short silence while Sally continued her sticky and satisfying duel with the bread and honey, and her mother and grandmother thought about Teddy. 'It's okay. But Teddy's not mad. He just needs healing.'

'He's the sweetest, loveliest man in the world. But even he—'

'Even he what?' Annoyed, Mercy slapped the plates down on the worktop. 'He wasn't here. Are you saying he came out of hospital and all the way down here without anyone seeing him and strangled Jane?'

'No, love. That isn't what I meant at all. Just that you can't escape the truth of it. We sent a dozen young men to the war and they could slaughter or a pig or a chicken, or put a dog out of its misery. But now they've all come back and every one of them will have killed a man. If they didn't, they were taught how to do it. And if that doesn't scare you, it should. A village full of men who can kill you.'

A village? There were millions of men in England with blood on their hands. Perhaps remorse and regret was something of what underpinned Teddy's crisis of nerves. 'But not him.'

'No. At least we know he's innocent,' Carrie said mournfully.

'I'll get my supper later.' Spending time with her mother would mean talking about Teddy and that, in its turn, would lead to thinking about him. It was bad enough knowing she'd have to retreat to the double bed in the back bedroom and lie awake missing him, knowing that he would be curled up in the cold room in the Edinburgh hospital missing her. There was no company, no friendship, no solace for him. 'I'll take Sal up to bed.'

'I'll do it if you like,' said Carrie, but she stepped back from the debate as though she understood. 'I thought we could have a quiet bite together when you come down. Just the two of us.'

Was a drunken husband harder to bear than a frail, absent

one? Their eyes met for a second, mother and daughter in shared sympathy. 'A bit later, if that's okay. I want to pop into the office when Sal's in bed. I just need to check over the week's accounts. I'm behind with everything this week. And you know how it is.' The longer she left George's work unchecked, the longer it took to unpick and correct it.

'Sometimes I think there would be less for you to do if he did nothing.' Carrie shrugged and turned away.

Sally's bedtime routine, at least, offered her some of the comfort of routine. Washing, hair brushing, story time and a quick prayer against ghosties and ghoulies and long-leggedy beasties did the job and Sally, exhausted by a day being shuttled between her grandparents, was almost asleep before the ritual was finished, too far sunk in dreamland to add the amen. Mercy stood and looked at her for a moment, settled in the bed in the corner of the room they shared. For all her misfortune, she had many blessings and Sally, a soft-haired, pink-cheeked rosebud of a child nestled into the pillow, was the biggest of them.

Blanche must once have thought that about Annie and Edward and Flora. She leaned down one last time and straightened the pink bedspread, pulling it up to Sally's chin. From the bedside table, Teddy's photograph smiled down on them like a benevolent spirit. As she always did, Mercy blew him a kiss as she left the room.

Craving silence and isolation, she managed to avoid her mother as she headed back through the house to the office. For all his faults, her father was neat and tidy, in outward appearances at least, despite the muddle that too often overtook his mind. Knowing that everything had a place and putting it there was something he could handle, even in the confusion of drink.

She crossed to the shelf containing the most recent of the account books and took it out, setting it down on the desk and sitting down in George's heavy rosewood chair to open it. Her father's Waterman fountain pen lay uncapped on the desk, hastily abandoned, but when she opened the ledger, there were no recent entries.

Mercy tapped her finger on the book. In these days of uncertainty, the tiniest thing warranted attention, everything a potential slip which could hang a guilty man or save an innocent one. She reached for the blotting pad and turned it over. Yes, he'd been writing a letter, though the smudges on the blotting paper weren't clear enough to suggest what it was about.

Deep in thought, she closed the book and as she did so, a ragged edge to the pages caught her eye. So that explained the convulsive twitch with which her father had closed the ledger when she'd interrupted him earlier. Maybe it also explained his sudden fury. She tweaked out the sheet of paper — a scribbled note.

Dear Guy, I will place the notice on trembling a little, she turned the ledger upside down, holding it by its spine, and shook it. A folded paper fluttered out from it and onto the desk.

It was a quarter page torn from *The Times* and she knew immediately that it must be the one that had gone missing on the day of Jane's death. She scanned the Court Circular. Their Majesties had been at Sandringham, receiving decorated members of the armed forces. Was this significant?

Her father had no interest in royalty that she knew of, and Guy no connections with them. What else was on the page? She turned it over. There was a list of a dozen different personal announcements, which she read without recognition.

The engagement is announced between the Hon Freya Grafton and Sir Barnabas Wilson of Cornwall… Thank you, St Jude, for the restoration of what I thought was lost… Lady seeking a companion for travels to the Levant, reply Box no 4259… Come into the Garden Maud… Forgive me my dear heart, for what I failed to do. One day I will come to you. Contact me via box 2136…

She laid the paper down. How could the lives of strangers

matter to Guy and to her father? But matter they must, because why else would Guy want this piece of paper kept, why else would her father shuffle it away before she saw it?

Her duty was clear; she should hand it over to Inspector Livingstone and leave it to him to shake the puzzle like a tangled coil of rope until the knots loosened enough for him to pick it apart, but if she did that, what would be the cost? Whatever he said, her father had not been wandering the grounds of Waterbeck Hall: he'd been sound asleep in the kitchen as she and Frank had seen him.

'You're protecting Guy,' she said to his shadow. 'That's what you're doing.' But why? What possible benefit could there be to him to compromise what remained of his good name for someone else?

If she'd known Guy better, she might have asked him outright, but he'd been the oldest of the four Waterbeck children, more burdened by the responsibility of his inheritance and more distant because of it. By the time Sir Henry and Lady Blanche had moved with their family into the estate house and given up the main Hall to wounded soldiers, Guy was already in uniform, severe and remote while his siblings fell into an easy and comfortable relationship with their employees and accepted them as friends. For a moment she sat and stared out across the courtyard, almost expecting to see the inspector driving along in his black car with a posse of policeman and jangling handcuffs, but the Hall lay somnolent in the evening sunshine that had followed an afternoon's rain.

Guy was a mystery. It was obvious that he'd changed, that he'd lost faith — not just in God, though as she sat behind him in the Waterbeck pews at the church she could tell by the way he rolled his eyes during the readings and barely allowed the communion chalice to touch his lips that he had no time for fables and frippery. Guy had lost faith in everything.

Jane had taken a shine to him, from early on, as a matter of course. It was the blatant play she'd made for him on his last leave that had tested even Carrie Smart's charity too far. Guy's relationship with Kitty was strangely remote, too, even though Blanche seemed desperate for an engagement and Kitty herself was eminently suitable. It wasn't inconceivable he might have taken advantage of Jane that evening at the party and — who knew — before, but that was as far as she could go without incredulity getting in the way. To go further — to kill Jane her to protect himself from discovery, or from a fear of blackmail and the end of the marriage Blanche was so carefully plotting — was beyond belief.

If Flora had still been alive, she'd have handed the problem over to her. There had been eight years between them, but they'd been as close as sisters and the strong-willed, capricious teenager would have teased or hounded the answer out of her brother in the space of an afternoon. In the cool office, Flora's absence troubled her more than she'd thought. She folded the cutting back in quarters and replaced it in the pages of the ledger.

CHAPTER TWENTY

MERCY

'And how is Teddy?'

Blanche was in the garden, sitting on the swing the gardeners had constructed below the mighty horizontal branch of an old oak at the far end of the stretch of mown grass that rolled down the long slope to the shrubbery. She was wearing a white dress and straw hat with a pink silk rose at the brim, pushing the swing lazily backward and forwards with one foot, like a child. From a distance she looked for all the world like one of her lost daughters, until Mercy got close enough to see the sadness in her face, the wrinkles beneath the immaculate makeup and the silver threading her dark hair.

Blanche seemed unusually melancholy, she thought. 'There's no change. But he's moving closer to home.' Briefly, she ran once more through the update she'd had from the doctor, how Teddy would no longer be a military patient but a civil one.

'Certified,' said Blanche, whose melancholy didn't take the edge off her trenchancy. 'Oh, dear. I'm so sorry. We'll do everything we can for him.' She pushed the swing backwards and forwards, showing no sign of impatience. 'Was there something else?'

When there were no guests the Waterbecks ate Sunday lunch late, not until after two o'clock, and Mercy had timed her arrival carefully for the dead hour in which the servants prepared the meal and Guy and Sir Henry contented themselves, in separate rooms, with the newspapers, knowing she could catch Blanche alone. 'Yes.' She'd been holding the cutting from *The Times* in her fingers and Blanche's sidelong look indicated she must have seen it. 'I found this.' She held it out.

A breeze riffled the cutting as Blanche put a foot down to stop the swing and reached out a hand for it. 'This is what the inspector was talking about, I take it?'

'I think so.'

'It looks innocent enough to me. Where was it?'

Over the war and the couple of years that had succeeded it, Blanche and Mercy had grown close. Since Jane's death, that friendship had cooled like a late frost. 'My father had it. It was hidden in one of the ledgers.'

'Hidden? Are you sure? Maybe he put it there by accident.' Blanche folded the paper, affecting a lack of interest, but her fingers twitched at it. 'I wish I could bring myself to go back in my garden. But it will be a while yet before I can.'

The paper had been on Mercy's mind and on her conscience all night, and it had taken her all her courage to bring the matter to Blanche, concluding she was the one who could best be trusted for advice. Now her friend and mentor was deflecting her interest, undermining the significance of her discovery. 'I thought you should know. My father has been placing notices in *The Times* on Guy's behalf. I'm sure of it.'

Why? How do you know? Which notice? All the expected questions flashed across Blanche's expression, but she asked none of them. 'Whatever the explanation, I'm sure it's entirely innocent.' She turned her head to peer, gravely, at a robin that had skipped along the branch and jumped down to the ground between them.

There were, it seemed to Mercy, degrees of innocence, just as there were degrees of guilt. This deception might be innocent in itself, but not if it protected the guilty. The first stirrings of doubt troubled her. She'd been so sure Blanche would listen to her and she'd never expected the blank glance that implied at best disinterest and at worst hostility. She ploughed on. 'There's something else. Dad is lying about where he was on Monday night.'

'Is that right?'

'Yes. He says he was with Guy, but he wasn't. He was in the house all evening. I took him there myself early on and left him in the chair.' She took a deep breath. 'You saw me.'

The paper crunched in Blanche's fingers as she curled her hands once more around the rope and pushed the swing into a gentle arc. 'I saw you leave the ballroom, but I couldn't swear to anything more. And I imagine you've told the inspector your version already. We should leave it at that. I don't think we should interfere in the case. It's a criminal act in itself.'

'Yes, but if Dad—'

'The last thing anyone would want is for George to go to court for lying. I'm sure he knows that. So maybe he genuinely remembered where he was.'

The swing swung. Blanche smiled dreamily, lowering her eyes to avoid Mercy's gaze. In that moment Mercy saw something — a shiver of guilt on Blanche's face, a glance towards the sitting room where Guy was a shadow at the window. 'It was you!'

'I beg your pardon?' said Blanche, in a voice that would freeze flame.

'It was, wasn't it? You asked Dad to lie.'

'I remember you asked me to intervene to protect Tom,' said Blanche over-sweetly, 'and I think I told you then it would be inappropriate. Yet now you suggest I have decided to intervene in a criminal case. Extraordinary.'

And no denial. Those first fears were confirmed, and Blanche would act in her own interests. Why had Mercy ever thought otherwise? 'I asked you to make sure Tom got all the help he needed.'

'We remember differently.' Blanche curled a manicured hand around the rope on which the swing was suspended. 'Shall we talk about something else? What about Teddy? When does he move to Carlisle? Perhaps you could tell whoever is in charge at the asylum to get in touch with me. I know very little about these places, except for that poor woman from the village who went there about fifteen years ago. We paid for her to be a private patient.' She lifted her head, a challenging look. 'It would be so much better for him than having to rely on charity.'

It would be charity, but of a different sort, and it would spare Teddy from the further suffering. Mercy knew nothing, first hand, but the Garlands asylum in Carlisle was reputed to be a place where you'd only find refuge if you'd been rescued from hell. 'And would that come at a price?'

'I don't know what you mean.' Blanche wouldn't look at her, but swung on serenely.

'It would be conditional, wouldn't it?' Never an angry woman, Mercy was increasingly resigned to her lot and the troubles life seemed determined to deal her but Blanche, who had offered her friendship, had managed at last to rouse her to fury. 'It will be conditional on me staying quiet, won't it? On not saying that Dad was lying? Won't it?'

'If you think your father was lying, you should take it up with Inspector Livingstone,' said Blanche, her voice suddenly hard, 'though naturally there will be consequences for him and for you. Of course, we couldn't continue to employ a convicted perjurer, even if he wasn't jailed. You must think about what you would do then.'

She'd ask Frank to help. The thought flashed across Mercy's mind, uncontrolled, before she dismissed it. 'We'd manage.' But she was wavering. No-one would employ George as the drunkard he was, let alone the criminal he might prove to be. How would she provide for Sally? And what would become of Teddy?

'Then you must trust your own conscience. And of course, you don't need to accept any charity from me.'

If she agreed, it would make her complicit, and what if it turned out that Guy had killed Jane after all? Or, worse, what if the wrong man was hanged? She had to fight her corner. 'All I'm interested in is justice for Jane.'

196

'As am I. I'm glad we agree. And therefore, we must act as if this conversation never happened.'

And yet, and yet. If you believed in justice, you had to uphold it. 'I won't exchange Teddy's well-being for someone else's lies! If the inspector asks me, I'll tell him what I know.'

'As of course you should.'

Somewhere in the distance, the pop of a shotgun indicated the gamekeeper was out after vermin, or a rabbit for the pot. The two women stared at one another. Blanche had chosen Guy above truth and justice, but Mercy wouldn't lie.

Nor, though, could she speak out if no-one asked. Other people's futures — her parents', Teddy's, Sally's — weren't hers to sacrifice. 'I'll get home,' she said tersely. 'Mam will have lunch ready.'

'If you change your mind,' said Blanche, with the expression of one who has won a distasteful victory, 'do tell the director of the asylum to get in touch with me.'

Mercy didn't answer. Fine folk are only your friends while it suits them. Teddy had observed on her friendships with the Waterbecks. Now, belatedly, she saw how right he'd been.

CHAPTER TWENTY-ONE

BLANCHE

When Mercy had gone, Blanche sat for a long while on the swing, holding the newspaper cutting crunched up in her hand. In the distance church bells rang out, though she didn't know from where — Penrith, perhaps, and a late morning service. She went to church out of obligation and since the death of her children, just when everyone in Waterbeck had thought it safe to thank the Lord for His mercy and their deliverance, she had increasingly found reasons to get out of attending. Today she hadn't roused herself for the short drive down to St Mary's, reluctant to engage with a God who clearly wasn't on her side.

She slipped down from the swing and walked with narrowed eyes towards the southern front of the Hall, its creamy limestone delicious in the summer sun. It would be a long time before she forgave the Lord His first cruel trick, and now He threatened her with another.

'Weren't three of my children enough?' she asked rhetorically. 'Are You determined to have Guy, too? Hasn't there been enough blood?'

She didn't want to have to fight against Fate. Trusting in the intervention of God would at least mean she didn't have to choose between friends and family, but like everyone else, the Almighty was proving unreliable. That left her with no alternative. She paused and scanned the tall windows of the house to see if there was any sign of Guy inside. He'd been avoiding her for the past few days, or so she suspected. On Friday he'd been out walking the estate, something he never enjoyed but which kept him out of her sight, and then he'd gone into Penrith to the Conservative Club and not come back until late. The next day he'd motored over to see Kitty and hadn't turned up again until after lunch, disappearing into town immediately afterwards.

Mercy's expression, first shock and then disgust, at Blanche's attempt to buy her silence, hurt, but not enough to change Blanche's mind. It didn't matter that Arthur Henderson had assured her of Guy's safety. As long as he refused to say where he was, he was at risk, and the notice in *The Times* hinted at something that might yet implicate or condemn him. Thank God she'd had the sense to strike that desperate deal with George.

Her mouth twisted in distaste. She was, at heart, a decent woman, and the deal had not been struck between equals. She'd forced it on him with the same threats she'd issued to Mercy, and though her father would doubtless have been proud of her, she couldn't be proud of herself.

A twitch of movement in the drawing room betrayed Guy's presence. She almost ran the last few yards to the house and in through the French windows, for fear he'd give her the slip once more. Disappointment at his mendacity fought in her heart with the love she felt for him. He had sworn he'd met no-one, or she thought he had (the form of words he'd used wasn't clear in her memory). Now she understood he hadn't been honest with her, or that he'd led her on. It was time to challenge her son again.

Her declaration to Kitty still stood and she would do whatever it took to save him, but she was pragmatic enough to remember another lesson learned from her father — that the more complete your knowledge, the better able you were to reach a practical solution to a problem. Guy would have secrets, like everyone else. People did, and — she'd learned this as her children grew to adulthood — sometimes when you thought you knew them all, they acquired new secrets along the way. She steeled herself. 'Guy, darling. Do you have a moment?'

She'd surprised him. He'd been absorbed in *The Sunday Times* and, at her approach, he started visibly, then folded the newspaper as quickly as he could and tossed it onto the table with the greatest show of not giving a damn.

'Mother.' He stood up and walked towards the picture windows, drawing on the pipe he used habitually to smoke, daring her to challenge him. Her heart twitched. Another piece of Guy's youth had gone. Somewhere in the army, he'd learned to hide not just what he was feeling, as she'd told the Chief Constable, but what he was doing and why.

'I just wanted a quick word with you before lunch.'

He breathed out a mouthful of smoke, thick and mature. She suppressed a sigh. It was as if he was ageing before her very eyes.

'Why don't we step outside?' he offered, laying a hand on the door of the French windows.

The distraction failed. Blanche picked up the newspaper in as casual a manner as Guy had discarded it and stood with it folded between her hands as if it held his secrets and she could absorb them through her fingertips. 'Yes, of course.'

His eyes shot from the newspaper to his mother, and they showed the first trace of apprehension. 'What is this, the Inquisition?'

'I want to talk to you seriously, Guy. Of course, I don't believe you're in any way involved in what happened to Jane, but I need you to be straight with me and I need you to be honest. Where were you at the time she died?'

He put his shoulders back a little and drew on the pipe and then — so suddenly that it almost made her laugh — he was his Hardacre grandfather again, measured, careful and immovable. 'I went into the grounds for a walk.' Suiting his action to his words, he opened the French windows and stepped out onto the terrace. Waterbeck Hall was gloriously set, with a view to the ridge of Helvellyn in the south, but that afternoon the fells were lost under a low-lying bank of cloud.

They strolled for a moment in silence, until they reached the true isolation of the middle of that rolling lawn, and Blanche looked back at the Hall that was her home and finally understood despair. Nothing was permanent. Then she pulled herself together. There was always a positive viewpoint, 'always a best if you can make it'. That was another of her grandmother's homespun phrases.

'Now, Guy. You must be honest with me. What's going on?' She tapped the folded newspaper in her hand in what she hoped was a manner that brooked no dissent. 'This morning Mercy brought me the cutting out of *The Times* on the day Jane died. She found it in her father's office, along with the beginning of a note to you that implied he was putting an announcement somewhere. Do I have to do the detecting here? You've been using George to put notices in the newspaper on your behalf. Why?'

He stared at her.

She fished in her pocket for the folded cutting. 'Come into the garden, Maud,' she read. 'Guy. This is not my first rodeo. Who had you arranged to meet in the garden?'

He put his hands in his pockets and said nothing.

'Clearly it can't have been Jane. She wouldn't read *The Times*, and it's a cumbersome way of arranging to meet her when you could have spoken directly to her. The same applies to any of the local women. And I recall you specifically didn't wish Kitty to be invited. So, who did you meet?'

'Nobody. I was entirely by myself.'

Blanche drew in a deep breath. 'Did you intend to meet someone?'

Another long thoughtful draw on the pipe, another moment of contemplation. 'Yes.'

'Then you must tell us who that person was and we can get

them to verify they were there.' She was pretty sure Arthur would be as good as his word and say what was required, but she wasn't nearly so sure of the inspector. Nor, indeed, did she trust Kitty's radical sense of social justice, let alone if it emerged that Guy was interested in another woman. 'I need the truth so we can establish your innocence.'

'Impossible.' There was no hesitation this time. He'd thought this through.

'Not impossible,' she wheedled. 'Difficult, perhaps. I can understand that. Tell me who she is. I'll talk to her. Discreetly, of course. Her name needn't come out.'

'No, Mother.' This was a new Guy, desperately ill at ease and yet steadfast. 'I've said all I have to say. It's a matter of honour.'

'Is she married? Is that it?'

'I've told you. I've nothing to say.' His lips were set in a narrow line. 'I wish you hadn't interfered. Yes, George was sending the notices to *The Times* so that they weren't linked with me. Yes, you are right in your suspicion that there is someone else. But I can't give an alternative version, at this juncture, can I, even if I wanted to?'

'Why not?'

'I spoke to George yesterday. He was delighted to tell me he could vouch for my whereabouts on the evening of the party.' He almost spat.

'All the better.' Blanche found her breath shortening in her chest.

'Really?' Regardless of the possibility of being overheard, he raised his voice. 'You made him lie for me. What happens if it comes to court? When he stands up and lies under oath and it comes to my turn in the witness box? I can't lie. I'm a man of honour. I chose to stay silent and take the consequences, but he's a good man and you've made him into a liar!'

Blanche was affronted. 'He isn't lying for me. He's lying for you.'

'I didn't ask him to. I didn't want him to.'

'Guy.' She strode right up to him, as close as she could, but he stepped back. That was a slap in the face. He didn't trust her. 'You're all that matters to me.' She'd sacrificed her friendship with Mercy for him, already bitterly regretting it but knowing she would do the same again. 'If you'd told me the truth, I wouldn't have needed to do it.'

'I told you the truth. I met no-one.'

So, Blanche guessed, from the bitterness in his eyes, the woman hadn't turned up. Perhaps she'd ended things. Perhaps there was a husband or a stern father or... oh God, she said to herself, now sounding like her mother. Does it never end? You could bend over backwards to do the best thing for your children and at the end of it they pursued their hearts' desires and someone — usually their mother — ended up picking them up and putting them back together again. 'Guy.'

He'd turned away from her, blinking towards the afternoon light. 'What?'

'If I had known about this,' she waved the cutting at him, 'I wouldn't have asked George to become involved.'

'Mother.' He smiled at her. 'Don't be an idiot. I didn't do it. I'm not at risk.'

She didn't answer immediately. It wasn't that she might alarm him, because how could she alarm someone who'd seen what he had seen? But she didn't want to reveal to him how all-consuming her love for him had become since the loss of his siblings. 'All I want is for you to be happy.'

He lifted a sceptical eyebrow. 'It seems to me all you want is for me not to hang.'

If he hanged, none of them would ever be happy again. 'Will Kitty make you happy?'

'Would it make you happy if I married her?' He smiled. 'I don't know. Maybe if we tried. Maybe if I didn't care about someone else. Maybe if she wasn't still so crazy about her husband.'

'It's natural to grieve.'

'She's deified the fellow. I met him a couple of times. A jolly pompous chap, blinding us all with his intellect. A bore who knew everything about everything. An Edinburgh lawyer who thought we're yokels who tie up our trousers with string. And yet you listen to Kitty. "Freddie said this" and "Freddie thought that" and "Freddie would have done the other".'

Blanche reflected on Kitty. 'She'll get over it.'

'Maybe she will. Maybe she won't. But can you really blame me for looking elsewhere?' And he smiled and leaned forward to kiss her cheek, a cloud of pipe smoke and hair oil, and walked away.

What have I done? Blanche asked herself, as she watched him go. What have I done to Guy and George, and to Mercy and to myself?

Only time would show how great the damage she might have done.

CHAPTER TWENTY-TWO

MERCY

'I was telling Uncle Arthur,' Kitty said, with a sigh of irritation, 'and in fact, I must have told him two or three times. The local police here have very limited capabilities. Of course, he's as bad, in his own way. He has this same ridiculous pride. Oh, we do things our Cumberland way. We're different. We don't need to bring in the Yard. Well, I told him that we do need to bring in the Yard, because that man Livingstone can't seem to make the leap of imagination he needs if he's to catch who did it. If we don't have people on the job who know what they're doing, he'll feel under pressure and then they'll catch the wrong man. And that would be terrible, wouldn't it?'

Mercy's head had been full of other things, quite apart from the George's situation and the breakdown of her friendship with Blanche. The work of the estate had to go on and her father's mind clearly wasn't on the urgent question of how many people they would need for the upcoming harvest. She closed the ledger she'd been pretending to read. For the previous five minutes she'd allowed Kitty to ramble on, but it was difficult to resist a direct question and anyway, the idea of hanging the wrong man was more than terrible. What if it were Frank who fell foul of Blanche's determination to protect Guy? What would she do, having lost Teddy in all but fact, if she were to lose Frank as well? 'It would be unbearable.'

'And so I keep saying. There are scientific developments going on all the time. Freddie was very keen on forensic science. It's developing all the time. It prevents miscarriages of justice. But no-one in the local force even seems faintly interested.'

'What does Sir Arthur say?' asked Mercy, feeling some input was required of her.

'Oh, he just nods and says, very interesting, my dear. If I were Freddie, or even just one of the men at his club, no doubt he'd see what sensible ideas these are. All you need is a camera and some powder. It frustrates me so much. There would have been fingerprints at the scene of the crime, I'm sure. There always are. But no-one wanted to look for them.' She breathed out a long gusty sigh, and helped herself to a cigarette from the box on George's desk. 'I'm surprised Lady Waterbeck hasn't expressed an interest. I'd have thought she'd have been keen. Why, Guy has a camera and although I'm not sure exactly what powder we'd need, I'm sure there would be something around that would do. But when I was telling her about it this morning, she waved me aside just the same as Uncle Arthur. But at least she didn't call me my dear.' She inspected her cigarette. 'Well, not in the same tone.'

Blanche wasn't interested in anything that might bring the wrong answers. The disappointment which had lodged in Mercy's heart since their conversation of the previous morning flared up into a sense of betrayal. Blanche was prepared to let an innocent hang for the sake of a man who ought to be able to stand up for himself.

On reflection, she knew George had a deep fondness for Guy. He probably hadn't needed a lot of persuading to co-operate with the false alibi. 'Perhaps Blanche trusts the police.'

Kitty arched a painted eyebrow. 'Oh. I didn't think she was that naïve. In fact, I would have said the opposite.' She got up and headed to the doorway. 'I'm sorry. I realise you have a lot to do. You know how it is. Sometimes I get so terribly frustrated that no-one listens to me just because I'm a woman. I'm sure it's the same for you.'

'I'm used to it by now.'

'I daresay I'm not helping. I'll head off. But I'll keep on at Uncle Arthur and you can keep on at Lady Waterbeck and between us we'll get the police to solve it. Because obviously I can see it might be very messy if one of the villagers is hanged, but we owe Jane some justice. They rather seem to have given up, now they've finished putting the fear of God into us all.' She stared out of the window a moment longer. The driveway outside Waterbeck Hall was empty but for Kitty's own motor and there had been no sign of Gordon Livingstone for the last few days. It seemed, already, that the trail had run cold. 'I wonder what clues got lost or destroyed on the evening of the murder? Really, it breaks your heart.'

Stubbing the cigarette out in the ashtray on the desk, she stalked out of the office with a toss of her blonde head and a flash of her ever-present amethysts. A moment later she reappeared on the front steps of the Hall with Harold in her wake, then headed to her car, turned it and bumped off down the drive. A moment more and the place had descended again into silence.

Mercy sighed. It had been impossible to concentrate even before Kitty had arrived with her long stream of complaints. And she was tired. Blanche's cold devotion to Guy had gnawed at her, with its risk of collateral damage — to Teddy if she told Livingstone the truth about Guy, to Frank if she didn't — into the small hours of the morning and she'd barely drifted off to sleep before Sally had woken, like a bird, with the sunrise. Dealing with the estate's correspondence had taken her far longer than she intended and over lunch Sally had been whiny and tired.

She owed herself a break. If Blanche or Sir Henry thought she should be in the office, they could take it up with George, who was officially responsible for getting the job done. A walk would clear her head for the rest of the day, give her a chance to rationalise Blanche's sharp rejection of what she'd thought was the bond of trust between them, and allow her to try to come to terms once again with that ever-resurgent guilt she felt about Teddy.

She shook her head over him. His state of mind had shaken her more than she liked to admit, and the finality of the doctors' diagnosis had scared her, a nightmare stretching away to infinity. At least if Teddy was in Carlisle, he'd be closer. Perhaps, then, some other people might visit him and he'd feel less isolated, less abandoned. In time, when Sally was a little older, father and daughter might be able to build some sort of relationship.

Taking care to avoid the places where she might encounter Blanche, she picked her way down the path through the woods, listening to the birdsong in the green canopy above her. She wasn't without sympathy for Blanche. How could she be, when she'd suffered herself from the loss of her close friend Flora and watched Blanche, strong for everyone around her, bid farewell to her children when she must have been dying inside? But if Blanche didn't trust the law to protect Guy, it surely meant she believed he might be guilty.

Even that didn't make sense. There was a flaw in the theory that Guy had killed Jane for her silence. He didn't need to. Jane had never been greedy, taking pleasure in simple things, and she could have been easily paid off with very little, if she'd so demanded. And in any case, why go to the effort of an ad in the personal column of *The Times*?

It wasn't hard to lose people in the woods around Waterbeck Hall, certainly not hard to lie with them on a summer evening without anyone noticing. With a pang, she recalled the bright afternoon before the shadow of war had descended on them, when she'd finally allowed herself to give in to Teddy's pleas and her own desires.

Up there in the woods, where a path cut up along the edge of the cornfield and into the trees, there were memories of good times and bad. She hadn't been up there since the time they'd sent him home and he'd run away. This was where he'd fled. She chose to shift her mind to the better times, when the kisses he'd bestowed on her had taken them to the end of a delicious road. She'd passed the stile that would have taken her on to it a couple of hundred yards earlier, but just where she stopped there was a slump in the dry stone wall. She'd noticed it earlier and made a note to get it fixed, but just now it was handy enough. To the detriment of her black leather shoes, and at the cost of a long ladder in her stocking, she scaled the wall and tramped up the path and into the woods, determined to retrieve the good memories of the place and obliterate the bad. Instinct led her straight to the spot where she and Teddy had once kissed and made love. Afterwards they'd done what young lovers always did, pledged their hearts and souls to one another for ever and carved their initials deep into the flesh of a young oak to seal the bargain.

The tree was six years older now, with new growth bulging over the deep cuts they'd made. Mercy stared at it for a moment. It wouldn't be hard to restore it. She traced the letters with her forefinger — TA + MS and a heart beneath — and scraped experimentally at the heart with a fingernail. It was no good. She'd need to come back with something sharper.

In the dim stillness of the wood, a twig cracked. She spun on her heel, but there was no-one there.

Visiting Teddy always put her on edge for the day or so immediately after, as if some of his nervous crisis somehow transferred to her. In the cool green of the woods, there was no need for paranoia, and yet she was sure someone was watching her. Was it Jane's ghost, restless and unsatisfied, creeping around in the trees, or the part of Teddy's spirit that must live in these woods, the only place he was free? More slowly, she turned through a complete circle. Green ferns and long grass rippled in the breeze, the tree branches swayed, a bird dipped from one branch of a tree to another. Waterbeck Wood was a shimmering background of constant movement, of changing light, a magical, haunted place.

'Hello!' she called out, to give herself courage she shouldn't require. It was superstition. Jane's soul was unshriven, but there was no reason for it to walk here, no call for the dead woman to track her steps. 'Is anyone there?'

The cry startled another bird, and another — magpies, this time, lifting off in near-vertical flight and shouting at her as if irritated by her intrusion. She tried again. 'Hello!'

'Hello!'

An answering cry, a familiar voice. The relief that washed over her was unexpected as she turned towards the sound. 'Frank! I thought someone was following me.'

'Not quite following you,' he said, crashing through the trees towards her. 'I saw you disappearing over the wall and wondered what you were up to. So I thought I'd come and find out.'

Honesty hurt no-one. 'I needed to get away.'

'Not a good day, eh?' He bent down and snapped a blade of grass, winding it round his fingers as if to keep them occupied. 'Do you want me to go?'

She hesitated. 'No. It was just that I was thinking of Teddy.'

'I understand.' He hesitated. 'I'd keep visiting the old chap myself, but you saw how it was. He doesn't want to see me.'

She nodded. 'I used to love this place,' she said to him on impulse. 'Now it has dreadful memories.'

His eyes strayed over her shoulder and he could hardly fail to see, and understand, the message on the tree trunk. 'Is that right?'

'The time Teddy ran away. When he couldn't cope.' The time he'd hit her turned into a man she didn't recognise. 'This is where he came.' She'd known that would be the place, and that was where she'd come, calling him, searching for him, but he hadn't replied even though she'd sensed his presence. He must have been there, creeping about, too scared to come out and speak to her. 'We found him after three days. So sound asleep I thought he was dead.' She tilted her head towards him defiantly.

'For a moment, I thought it would be better for everyone. But then he woke up, and he cried and cried and cried, and the doctors gave him something to make him sleep again and took him back to hospital.'

His silence was comforting and for a moment she thought, even hoped, that he'd reach out and fold her into a healing hug, but he kept looking over her shoulder and winding the grass stem until it snapped. 'Poor old bugger. No wonder you wanted to run away.'

She was glad of his company. She could no longer trust Blanche, but she knew she could always rely on Frank. After all, she'd known him as long as she could remember. It was easy to pour out what had happened, the conversation she'd had with Blanche, the threats, the injustice of it.

'The system protects its own, eh?' he said thoughtfully when she'd finished. 'Don't you worry about me, Mercy lass. I can look after myself. Your job is to look after Teddy and Sal. No-one else. Your da can look after himself.'

'But I'm afraid.'

'What of?' He laughed.

'For you. Whatever he says, that inspector is desperate to be a hero. How can he be a hero unless he catches criminals?'

'Aye. Well, I'm not worried.' She saw him turn around as if he were looking for a way to escape.

'If they arrest you, I'll tell them what Blanche did. I won't let you hang.'

'Let's just hope they find out without you needing to do that.'

That moment of chill, that sense that someone was watching her, had reminded her just how hard it was to be lonely. Not alone, because she was never short of someone under her feet or wanting something, but without that easy, silent understanding everyone should have. 'I'm so glad to see you, Frank. It hasn't been much of a homecoming for you.'

'Maybe I'm going to turn into everyone else's bad memories,' he said moodily. 'I'll move on soon enough. As soon as this is done.'

I'll miss you. It didn't seem appropriate to say that out loud. 'Aren't you happy here?'

'I've realised how big the world is, that's all. I've outgrown Waterbeck. I don't know how I can live here now.'

'Nobody blames you for what happened to Jane.' They'd started walking by mutual consent, picking out the path that led through the woods and would bring them out at the back of the Hall, bypassing the village.

'No. But you'll think less of me. I didn't kill her, but old Tom was right to say what he did on the night of the do, and right to accuse me. I've seen more of Jane than I ought to have done. But I didn't see her that night, and I didn't kill her.' He'd picked his way ahead of her, and his voice floated back towards her as if from a greater distance. 'I didn't want to tell you that, about me and Jane, but you ought to know. I lied to that inspector about it, but he found out. Tom told him and Jane told Tom. So we've no secrets.' He crashed onwards.

Mercy hurried on to keep up with him. Did it really matter to her what Jane and Frank had done in the dark? 'You didn't have to tell me.'

'No. But you'd have thought worse of me if you'd have found out some other way. That doesn't make me any less of a liar.'

They were through the woods by then, crossing a lonning marking the edge of the Hall grounds where their ways parted. 'We're friends. Friends don't judge.'

'No.' He paused, turned away. 'I'll see you, then.'

She headed on rather than watch him leave. To the left, a few steps further along the lonning, a tumbledown barn squatted like a watchtower over her, crusted with ivy. As the sun drifted out from behind a low-lying cloud, its declining rays sparked off metal.

She stopped. The flash of light came from a pile of ferns and brushwood, heaped up as if for a bonfire. With one foot, she flicked some of it aside. A wheel. A set of handlebars. The bright, bulging metal of a fuel tank.

A motorcycle. She frowned at in perplexity. No-one in Waterbeck had a motorcycle and if they had, they'd surely have had no need to hide it. So whose could it be?

There had been a motorcycle in the distance on the night Jane died, drowning out the sound of singing from the party as it roared its way along the road towards Penrith. 'Frank! Frank!'

He came crashing back up the path and appeared by her side. 'Something wrong?' And then his eye lit on what she'd found. A low whistle broke from his pursed lips. 'Ey up. What's this?' Two strides took him towards the wall of the barn. He reached to clear the rest of the camouflage.

Something sparked in Mercy's mind. Her hand flashed out, pushing him back until he overbalanced and rocked back onto the path. 'Don't touch it!'

'Why not? It's a motorcycle. A Triumph. Trusty Model 8. Damned if I know what it's doing here, but it's not going to kill me.'

But it might. 'Kitty says—'

'Oh, her. Knows about motors, does she?' But he stayed off the path and dug his hands in his pockets.

'No. But she knows about fingerprints. She says you mustn't touch things.'

'There's no harm in touching this.'

'I heard a motorcycle on the night Jane died. Just after we found her. Maybe it was this one. And so maybe...'

'I heard it, too. A Triumph, it was. Just like this.' Belatedly, his face creased in thought and he stalked around it, viewing it with narrow eyes as if it he didn't like the story it was telling him. 'I'll lay you a guinea to a penny it's the one lifted from my mate in Penrith that day. You can tell one make from another if you know. When I was in the army, I learned a lot about the buggers. The Triumph runs sweet as a nut. I'll have one myself in a few months, if I can haggle for a cut in the price.'

'It was heading out of the village. If it was the man who killed Jane, then he might have been running away. But if it was going to Penrith, I don't understand what it's doing here.'

'I'll guess. The fella roared up the road a bit, came back later on, next day maybe, then dumped the bike and made off over the fields. And if they found the bike somewhere else, Carlisle say, they'd know where he went but this helps nobody. You'd need a hell of a brass neck to do that, but maybe he'd not be worried that anyone would be looking for him so soon.'

'Then we should be looking beyond the village. An outsider?' There were too many army men in the country, all of them with a new approach to fear and the law.

'Looks like it. We'd better tell that inspector, hadn't we?'

'I'll tell Kitty too. Because she'll know how to make them leave it alone. She'll know what to do, who to talk to. If they get fingerprints… they may be able to find out who he was.'

'You'd better get on and call her, then,' he said, and offered her his hand to get over the stile.

CHAPTER TWENTY-THREE

MERCY

Mercy was in the office dealing with correspondence. It was three days since she and Frank had discovered the abandoned motorcycle on the estate and brought the inspector back to the village like a second wave of the Spanish flu. This time there had been a lot more sense of excitement, a much greater feeling of progress, and Kitty had fluttered around the place talking about forensics and fingerprints and evidence and the last lecture she'd been at with Freddie to hear Sir Harvey Littlejohn, as if they hadn't all heard her the first time she'd told them. Blanche, usually a regular visitor to the estate office, had remained absent.

Today Mercy was paying the bills, writing out the cheques for Sir Henry to sign, but the flurry of activity about the Hall made it impossible to concentrate. Through the window she'd seen Guy stroll out to the Rolls with a broad smile and a casual air and drive off without a care in the world, with Kitty looking smug by his side. Then another car had arrived and two policemen had got out, calling at the front door and driving off again, but not back down to the village. She'd seen the gleam of polished chrome through the trees as the car headed up towards the plantation where she and Frank had found the motorcycle. Then the inspector had driven up to the Hall, puffing on his cigarette and looking as if he had all the time in the world, and Blanche herself had appeared on the doorstep to admit him. Something was afoot; no doubt she'd learn about it in due course.

She wrote out the last two cheques and placed them in a brown card folder ready for Sir Henry to sign. As she did so, she heard footsteps in the corridor that linked the office to the main building, and Millie popped her head round the door. 'Her Ladyship wonders if you could join her in the parlour. The inspector is in there with her.'

Mercy's stomach clenched. Did that mean they'd arrested someone? Why would they want to speak to her? And anyway, she reminded herself, Frank was in the clear. He hadn't touched the motorbike. 'Did she say what it was about?'

'No. But I'll say one thing. Her Ladyship's looking ten years younger than she was before he arrived.'

Then it was good news, for Guy, at least. By chance or otherwise, Blanche's manipulation had paid off. Locking the cheques in the desk drawer, Mercy wiped inky fingers on her handkerchief and got up. 'I'll be right along.'

'I'll tell her.'

Millie was still a child; she couldn't keep her steps in check and went skipping off down the corridor, bubbling with excitement. She'd be the one to hear the news when it broke, and the one who took it back to the village when she went home that evening. Excitement drove her. Less sure of the outcome, and remembering Blanche's determination that maintaining everyone else's reputation and innocence was second to Guy's, Mercy was slower of step. She knew now what Blanche was capable of and how easily she would abandon the pleasures of friendship for the powers of rank.

Blanche was seated on the chintz-covered sofa in the parlour, silk-stockinged legs crossed at the ankles, with the inspector installed in an uncomfortable-looking armchair opposite. A tray of tea things sat on an inlaid cherry wood table between them. Outside, in the distance, the gardeners worked away at the herbaceous border and the sound of birdsong came in through the open window.

'Mercy.' The room illuminated under Blanche's smile, as if she were declaring all disagreements between them void. Millie was right, and she looked as if the cares of the world had been lifted from her shoulders. 'Do sit down.' She patted the cushion next to her as she would for a dog. 'The inspector has some news for us, and a couple of questions to ask you. A serious matter, of course, but really nothing to worry about.'

If Blanche thought she would lie, she was mistaken. Mercy steeled herself to hold to the truth and sat, politely, on the edge of the sofa at the far end from Blanche and looked questioningly at Livingstone. Yet again, it seemed, the man was adjusting his approach according to the person to whom he was speaking, and today he wore a cloak of deference. 'Thank you, Lady Waterbeck. Yes, Mrs Appleby. In the past few days, since you and Holland uncovered the motorcycle in the woods, we've made considerable progress in our investigation.'

He looked relieved at that. There must have been pressure mounting on him, with a dead woman and three obvious suspects, not one of whom he'd been able to identify as the killer. The whole scene had the genial sense of an afternoon tea party. It didn't seem to matter that nothing was concluded, that Jane was dead and someone must hang for it.

'I'm glad to hear it.' She smoothed down her skirt, waiting to be told who they'd charge. Not Guy, for certain, but Blanche might equally be smiling to hear that it was Tom or Frank or George.

'Shall we have some background, Mr Livingstone?' asked Blanche briskly. 'Mercy, the inspector has been giving me the details. So clever. They were able to identify fingerprints on the machine. It's quite extraordinary what they can do. They took photographs and sent them down to London and the police officers at Scotland Yard did the rest. They took a look at the prints and they think they have a match with a wanted man.' She took a deep breath and stretched out a hand to touch the petals of a lily in a tall vase on the table. 'I'm happy to say it's not one of us.'

Sunlight danced across the hall floor. Everything suddenly felt remarkably optimistic. No-one they knew would hang. They were still a thankful village. 'Do we know who it is?'

'We think so.' The inspector took up the story, more briskly now. 'The prints match those we have from another crime. They belong to an itinerant conman, a deserter from the army back in 1916. He's left a swathe of broken hearts and empty bank balances across southern England over the last couple of years, and latterly it turned nasty. He's wanted for killing a couple in Lincolnshire a few months ago. There are similarities between the cases. As far as we can reconstruct what happened, he seduced the wife, and the husband found out. When confronted, the fellow killed them both. The police had been alerted by a smart neighbour, and the villain took a shot at the policeman, too. The officer died. Our man has been on the run ever since.'

'Utterly dreadful,' cooed Blanche. 'How extraordinarily lucky we've been, given that we've had a mass murderer in our midst.'

'My men are checking the woods as we speak,' Livingstone said, trying to keep a smile off his face, 'but we suspect he was living rough for several days before Mrs Freeman's murder. He will have arrived and escaped unseen.'

Mercy cast her mind back. The newly broken-down wall. The missing chicken that had so upset Beth Blunt. And there were rabbits and birds in the wood. For any man with survival skills, nature's bounty was easy to access and offered plenty to sustain him. 'And now?'

'Oh, he'll be long gone now. These fellows always disappear. We'll be putting out a hue and cry for him good and proper, across the country. He's killed three times, one of them a policeman, and he'll hang for that, so he'll not think twice about killing again. He'll pop up again, for sure, but it'll be in Cornwall or Scotland or the continent.' He reached out a hand for a biscuit from the plate on the table. 'In the meantime, I want to know if anyone saw anything suspicious. I've shown Lady Waterbeck a photograph — a poor one, I concede, but the only one we have. I'd like you to look at it and tell me if you saw anyone resembling him in the days before Mrs Freeman's death.'

He nodded to Blanche, who passed Mercy the photograph she'd been holding. Looking down at it, Mercy saw a studio portrait of a man in an army uniform, one hand on a table. The peak of his cap cast a light shadow over his eyes, but there was no hiding the smile that lurked on his lips, and when she peered closer she recognised, too, the impish look in his eyes.

William Edmundston, the handsome soldier who'd charmed her with so little effort on the bus into Penrith and sent her so cheeky a postcard, was a murderer.

Her stomach lurched. At another time, in another place, she might have been the one to feel his hands around her throat as he choked the life out if her.

'Mercy, my dear. You've gone pale. Are you all right? Shall I send Millie for some brandy?'

'You recognise this man, then, Mrs Appleby?'

Ignoring Blanche's offer, she turned instead to Livingstone. 'Yes, I do.' A deep breath. 'I met him on the bus on the morning of the day Jane was killed. I was on my way to Edinburgh to visit my husband and he engaged me in conversation.'

'What did he say to you?'

'He told me his name was William Edmundston.'

'An alias,' Livingstone said, 'though one he regularly uses. His real name is Clifford Rowe.'

'He said he was a soldier in the Royal Artillery. He was on leave, and visiting his sweetheart in the area. He was very talkative.'

'Of course he was,' Blanche said, bracingly. 'I expect he wanted you to know as much as possible of the story he was trying to sell. Isn't that the way these criminal minds work, Inspector?'

'Certainly some of them, Lady Waterbeck. Tell me, Mrs Appleby, did this man volunteer this information?'

'Yes. I gave him no encouragement. He sat next to me without invitation and asked me my name, and told me about himself. And later I received a postcard from him, from Carlisle.'

'Classic modus operandi,' the inspector said, smiling. His wall eye rolled alarmingly. 'No doubt he was hoping to establish his alternative personality.'

Something occurred to her. 'But he got on the train at Penrith. That was before Jane died. He wasn't in the village.'

'Did you see him get on the train?'

She thought back. She'd turned away from him, as she recalled, because that cheeky smile had seemed to tease her. Her face flushed red at how foolish she'd been, at how easily she'd been flattered and, yes, attracted to him. 'No. I walked with him to the station, but I went to the northbound platform and didn't see him go in.'

'And the motorcycle was stolen in Penrith that afternoon.' He turned back to Blanche. 'It's clear enough. He came back to the village and indulged in an assignation with Mrs Freeman. Perhaps he'd formed a relationship with her while on the run. And then she must have said something. She realised that something didn't ring true, perhaps, or refused when he asked her for money or some other assistance. And then he must have done the only thing he could do to prevent her from giving him away, and killed her.'

'I can't believe… he seemed so nice.' He had been kind and for a moment she'd compared him favourably with the wreck of a man Teddy had become. She looked away from Livingstone in shame.

'Yes. He's an accomplished confidence trickster. We know that. He paid you those attentions precisely so that you would remember him, remember when you saw him, and where. There's no embarrassment in falling for it, Mrs Appleby. In his career as a fraudster, Rowe has pulled the wool over very many eyes, including those of some high-ranking officers in the army. The first man he swindled was a local magistrate.'

Mercy took a sidelong look at Blanche, who was tapping elegant fingers on her lap and smiling with satisfaction. It was chance that had delivered the identity of Jane's killer. Without that, they would have been unpicking a mesh of lies and silence, trust reinforced between some and lost between others. Blanche had disappointed her. She was tired, and she wanted to leave. 'Do you need anything more from me, Inspector? I have plenty of work to do.'

'I'll take a formal statement from you, Mrs Appleby, and then you can get back to work. Thank you. You've been most helpful. Your observational skills have proved instrumental in what I hope will be the conclusion of this affair. All we need to do now is track him down, and I think that's something I can pass on to my colleagues at Scotland Yard.'

CHAPTER TWENTY-FOUR

BLANCHE

An hour or so later, Blanche made her way through the linking door to the office with a smile brighter than the sun. 'Well, Mercy. Here we are. I've put the inspector in Henry's study so he can use the telephone, but I doubt he'll do anything other than call as many relevant authorities as he can think of with the news of how clever he's been. So now it's time for us to mend fences.'

Mend fences? Mercy stared. Had Blanche forgotten the conversation they'd had? Had she forgotten the implied threats as to the damage she could do to the whole Smart family, and to Teddy, if her request for silence wasn't met? Mercy had thought they'd forged a friendship through the war and its aftermath, but in times of crisis that counted for nothing. What counted was power and rank and money, and all of those weighed in behind Blanche. 'Yes. There are fences and walls to be mended around the estate. I don't think the police were very careful with them.'

It was Blanche's turn to stare, but there was genuine surprise behind it. She must know what she'd done was unscrupulous, but she was equally clear she felt she'd had no alternative. 'That wasn't what I meant.'

Mercy, who had managed to avoid her for the past few days, had half expected to be confronted with expressions of regret when the matter was over. It was easy to be generous when you'd won, like the cheating wrestler offering a hand to his defeated opponent. 'I understand what you meant. It doesn't alter what happened.'

'I don't think you do, or you'd be more understanding. You'd know I had no alternative.' In the doorway, Blanche shuffled backwards a little. 'I'm sorry if you feel I put pressure on you, but I'm astonished you can't accept my doing so. You're a mother, too. Think of Sally.'

Sally was a small child who knew no wickedness beyond a toddler's happy mischief, and Guy was an adult with men's lives on his conscience. 'They aren't the same.'

'Nevertheless, I do regret what I was forced to do. It wasn't what I would have wanted.' Blanche got out an embroidered handkerchief and turned it in her fingers. A pale pink letter F adorned a corner.

She carried Flora's handkerchiefs with her. Against that gesture, knowing or unknowing, Mercy was powerless to hold a grudge. 'Then we won't mention it again.'

'You say that as if you don't mean it.'

'I do mean it.' But it would take her time to think as kindly of her friend and employer as she used to do.

Blanche twisted the handkerchief again, then turned and looked out of the window. 'At least now we can bury poor Jane with decency and turn our collective good intentions on Tom without fearing we're giving help and support to a killer.'

'Help and support? You mean like I did to William Edmundston?' Mercy laid her pen down and turned a mutinous face to the woman on whom her livelihood depended.

Blanche looked taken aback. 'No, sweetheart, not like you did. All you did was believe the story he told you. The inspector was telling me some tales about this man and you can rest assured. He'd have sweet-talked every one of us.'

Mercy was mollified. 'I can't help thinking… if only I'd noticed something strange about him. I could have reported him to the police.'

'What was there to notice?' Blanche asked, almost rhetorically.

'He hadn't killed Jane by then.'

'If he'd been living rough in the woods, I should have spotted it.'

'I know a little about living in the woods. Second hand, of course. When I was a small child, there were trappers who came into town and they were neat as a needle when they wanted to be. If he's been in the army, he'll know how to spit and polish under the toughest circumstances. I expect the police will find a shelter way up in the woods. Maybe he even hid up there after he left the motorcycle. I really don't think you've anything to reproach yourself for.' Blanche picked up the folder with the cheques on it, which lay open on the desk. 'Are these done? I'll take them up to Sir Henry and get him to sign them. And tell him the good news, of course. We can all sleep a little more soundly in our beds tonight.' She hesitated. 'Perhaps you want to go down to the village and tell Tom. And Frank, of course.'

'If that's all right.' She could take Sally down to Frank's and they could choose the kitten he'd promised.

'No-one's going to get any work done today, are they, with all this excitement?' She paused. 'I keep thinking about Tom. Without Jane's wage coming in, he'll struggle. We'll have to see what we can find for him. But there's so little he can do with just the one arm. Help with the sowing in the springtime, perhaps, and work some of the more biddable horses. But even they'll be replaced by machines in time.'

'I'll ask my father if he has any suggestions,' Mercy said to her, and the devil in her couldn't resist adding a barb. 'No doubt he'll be relieved not to have to lie any more.'

In the act of turning to leave the room, Blanche paused. For a second Mercy thought she'd overstepped the line between them, even though their friendship had outgrown that which existed between employer and employee. Blanche always claimed she liked people to speak their minds, but when she didn't like what she heard, she tended to remember her rank.

'No. That's fair play. Perhaps, after all, I didn't behave so well in the affair myself.'

'You did what you thought was right.'

'He's my only child. You know how it was when we lost Edward, Flora, and Annie. Maybe I was a little mad.' Blanche's mouth was set in a hard line that showed no regrets, but at least she admitted her fault. 'If I'd lost Guy, it would have destroyed me. It would have destroyed Sir Henry. And the house, the village. There's no-one else. It would all have gone to some fifth cousin of Henry's in Canada. All sold, broken up. There would have been so much change.'

And this was meant to justify the risk to an innocent man's life? If, for whatever reason, Guy had killed poor Jane, Tom or Frank could have gone to the gallows declaring their innocence and leaving devastated friends and ruined reputations behind them. 'I think we'd have survived it,' she said quietly. Because they'd somehow survived the war, and the great changes that seemed to terrify Blanche so much were happening elsewhere. Sometimes the little people benefited. It was a revolutionary thought. She was almost shocked at herself. 'The innocent will go free. That's what matters.'

'And all we need now is for the police to round up Clifford Rowe,' observed Blanche, and left the office.

CHAPTER TWENTY-FIVE

MERCY

Mercy's first call was to break the good news to Tom. The cottage he'd shared with Jane was in the centre of the village, one of a terraced row of rich red sandstone homes a little way along from the post office, with a postage stamp of a front garden for flowers and some ground at the back for vegetables. Even in the week or so since Jane's death it was showing signs of neglect — the curtains pulled aside too hard so they hung unevenly, dirt on the front step, a flush of couch grass sprouting up around the roses in the front garden. Jane had loved her garden and, whatever her faults, had been an excellent worker up at the Hall and no slatternly housewife at home. While some of the energy she had left for her leisure hours might have been directed towards immoral liaisons, the rest of it was dedicated to keeping her cottage and its garden sparkling and neat.

Even those villagers who liked her had judged her harshly for her lack of godliness rather than kindly for her exemplary cleanliness. With a wry smile, Mercy pushed open the gate and took the two steps along the short path to the door. 'Tom, it's Mercy. Are you home?'

No answer. She pushed open the front door and stepped inside. The house was dim and smelt of wood smoke and burned food, but she could see through to the kitchen where the back door stood open. 'Tom!'

He was in the garden, stooping to pluck at the weeds in the

vegetable patch with his good arm. 'Come to see the local villain, have you? Come to poke me with a stick and see if I bite?'

'We're on our way to see Frank,' she said, 'to pick up one of his kittens. But I thought I'd call in on you on the way. The police have been up at the Hall.'

He straightened up. A rush of goodwill coursed through her as she looked at this damaged giant, remembering how Teddy had described the moment when Tom had saved his life, breaking their enemy with his agricultural strength. 'No good to me, no doubt.'

'It's very good news,' she said, seeing his sour expression. 'Really it is. Inspector Livingstone went to tell Lady Waterbeck about the motorcycle Frank and I found. They think they know who killed Jane.'

He straightened up. 'Do they, aye? For his sake, let's hope they get the bastard before I do. Make us a cup of tea then, Mercy, lass. I've time for a blether.'

She stepped back into the house, leaving Sally in the garden. The kettle was on the range, hissing away and there was barely any water in it, but she squeezed enough out to make the tea in the dainty Coalport teapot that had been a wedding present from the Waterbecks, and fill two of the matching cups. Tom struggled to manage a saucer with his missing arm, so she took cups only out into the garden where he was standing in the sun, contemplating the frothy green line of the carrot crop he'd been thinning out. 'Here.'

He tossed the rejected seedlings onto the heap next to the vegetable garden, alongside potato peelings so rough and chunky they told the tale of a one-armed widower struggling to cope. Guilt overwhelmed her. Like everyone else, she'd been so concerned about who'd killed Jane that the difficulties of the man who hadn't had been overlooked. They should all have been better than that. If Blanche wanted to help him, the first thing she should do was try to persuade him to accept a little charity. A few meals would be a start. 'That's a good cup of tea, lass.'

On the grass between them, Sally was enraptured by a butterfly, reaching out towards it with a chubby pink hand. They sipped companionably as she played, as the butterfly lifted off and settled again. Tom watched her with a solemn expression. He and Jane had been married since before the war and had no children. He had suffered more damage than she could imagine — bereaved, accused and abandoned. 'If there's anything I can do for you while I'm here, let me know. Perhaps something in the kitchen.'

He shook his head. 'I can struggle on a while yet. Tell me about the bugger that took my Jane.'

Mutinous, stubborn, angry Tom would never forgive or forget. 'He's a conman and a murderer, wanted for at least three killings down south. The police think he'll have fled the county as soon as the deed was done. He could be anywhere. They may well never catch him, but there's still a chance.'

'Jane did nowt to deserve that.' He perched himself on the wall, cradling the cup in his hand and looking down at it, misty-eyed. 'Like a bitch on heat all the time, but that was just how she was made. If I wasn't such a ghost of a man, it would never have happened. When I lie awake in my bed at night, I think it would have been better if they hanged me for it. If they'd taken me off to jail, I wouldn't be left living like this.'

Livingstone's reassurances had been all very well, Mercy reminded herself, but he hadn't showed any confidence in actually running the wanted man to earth. Rather, he'd seemed delighted by the prospect of handing the job over to someone else. Perhaps her father was right when he said the man wasn't as clever as he thought. It didn't matter how smart you were in your deductions when you made them after the event, long after the horse had bolted. 'They'll catch him.' She hoped she sounded convincing. 'He said something about Scotland Yard.'

'And do they know where he is? Know what he looks like?

Master of bloody disguises these guys, one day turning up on your doorstep like a vicar and the next like a travelling salesman.'

'Did anyone like that come to the cottage?'

He shook his head. 'No, but Jane was out and about often enough. If he'd have gone up to the Hall, she'd have met him there.'

'I don't think he ever did go up to the Hall,' said Mercy, sipping at her tea. The china was so fine the sunlight shone through it. Jane had been justifiably proud of it. Mercy and Teddy had a set, too, from the same source, though because of their closeness to the Hall, their tea set had a matching dinner service. Not a piece broken, she thought as she watched Tom clench his hand around the cup. She and Teddy had joked about that, about how far into married life they'd get before they started throwing the crockery at one another. 'I'd have recognised him. I met him. He was on the bus when I went up to see Teddy.'

Tom's attention sharpened. 'Was he, now? So, what was he like, the man that killed my Jane?'

She took another sip. Even knowing William, as she still thought about him, had killed goodness knew how many people she couldn't forget the warmth of that smile. Maybe, after all, she'd touched his heart with the tale of woe he'd encouraged her to unload. She stopped herself. That was the evil genius of the trickster, persuading everyone they spoke to that they were different, special. 'He was average. That's the funny thing. Average height. Average build.' Maybe that was deliberate, so when choosing to reveal himself in public, he was as unremarkable as possible, his face a blank canvas that could be transformed with the addition of a fake moustache or a painted-on scar. 'Fair hair, clean-shaven. He was dressed like a soldier and said he was on leave, but he wasn't. He was a deserter.'

'Was he good looking?'

'Tom. Don't torture yourself.'

His fist tightened again on the cup, and it gave way. What was left of the tea cascaded to the ground at his feet with the shards of china and he was left holding nothing but the delicate handle. A scarlet slash of blood spread across his finger.

'Don't bother,' he said, twisting his handkerchief around the wound as Mercy moved to help. 'Tell me everything about him. Every last little thing, the good and the bad. So that if I ever meet him, I'll recognise him and if the police don't make him pay, then I will.'

A bee descended to investigate the spilled tea and the broken cup. Wary of Sally's interest, Mercy scooped her daughter up and held her close. The intensity of Tom's stare was discomforting, but not as much as her own feelings when she thought of William, the offer of friendship she'd been so glad to accept and the postcard with its now-chilling note. I know we'll meet again.

But there was comfort to be had from the idea that William killed out of perceived necessity, not for pleasure. She told Tom, as simply and as honestly as she could, more about her encounter with Clifford Rowe, also known as William Edmundston, and the fifteen minutes she'd spent in his company.

'Jane was out early that morning.' Tom tossed the handle of the cup over the wall into the field behind him. 'Didn't say where she was. Now I reckon I know. Arranging to see him. Clever bugger. Made sure you saw him leave. But it didn't work, did it? Stupid thing to do, leave the motorcycle.'

'Maybe he meant to come back for it and never got the chance.'

'Aye. That'll be it.' He bent down to the vegetable plot again, to indicate the visit was over.

'If there's anything I can do for you, you'll let me know? I'll get Mam to bring down a bite of stew for your supper. We always have plenty.'

'You're a good lass, Mercy. Aye. That would be grand.' Untwisting the bloodied handkerchief, he felt in his pocket and fished out a sixpence, reaching out and folding Sally's fingers around it. 'Buy the lass a sweetie.'

She'd have refused, aware he could ill afford it, if it hadn't been for the price she knew he'd placed on his pride. They left him to his struggle, though with Mercy still running through things she could do, things the village could do, to help him as she walked through the cottage. In the front garden a thought struck her, and she picked half a dozen roses from the bush by the front door, slipping back inside to place them in a vase and leaving them in the dusty living room in an attempt to brighten the place up. She hoped he'd see them and give them some water. With Sally still clinging to her hip, she had to manage one-handed, the first glimpse of how difficult his life must be.

It would be a long time before any light flooded into Tom's life. With this sombre thought in mind, she strolled out of Waterbeck and up towards Frank's cottage. 'Come on, Sal. You give me that tanner to look after, and we'll go and see if Frank's in. Maybe he'll let you choose your kitty.'

The Hollands' cottage looked more alive, with curtains stirring at the window and a streak of black that must be the mother cat disappearing around the edge of the open front door. There was no answer when she lifted her hand to the knocker, but when she pushed the door fully open and went into the kitchen, there were signs that someone had been there — a loaf of bread sitting on the worktop, a pat of butter in the dish beside, a cut of ham with a chunk sliced off.

She wrinkled her brow. The place had a look of recent abandonment to it. She hadn't expected Hetty Holland to be there — Frank's mother worked up in the dairy on the estate — so Frank must have seen her coming and be trying, for reasons of his own, to avoid her. With a little shiver, she thought of how, in a different set of circumstances, she might have found herself complicit in Frank's arrest. William could have done so much more damage beyond the harm he did to Jane.

But she would never have allowed Frank to hang. If it had come to that, she'd have told the truth and let her father and

Guy sort out their lies, left it to Blanche to defend her son alone and paid the price for it in friendship. Nevertheless, though she owed him an apology as well as good news, she was irked by his behaviour. Frank was her friend, and a lifelong one, as close as a brother. She wouldn't let him get away with avoiding her.

'Kitties!'

Sally, delightedly, was pointing out through the open back door. Still clutching her daughter, Mercy went into the garden and found it empty apart from a crazy circus of tiny stripy felines among the beetroot and potatoes. The back gate swung open and fifty yards away a figure was walking quickly off along the path that followed the field edge, distinctive in flat cap and the brown jacket that belonged to Frank's demob suit. He must have got back from town or wherever he'd been — on business, probably, if he was dressed like that — and not been ready to see her.

'Frank!' she called after him. 'Come back! I need to talk to you!' And then, as he hesitated, so that she knew he must have heard and yet moved on, she shouted again. 'I've some news for you!'

His pace quickened. He was dodging along the edge of the field now, from hawthorn bush to elder bush, away from the village where the road curved round towards the estate. He clearly hadn't thought it through, because the path would eventually take him out on the main road and if he doubled back to the cottage and she went along the road, she'd cut him off.

'Let's go and find him, shall we?' she said to Sally, putting her down and taking her hand and they re-emerged onto the road. 'He's no business running away. And I want us to choose that kitty. What about the little ginger one? Did you see it?'

They walked as briskly as possible, given Sally's short legs, a dignified amble along to the curve of the road where Frank would emerge from the woods. And there he was, his figure just visible as he bobbed through the trees, a whistle on his lips.

'Frank Holland!' she called with confidence. 'Come here! You don't get away from me that easily.' For God's sake, why was he making such a song and dance of it?

When, a second later, he emerged from the woods, the world stuttered to a stop. The brown jacket was Frank's, and the well-worn cloth cap, but it wasn't he who wore them.

Mercy was face to face with William Edmundston.

CHAPTER TWENTY-SIX

FRANK

The army had kept Frank fit, but no drill instructor could have pushed him as hard as his own desperation. The inspector was up at the Hall, they'd said in the village, and so that was where he headed, pounding up the driveway with his breath snatching at his throat until the world around him rocked. He ran with blood throbbing in his head and white lights dancing in front of his eyes. He stumbled, fell, scrambled up and kept on again, until sweat dripped from his face and soaked his shirt as he burst across the courtyard and realised, as he finally stumbled to a halt by the inspector's car, that he hadn't breath left to shout for help.

He staggered up the steps and leaned on the bell pull with all his weight, sending it jangling crazily inside. When no-one answered, he tried again, as if its mad ringing could somehow impart his desperation.

Footsteps. The door opening. The butler, his face frozen in outrage at such behaviour. Still unable to speak, Frank shouldered the startled man aside and burst into the cool marble of the hallway, where he staggered to a confused halt. The corridors were lined with doors, all of them tall and elegant, all with gold leaf picking out the paintwork, all of them closed against him. His encounters with the Hall had been limited to that fateful party and the subsequent interview with the inspector, and now he was inside, he had no idea where to go.

'Holland! How dare you burst in here!' In his outrage, Harold attempted to lay hands on him as if he had a chance of manhandling him out, but Frank shook him off with ease. To his left, doors opened. Blanche popped her head out from one, startled, and Gordon Livingstone appeared at another.

'Frank!' cried Blanche, expression as appalled as Harold's, but surely not for the same reason. 'Has something happened?'

He was regaining some of his composure now, though very little of it. Enough, at least, to save a life, or so he hoped. 'It's Mercy.'

'What?' said the inspector sharply and Blanche, growing suddenly pale, took him by the arm, steered him into the study and deposited him in a leather armchair.

'Frank,' she said, turning to pour him a glass of brandy, 'get your breath back. Has something happened?'

By the time she placed the glass in his hand, he felt foolish. 'No. Not yet. I thought I'd better warn her.'

'She's not here just now. She went down to the village to see you.' He couldn't suppress the groan. 'But she went to Tom's first.'

So, there was hope. He sipped the brandy, and it burned its way down his throat. This wasn't how he'd hoped to be sipping fine Cognac at the Hall. The tricks life played. 'I'd a fellow come to visit just now. A stranger.'

'A stranger?' echoed Blanche. The inspector, though silent, was watching him intently.

'Aye, and yet not a stranger. He came along and asked directions up to the Hall. Wanted to talk to a friend he had up there, he said. A Mrs Appleby.'

'Mercy is allowed to have her friends,' observed Blanche sweetly.

She thought he was jealous. Maybe he was. 'So she is. I'm one myself. But this gadgie… there was something about him.'

'What do you mean?'

His breath came more easily now. 'He said he was an old soldier, so I invited him in for a cuppa. There was something familiar about him and when I was in the kitchen, it came to me. I saw him at the party.' He jerked a thumb to the courtyard. 'I was standing in the hallway and looking out and I saw him. Saw his face. A chap I'd never seen before. I reckoned he must be someone new to the place, but I never saw him again until today. And suddenly he was in my kitchen, clear as day, not knowing the village.' And asking where he could find Mercy.

The effect was electric. Blanche turned to the Inspector. 'Surely to God it can't—?' But he was already turning away from her, lifting a brown cardboard folder on the desk, taking out a photograph. 'How could you forget to tell me that?'

He'd forgotten because all he'd been thinking about on that evening was Mercy. He'd had no time for Jane. He shook his head.

'Have a look at this, my man.' Livingstone thrust a photograph towards him. 'Is this him?'

It wasn't the clearest picture, and Frank had been careful not to attract too much attention by staring. The man he'd left sitting in his mother's small front room had lacked the smartness of the soldier in the photograph and had sported a week or so's growth of dark stubble, but there was no mistake. 'Aye, that's him.'

'But why has he come back?' said Blanche, almost in fury. 'What can he want with Mercy?'

Wasn't it obvious? 'Come to prey on some other poor woman, as he sees her.' Frank got up, not sure what he could do but knowing he must do something. He directed his rage at Livingstone. 'You'd better get off your non-uniformed arse, my man, and get down and arrest him.'

'I shall telephone to Penrith for some support—'

'Aye, and how long will that take? We need to go and find him now, not when some copper's finished his tea break. Now, before he kills again.'

'The man is a cold-blooded murderer. Man, woman or child, civilian or police officer, it means nothing to him. It would be madness to approach him unarmed.'

'All the more reason why you'll have to stop him before he

harms anyone else!'

Blanche had turned away and crossed the room as the two men faced each other across the desk, Frank in red-hot fury and the inspector coldly stubborn. 'We'll issue weapons to the officers who will arrest him.'

And how much longer would that take? 'I knew you were a coward,' Frank hissed at him. 'You can always tell. Too scared to fight, but brave enough to hang a man from a distance. You'd have hanged me if you could. But the man who deserves it is in the village right now. Go and get him.'

'It would be the height of stupidity. I would be a lamb to the slaughter.'

Frank thought of Flanders, of a July dawn stripped of birdsong when he and Teddy, Tom, Jesse Turnbull and all the rest of them had followed Guy Waterbeck out of a trench and into no-man's-land, shoulder to shoulder in a thin khaki line. A vein of pure fury throbbed in his temple. 'You selfish, cowardly bastard! Don't you dare talk to me about lambs to the slaughter!'

In the ensuing silence, during which he struggled not to wipe the look of virtuous self-righteousness from the man's smug and cowardly face, Blanche re-crossed the room. Between them on the desk, she placed a Webley revolver.

'It's Guy's,' she said, sweetly. 'Loaded, of course. I'm sure if he were here, he would already be on his way to rescue a young woman in danger and apprehend a murderer. Frank makes a good point. He and Guy, and many other fine men, know all about putting themselves in the way of danger. So, it's over to you, Inspector. It's your time to be the hero you say you never had the chance to be.'

Livingstone stayed still, staring at the gun, and his face faded to grey. He said nothing.

The grandfather clock in the hall echoed the half hour.

It was that, the reminder that time was running on too quickly, that spurred Frank on. 'So, it's down to me, then, is it?'

In the homecoming church service on the day of Jane's death, the vicar had preached about swords and ploughshares. Frank was too pragmatic to be a religious man, but that message had sat comfortably with him. He reached out for the gun. The metal rested heavy as a nightmare in his hand, cold and sharp as a November frost.

'Right,' he said, 'if you'll not do it, I'll do it myself.'

He must face another enemy once again. Not for the King this time, but for the woman he'd always loved.

CHAPTER TWENTY-SEVEN

MERCY

'Hello, Mrs Mercy Appleby,' he said in that cheerful, musical voice that had touched her so easily the previous time they'd met. 'Didn't I tell you we'd meet again?' He stood back and looked her up and down. 'And this is… your little girl?'

She nodded.

'And her name?'

'Sally.' The name crept out of her dry throat.

'Sally. What a beautiful name. Hello Sally.'

'Miaow!' said Sally, and stared down at her feet, her face a glow of bashful pink.

'A beautiful little girl and a beautiful mother.' He turned back to her with that smile. 'Why so quiet? Didn't I say we'd meet again?'

They make you think they're someone else, she thought, her heart beating so she could barely think straight. That was how he did it. And then the moment of truth, the instinct for self-preservation, the understanding of how close she was to death. I mustn't let him know I know.

'So you did.' She remembered to smile, but she couldn't stop herself from picking Sally up, holding her close. Perhaps if he killed her, he'd spare her daughter. She would beg him to. She would do anything. 'Mr Edmunds, wasn't it?'

'Edmundston,' he corrected her, with that confidential smile. 'Don't look so surprised. If you do that, I'll begin to think I'm not welcome.'

When you knew what lay behind the charm, its power faded. She tried not to shiver as he stepped forward and lifted her free hand to his lips, a gallant gesture that brought him too close. There was a tang of the woodlands about him, the smoke that clung to his hair and clothes telling of a scavenged, damp fire built of unseasoned wood. Stubble shadowed his chin. He must have been living rough, then, but where and for how long? 'Oh, most welcome! But you surprised me. When I saw you coming through the trees, I thought you were someone else.'

'Someone you're very keen to see. I take it.' He teased her with a sly smile.

'Not exactly. Just a friend of my husband's. I had some news for him, and—' She stuttered to a halt.

'I must look very much like him,' he observed, keeping her fingers between his and his eyes on her face, 'if you were convinced enough to run along and cut me off.'

He let go of her hand and turned his attention to Sally. The long fingers that had squeezed the life from Jane Freeman stroked her soft cheek and Sally, in her sweet innocence, looked up at him with a smile.

'No.' It was a struggle to concentrate. 'You don't look like him at all. It's just that you're wearing a jacket just like his.'

He looked down at the sleeve of the brown suit in surprise. His khaki trousers didn't match the jacket. Now she'd drawn attention to something odd about him. She forced herself not to shiver.

'Oh, this? Some fellow in a cottage just outside the village gave it to me. I'm on my way to Keswick to see my sweetheart, but I've mislaid all my kit. I'm not sure how. Some cad made off with it at Carlisle station, I think. But you know how it is…' At last, with a shrug, he let go of her hand. 'When a good man needs something, something always turns up. The chap said he wouldn't be needing it. He was starting a new job next week.'

'That sounds just like Frank,' Mercy said with a weak smile.

'And is Frank your sweetheart, you naughty little minx?' he teased. 'Mrs Mercy Appleby, with the emphasis on the Mrs and your lord and master a long time in hospital a hundred miles away? Are you looking for someone better?'

'How dare you?' She went scarlet. Knowledge was a dangerous thing, but this was how she'd have responded to anyone else. No, she corrected herself, if it was anyone else she'd have slapped their face and left a mark for them to contemplate for a long time, but she had her daughter in her arms and she was dealing with a murderer. Who knew what might trigger his temper, or what Jane might have said to him to cause him to turn on her? 'Frank is a friend, that's all.'

'I meant no harm,' he said, showing all the signs of regret. 'Excuse my little joke. Tell me, did you ever get my postcard?'

'I did. I daresay that's the talk of the village as well. You know what folk are like.'

'I thought I was very discreet.' He twinkled that smile at her, and she breathed a little more easily. Another hurdle negotiated, another sentence that had fallen from her lips without giving her away. 'That's partly why I'm here. I know you'll understand. I know you'll help me.'

She met and returned his smile, but her stomach was churning. What was the penalty for helping a convicted felon escape? Surely it would make a difference if she was in fear of her life. 'Of course. What do you need me to do?'

'I haven't been entirely straight with you, sweet Mrs Mercy Appleby.' He paused a moment and whistled a few random bars. 'Doesn't that sound like an old folk song? Sweet Mrs Mercy Appleby.'

She must pretend to be charmed, so she laughed with him, flipping her hand up to her face in an exaggerated la-di-da gesture like the one poor Flora had used to mock her older sister Annie whenever a certain young soldier, temporarily resident in the Hall when it had been a hospital, had been mentioned. 'William. Don't. How many times must I tell you? I'm a—'

'Respectable married woman,' he finished for her. 'Yes. Yes. But to continue. I do have a sweetheart in these parts, but not in Keswick.'

'Is that so?'

'Yes.' He leaned in towards her again, conspiratorially. 'My sweetheart is in this very village.'

'She is?'

'Yes. I met her a few months ago when I was passing through, and though I've been away, somehow she keeps drawing me back. Now, you look like a woman who understands love. You look like someone who'll take pity on me. And you look so innocent, the sweet young wife with the even sweeter child.'

Oh,' she said, with a false giggle, 'yes. I understand love.'

'I know I can trust you.' Once more, he leaned in too close. Once more, he tickled Sally under the chin. 'Then will you do one thing for me?'

'If I can,' she whispered, her mouth dry, her blood icy at the implied threat.

'I want you to take a message to my love and tell her I'm ready for her. Tell her to meet me tonight after dark. I'll be at the gate of the estate. You'll do that for me, won't you, sweet Mercy?'

His look turned to a plea. Mercy's blood raced around her body, but her mind worked more slowly. What should she do? Agree, of course, get away as soon as she could with Sally and then call the police to pick him up at the appointed place. 'Of course I will. Who is she?'

'I always knew I could trust you. It's Jane. Jane Fleetwood.'

How could he not know? But if he'd been lying low, it would have been easy to miss the news. She stared at him in horror.

'Come,' he said, with a sharp edge of irritation in his voice, 'don't go all prim on me. I can read your mind, my dear, and I daresay you'll be no better than Jane when you've been without a man for a few years. She's tied to a man who's no good to any woman and violent with it, and the only difference between you and her that I can see is that you're spared the violence she had to put up with.'

And I have a child, she thought, agonised. I have a child he can use against me. 'I'm sorry. I can't.'

'Spare me the morality and take a message to Jane.' There was a trace of impatience in his voice.

'If I could do it, I would.' I will do anything to save Sally. 'I can't.'

'Of course you can. Drop a note off at the Hall. That's where she works, isn't it? And where you live, too. See, I know all about you, Mercy.'

He kept smiling and his hand kept moving, touching her own hand so that her skin felt clammy, gently twining one of Sally's soft curls around his finger until all Mercy could feel was fear, closing round her, crushing her. 'Haven't you heard?'

'Heard what? Has something happened to her?'

'I'm sorry.' Now she was apologising to a killer for bringing him bad news. Hadn't he shot a policeman in his escape? 'Jane's dead. She died the day we met on the bus. Someone killed her. At the party.'

In the silence, the wind wheedled a tune from the leaves of the big birch tree beside the road and the birds joined in. The church clock, always a little late, struck the half hour. 'Someone killed her?'

'Yes.'

'Who? Tell me who the bastard is and—'

'We don't know.' Her voice had slipped down to a whisper now. His shock was genuine and the implications of it hit her with a dizzying blow. If he didn't know Jane was dead, he hadn't killed her.

So, who had?

'It's all right,' he said, 'it's all right, Mercy. No, I didn't know. You can tell. But oh… poor darling Jane. At least she's been spared the rest of her life with the brute she married.'

'Tom loved her too,' she said, through a fog of tears, 'in his own way.' She felt in her pocket for a handkerchief and scrubbed at her eyes, not daring to allow herself to be blinded even for a second.

'Not as much as I did.' He turned on his heel, looking back towards the village as if he were of a mind to go storming back there. 'Then there's nothing more for me here. I'll get the hell out of here, but maybe we'll meet again some day. Maybe we'll bump into one another in the churchyard when I creep back to lay flowers on her grave.'

'I hope so.'

Something about the way she said it must have triggered his attention. Without warning, his hand shot out and seized her wrist — nothing tender. The iron grip of the manacle. 'What aren't you telling me?'

'Nothing! I swear it.' Her arm tightened around Sally.

'You're looking at me as if I killed her. You're not shocked, by her or by me. Who's been talking to you and what have they told you?'

'Nothing. I—'

'Did you tell them you'd seen me?'

'They were asking about everyone. About what we were all doing and who we saw. So, of course, I told them. Because I don't know who you are.'

Silence, but it lasted only for a second. 'You damned little bitch!' He let go of her wrist for a second and raised both hands, reaching for her throat. 'I'll kill you. And if you've told anyone about me, I'll tear your sweet little child apart in front of your eyes. Don't think I won't.'

'No! Not Sally!'

Sally broke out into a wail as he reached out for her. There was one half chance and Mercy snatched at it, holding Sally away from him with one hand and pushing at him with the other. She wasn't strong, but she had surprise on her side, and the desperate courage of a mother fighting for her child, a mother who would do anything.

She struck lucky. He rocked off balance, stumbled sideways and fell and even as she turned and began to run, she heard the crunch as he hit the ground, the shouted curse that showed his true, murderous colours.

'You bitch! Come back here!' The click of a revolver, so soft she could barely hear it over his shouting and the hammering of her heart, echoed in her head. Then the shot fizzing past her and biting into the stone wall that bounded the road.

She had no chance of outrunning him. Death was at her heels and all she could hope to do was save Sally. As she thrust her wailing child over the wall into the field, there was another shot, a bemusing, confusing sound that seemed to come from somewhere else entirely and somehow failed to touch her, and a third.

And a man's scream, and silence. No running footsteps, no angry shouts. No threats. No more shots. The birds that had risen in a cloud of irritation at the disturbance subsided again into the security of the birch tree as Sally's outraged howl emanated from the other side of the wall.

She would fight him to her last breath. With fear creeping across her skin, Mercy turned to meet either her death or her salvation.

William Edmundston, murderer, confidence trickster and thwarted lover, lay sprawled on the gravel road a bare ten yards away. His pistol clutched in his right hand, he pushed himself up, reaching out towards her, before slumping back to the ground.

'Mercy Appleby, save me.' Was it a whisper from a living man or a cry from somewhere between life and death? She stayed fixed on the spot while time passed, immeasurably, while the fear that had flooded her slowed and the blood which had pounded through

William's veins seeped out onto the ground in front of her.

At last, she was able to move. Was he dead? Was he pretending, only to rear up like a snake and seize her by the throat as she'd thought he'd seized Jane? She knew about shotguns and these neat little weapons of war such as the revolver in his hand were hardly strange to her, because many of the men had kept them as souvenirs, but she'd never touched one. Guy kept his locked away in his desk and Teddy had never brought his home. Had William shot himself? Or had the bullet, in some strange way, bounced off the wall and come back to reprieve her?

'Mama! Mama!'

He was a wicked man and a clever one. If he still lived and cheated the hangman, he would come back.

Mercy would do anything for Sally. He'd tried to kill her. He still might. She tiptoed reluctantly along the path to where he lay on his side. His face shone pale in profile, like a child's drawing. Lifting the gun from his hand, she pointed it towards him with her finger touching the trigger, but before she could shoot, the eyelids twitched upwards, and the light in his blue eyes went out for ever.

CHAPTER TWENTY-EIGHT

MERCY

'Mercy! For Christ's sake, lass! What are you doing?'

She spun round. Twenty yards behind her, rising from the other side of the field wall, Tom's heavy frame threatened to blot out the sun. In his good hand, he held a pistol. 'Tom! What—?'

'Do you want them to find you with a dead man at your feet? They'll hang you, Mercy Appleby. They'll think you did it. Do you want to die? Get over here!'

She ran towards him. 'No. It'll be fine. I can explain—'

'Give me the child and run.' He thrust the gun into his pocket and seized her by the wrist, half hauling her over the wall. 'Can't you hear? There's someone coming.'

The growl of an engine came down through the thicket of rhododendrons that guarded the approach to the Hall. They ran, he holding Sally easily against him with his good arm; she struggling over the rough ground. The three of them made it to the shelter of the woods as a shout came behind them. 'Tom. We should have stayed. That must be the police.'

'I'll not help them when they've not helped me.' His face was grim.

In the shelter of the deeper woods, clutched in their deep, suffocating silence, he sank down on the soft ground. Mercy dropped down to her knees beside him, lifting Sally from his arms and holding her close. Thank God, her daughter, bless her, was a placid child and her wail had faded into stunned silence. 'Tom. Are you all right?'

'As I'll ever be.' His face was blank.

'What happened? How did he miss?'

'Them Webleys,' he muttered. 'They kick like a mule. You never get the bastards first time. Should have known that. So should he.'

'Thank God you arrived. You saved my life.' She reached out her free hand to touch his. It was the second time he had killed for her. First it had been for Teddy, somewhere in the mud of Flanders, now for both Sally and herself, so much closer to home. 'Don't look like that.'

'You don't know what it is to kill someone,' he whispered.

A febrile light flared in his eyes, just like the one that had cursed Teddy on the night, he'd woken in the sweat of madness and seen no way out. You couldn't argue with it, but she had to try. 'Nobody will blame you for killing him to save my life.'

'It's not that, lass. It's not him I'll never forgive myself for.' There was a tear in his eye. 'If he hadn't been threatening you, I'd have taken him face to face. He'd have known it was me. I'd have got my revenge.'

How long, she wondered, had Tom been lying in wait, counting each passer-by, ticking off the innocent as he searched for the guilty? 'How did you know he was here?'

'I saw him in the village. Seen him before, a couple of times, and he'd given me that chat about a soldier passing through. All those lies about a sweetheart. It was my wife and all the time that bastard — the two of them — were laughing about me behind my back. I been waiting for him to come back.'

'He told those lies to me, too,' she said gently.

'Going to run away, they were. I heard what he said to you.'

'Maybe that wasn't true.'

'Aye. It was. I heard them laughing about it on the night of the party, sniggering in the corner. Then sneaking off to the

252

garden hand in hand. They didn't see me or they didn't care. God, I was so mad.'

She recalled his anger in the lonning on the night of the party. Jane had already been dead by then, but it hadn't been William Edmundston who'd killed her. "But why didn't you tell the police you'd seen a stranger?'

'Cup!' announced Sally, and held out a dandelion.

His eyes misted over. 'If they'd've got him, they'd've known it wasn't him. Then they'd've looked for someone else. Or else they'd've thought it was him and hanged him before I could get my hands on him. I wanted to sort it myself, like I should've done from the start.' He reached down for the flower that Sally still held out, and a fat tear rolled down his cheek and splashed onto the yellow petals. 'I'm not a clever man. I make mistakes.'

'So Jane—? It was you?'

'I couldn't help it.' He dropped the dandelion and covered his eyes. He was trembling. 'They were laughing at me. I'd have killed them both if I'd've been a minute sharper, but by the time I got to them he'd gone. It was just her doing up her dress. Laughing.'

After all that, it had been him. She thought of him outside the garden, his face ravaged even then with pain and anger. 'Oh, Tom.'

'I killed a lot of men, Mercy, and I can be forgiven for that. I'd kill that bastard of a lover again, in a heartbeat. But I never meant to harm my Jane.'

After all this, Radgie Tom had killed his wife. The silence deepened around them. Sally's brown eyes looked up at her mother in apprehension. As she looked at the huddled wreck of a man crouched like a child against the wall, Mercy saw Teddy, another man fashioned by fear and anger into a twisted caricature of what he used to be. 'You loved her, didn't you?'

'The sun shone out of her eyes. I was the happiest man in the world the day she said she'd marry me, the proudest man ever when I walked her out of the church as my wife. Now I'm a useless wreck of a man. A shell. I deserve to die.'

Jane, all dancing eyes and tender fondness for anyone or anything in trouble, had died because she was too soft-hearted, victim of a man who cared nothing for anyone as much as she was of a man who loved too much. In life or in death, Tom's punishment would be never-ending.

'Let me hold your wee lass,' he said after a moment.

Mercy swung Sally over and sat her on his lap, shushing her and trusting to her silence. Sally was tired and leaned her head against the rough wool of his jacket, her eyes resting on her mother.

'We wanted little 'uns, Jane and me.' He smiled down at her. 'A houseful of 'em. That was her dream. I don't know that I blame her for running away.' He pressed his cheek against the top of Sally's head for a moment and sat back. 'Now, take the lass home.'

She lifted Sally up. 'I can't leave you here. We need to think about what to do.'

'Nowt we can do.' He pulled the gun out of his pocket and sat with it on his lap. 'Take her away. She shouldn't have to see this. Nor you, neither.' A stubbly workman's finger, dirt under the snagged nail, traced a line along the barrel of the gun like a lover teasing his partner's spine.

Mercy understood. 'Tom. Don't.'

'They'll hang me because I killed her,' he said, looking at her as if she were stupid, 'and I killed him. At least I'll have my pride. God, but I wish the bastard had seen me do it.'

Kitty talked about justice as if it were as simple as two plus two. In the woods, with the wind gentling rippling the trees, justice was as many-layered and complex as the swaying summer shadows of the deep wood. It was a crime, a sin, to kill a woman, even as the accident he claimed it was, and he should hang for it, but he'd saved Mercy, and Sally, and Teddy. She owed him more than to turn her back while he blew his brains out rather than face the scaffold. She owed him his life, and she knew how to give it to him.

'They don't know what happened,' she said slowly. 'Do they? They think he did it. No-one but you and I know he came back here looking for her. Only we know they planned to run away together.'

He tilted his head, as if the pain and the effort had defeated him emotionally as well as physically. 'I have a conscience.' He turned half-closed eyes back to the barrel of the gun. 'You're a good lass. You know what your duty is. Turn me over and tell the truth.'

'If it wasn't for you, I'd be dead in the road by now.' He was right and she should tell the police everything she knew, but somehow, she sensed that Jane, who'd channelled her love towards her husband when he was able to respond and had only given it away when he couldn't, wouldn't have wanted him to die. Jane's soft heart meant she'd surely have forgiven him, would never have wanted him to hang. 'Don't you see? So why—?'

'There's him. They'll know it were me did that.'

If the police applied their common sense and observation, they would work out what had happened. They could all tell the difference between a shotgun cartridge and a bullet, and Kitty had said they could match up a spent bullet casing to a gun; but if they came after Tom, then Kitty, surely would be his advocate and Blanche, with Guy in the clear, would salve her conscience by going to fight on his behalf. 'If they do, we'll tell them the truth. Or part of it. That you saw me with him. That you thought he was going to kill me. No-one will hang you for saving my life.'

'They might,' Tom said in a dead voice.

'Give me your gun. I'll get rid of it.' The river would be the best place as soon as she had the opportunity.

He was beaten, and it was love that had finally broken him. He handed the gun over and when she got up and lent him her hand to help him up, he took it without complaint. 'What now?'

'We'll wait and see what they do.' She kept hold of his hand, and they crunched companionably through the woods, across the brittle seeds of last year's beech mast and a layer of young acorns stripped from the trees by a summer gale. 'Go home. If they come and ask you, tell them what we agreed. I'll do the same. Don't tell them anything more.'

May I be forgiven, she thought as she left him to head back to the village. When she turned to take a final look down through the trees, she got a clear glimpse of the road. Gordon Livingstone's car was there and a figure, jacket-less, leaning against the bonnet of the car with such cheerful nonchalance that even if she hadn't recognised it straight away, she would have known it was Frank. May we all be forgiven.

She headed down past the river and dropped the gun into it, not a perfect hiding place but one that would remove it from the reach of Tom's despair, at least, and the first of the autumn storms would wash it down to join the River Eden if the summer rain didn't get there first. And then, with Sally clinging solemnly to her fingers, she headed for the Hall.

CHAPTER TWENTY-NINE

FRANK

'Aye, well. This is a bit of a puzzle and no mistake.'

'Did you have trouble starting the motor?' asked Frank, tapping his fingers on the bonnet of the Ford, which had just drawn to a halt in the lane beside him. 'That must be it, or you'd have got here in time. You'll need to bring her in and get her looked at. I can do it for you. Special favour, like.'

Gordon Livingstone had recollected his duty and decided to give chase to the fugitive who had so suddenly landed in his path, but not, Frank noted with wry amusement, until well after the danger was past. He got out of the car and strode across to the body, ignoring Frank's sarcasm. 'Dead, eh? And before we got here.'

Frank noted the 'we' and shook his head, this time slightly less amused by it. He'd always had Livingstone down as the type who'd jump on the wagon as it gathered speed, once all the heavy loading was done. Now, with the implicit suggestion that the two of them were in this together, he realised Livingstone was looking to share the glory.

That suited him. The car had rolled up just as Frank himself had concluded his downhill sprint to find Clifford Rowe, aka William Edmundston, sprawled still warm in the sun; Livingstone must have seen that Frank hadn't had the opportunity to kill him. He waited while the inspector examined the corpse, turning his attention away. You could see too many dead bodies, even though this one looked curiously peaceful. Instead, he stared across the fields, scanning the distant woodlands for the figures he'd barely seen disappearing into the trees. Mercy was one, for sure, and her companion had moved with the uneven gait of a one-armed man. A bit of a puzzle and no mistake. Livingstone was spot on about that, but Frank, in a position to enlighten him, chose not to. There was a story behind it and Mercy would tell him later. In the meantime, the inspector could do his own work.

Yards away, Livingstone looked down at the body at his feet and bent down towards it, stretching out a distasteful hand. Frank made himself look to confirm what he suspected. Blood had seeped out from under the man and drained away into the gravel of the road. 'The laddie's still warm. Well, well.' His eyes flicked nervously across the adjacent field, looking for a man with a gun. 'Did it himself, maybe.'

The man was a coward after all, for all his pretence at being a quiet hero in his own world. 'Maybe that's one answer. But you can see what happened as well as I can.'

'Aye.' Livingstone was still frowning. His wall eye swivelled towards the village, towards the fields, back again. Mercy and Tom, by now, were deep in the woods, well out of sight.

'Somebody braver than you or me,' went on Frank, looking down at Guy's gun in his hand, 'took the law into their own hands, didn't they? Stopped this murdering bastard going back to the village to kill someone else. Who knows who that might have been? Someone in a position to catch him and lock him up. Maybe he realised you were onto him. Maybe it was you he was coming for, Inspector. Had you thought of that? You'd be driving down the lane on your merry way back to Keswick, thinking the case was a problem for someone else. And then... bang. And you're dead.'

Gordon Livingstone's shoulders twitched. 'He was a man with a hell of a record,' he said, as though that justified his cowardice. 'But there will be another inquest. Questions asked. Where the bullet came from. Your gun hasn't been fired.'

Frank reached over the wall and fired Guy's weapon into the air. As the Webley kicked back in his hands, a shudder of trauma came back to haunt him. The sheep scattered, the birds rose in complaint. The bullet would fall to earth three fields away, with luck in the bog by the beck or at the edge of the field, and before anyone could find it, the sheep would churn the ground into mud and it would be lost. 'It has now.' He handed to gun to Livingstone and his lips twitched into a smile. 'You'd better take charge of this.'

He'd meant it sarcastically, but even as he spoke, an idea formed in his mind, growing from a ridiculous thought into an elegant solution for everybody. He could see by the way Livingstone was staring at the gun that the same idea, or one very like it, had occurred to him.

'We didn't see what happened,' went on Frank, quietly satisfied he understood how the man's mind was working, 'but nor did anyone else. Ask no questions and no-one need know you were too scared to confront him.'

'His killer knows.' He rubbed his chin, still only half-persuaded. 'That person may come forward.'

'Not a chance. He'd have stayed to take the credit, if that was what he wanted. Why not just say you shot the fellow in self-defence, eh?' He grinned. After all that, he was offering the glory to a man who took pride in his collection of white feathers, making a coward into a hero for his own convenience. 'It'll tie it up nicely for your Chief Constable. That's what he wants, isn't it?'

Livingstone turned away in silence, but not before Frank had seen the expression on his face of self-doubt and temptation. He smiled. It surely wouldn't take long for the man to decide that justice was done and the truth of how it had come about was of less value to him than rebuilding his reputation.

'Hey!' Davy Robinson's bicycle came clattering round the corner, all boots and helmet. He skidded to a halt, jumped off, and flung it to the ground. 'I'd a call to come out, Sir. They said the murderer was in the village. I heard a shot.'

'The one just now? That'll be some lad shooting rabbits for the plot,' Frank said, to buy Livingstone a moment longer to fall for temptation. 'But there was a shot. Look what we've got here. This is Clifford Rowe. He killed Mrs Freeman. We intercepted him on his way back to the village. Thank God Inspector Livingstone was here to take him on.'

There was a pause.

'Yes,' the inspector said, with becoming modesty. 'Sometimes a man has to confront danger to save lives.'

Frank stepped away, leaving the field, but he couldn't resist a wink of understanding. Davy didn't see it, but Livingstone did. He'd always know, and Frank would always know, which one of them was the coward. And that, for Frank, was satisfaction enough.

CHAPTER THIRTY

MERCY

'Eh, Tuppence. Leave the lass to her granny just now.' George appeared in the doorway of the kitchen, through the link that led to the office. 'Her ladyship wants a word.'

It was almost suppertime in the Smart household, a day after the concluding incident in the story of Jane Freeman's murder. Mercy had been on her hands and knees on the rag rug in front of the range, tickling Sally until the child was helpless with laughter. She sat back on her knees. 'I'd better go.'

Blanche was normally a frequent visitor to the estate office, popping her head around the door several times a day in pursuit of this piece of information or that, a question about which fields were growing barley or when the harvest would be, but every question was only the preliminary to ten minutes chat about something or nothing. Over the past year or so, Mercy had come to take these little interventions for granted and a day without them was somehow bereft. It was bad enough being without Teddy, but their respective stances over the killing had undermined their friendship, too. And if it was like that for Mercy, with a solid and loving family behind her, with a child on whom to focus her love, her attention and her time, what must it be like for Blanche with Sir Henry so distant, Guy beginning to pursue a line of stubborn independence, and her three younger children in their graves?

Bereavement reshaped everything. At first Mercy hadn't

understood that, but now she saw that Blanche's loneliness and hers had a mutual solution. I didn't damage our friendship, she thought as she stepped past her father, through the early-evening haze of alcohol fumes he carried round with him.

There was an arrangement in the hallway, tall daisies and some exotic greenery from the hothouses cascading down the side of a green and white Chinese vase, reflecting a new, pared-down angle on Blanche's love of fresh flowers. She hesitated for a moment before approaching the drawing room. Blanche had the gramophone on and was playing Beethoven, a scratchy sound at odds with the beautiful evening.

She tapped on the door, not announcing herself. When annoyed, Blanche took refuge in stiff formality and Mercy was prepared neither to address her as Lady Waterbeck nor be reproved for being casual. She coughed.

'Mercy. Come in and sit down, my dear.' Reclining on the chaise longue as she listened to the music, Blanche looked relaxed and opulent. She wore a headband that looked as if it might be one of Kitty's and which suited her and made her look ridiculously young. When she turned her head, for a second, she was Flora, to the life. 'Such goings on. Who would have thought our inspector would turn out to be quite such a hero?'

Who, indeed? Mercy stifled a smile. 'I'm sure he's happy with the way it turned out.'

'I'm quite sure he is. He can go and burn those white feathers of his and the young women of the district can fawn over him and call him whenever they're in trouble, thinking he won't just hide behind a desk.'

Blanche's wicked sense of humour was back. It would be nice to giggle along with it, but Mercy herself hadn't been down to the village for the gossip, which had all arrived in the kitchen via her mother, and so she'd had no chance to speak to either Tom or Frank. Until she knew for certain the story that would go to the inquest, she couldn't relax as easily as Blanche seemed able to. She sat down on Blanche's comfortable old chair. 'I'm not sure he'd be the first person I'd call.'

'No, well, quite.' Blanche swung her legs round and sat up. 'I meant to pop in for a chat, but there's been so much going on. It does appear our inspector genuinely is quite brave and took on the killer single-handedly. Thank God this whole thing is over and we can leave it to die quietly.'

The clock ticked. In the distance, there was a clatter of cutlery as someone set the table for supper. 'Did I see Mrs Watson-Cooke's motor car here?'

'Yes. She came to make sure Guy was all right. Very touching.'

'Of course,' said Mercy after a fractional hesitation, 'he's perfectly all right.' Blanche, after all, had dedicated herself to ensuring exactly that.

'Well, I don't know that he is.' Blanche sat up and tossed over the copy of *The Times*, which had been at her elbow. It was open at the personal column.

GW, read Mercy, it can never be. Forgive me. Be happy. 'What does it mean?'

'Guy is in love with someone else,' explained Blanche. 'I don't know who she is. He won't say. That's why he wouldn't say where he was when Jane was killed. The woman never turned up and now, it appears, she's put a conclusion to it. Quite why they had to conduct their affairs of the heart through the columns of a national newspaper, I don't understand. It's not like Guy. The young lady must be something of an attention seeker. He's probably well free of her.'

Mercy folded the newspaper and replaced it. Poor Guy. She liked him, an inoffensive young man who yearned for a quiet life and yet could, or so it appeared, behave with quite extraordinary courage if it was ever required of him. 'Is he all right?'

'He came to show it to me, to set my mind at rest, but he seems to have taken it on the chin. When Kitty telephoned and asked to come over, he seemed cheerful enough. She's a very forceful woman, and I can hardly blame her if her heart is elsewhere, but if you can't have the one you love it's foolish to think you can't try for something with someone else, or at least I think so.'

Marrying for love didn't always work out the way you planned. You had only to look at Tom and Jane to see that, even at Teddy and Mercy herself, suffering in a very different way. 'I hope he's happy,' she said, and couldn't resist the tiny barb. 'There was no need to sacrifice anyone else for him, was there?'

Blanche put her head back and stared. 'I shouldn't have to tell you how much Guy matters to me. And I'm deeply sorry if anything I did caused you distress or upset.'

You bullied my father into lying to the police. You tried to bribe me about Teddy. You were prepared to see an innocent man hang. For a moment Mercy let the accusations hang in the air unsaid.

'You must understand. You have a child.'

Just twenty-four hours earlier up in the lane, with William Edmundston threatening Sally, Mercy would have done anything she could to save her. She'd been ready to shoot a dying man, and she'd gone on to conceal information from the police to save Tom and hide the identity of a murderer. She was no better than Blanche, no better than anyone else. 'I do understand.'

'You'd do anything for Sally, wouldn't you?' Blanche was watching her anxiously. 'Just as I would for Guy.'

'Yes. And if I ever have to put Sally first, I will. Above everything, above anyone.' Above Teddy, above her parents, above Blanche, even above herself.

'Then we understand one another.' Blanche looked relieved, though she'd neither offered a real apology nor had it accepted. 'It doesn't need to change anything, because nothing has changed.'

CHAPTER THIRTY-ONE

FRANK

When she went back to the house, the kitchen was in a state of uproar. Carrie was leaning against the scrubbed wooden worktop, laughing uncontrollably. George was sitting on the straight-backed wooden settle, glass in hand, giving off an air of benevolent good humour. On the rug in front of the range Frank sat cross-legged like a ten-year-old, with a covered basket on his lap, and Sally was sitting in front of him, stretching out a pleading hand towards the basket and squealing in anticipation.

'Not until your mam comes back,' said Frank, pretending to be stern. 'This isn't just for you. It's for her, too.'

'Please!' Sally wheedled. 'Please!' and then, the first to notice Mercy appearing at the door: 'Mama!'

'Are you causing trouble again, Frank?' she asked, amused.

He must have been there some time because there was an empty glass at his elbow. 'No, but I've brought you a basketful of it.' Vanquished at last, he let go of the lid of the basket and set it down in front of Sally. 'Go on then, lass. You've been patient enough. See what it is.'

They all knew. The tiny mews from the basket were all the clues they needed. Sally reached out a hand for the lid and before she knew it, a scrap of grey and silver emerged, blinding in the daylight.

'Miaow!' squealed Sally, enraptured.

'Good luck with her,' he said with a grin. 'She's the wildest one of the litter, but I reckon she'll make the best mouser. But a feisty lass deserves a feisty cat.'

He scrambled to his feet, dusting his hands down on his trousers. 'I'll be away. Can't spend all evening loitering in someone else's kitchen, disrupting bedtime.'

'I think you've disrupted bedtime well and truly tonight,' Carrie retorted, stretching out a hand to prevent the kitten taking off through the house. 'Thanks, though, Frank. The wee scrap will be a proper tonic for us all.'

'I'll see myself out.'

He headed for the door and Mercy, reluctant to leave the cosy domestic scene, nevertheless followed him. There was too much unsaid, too much she didn't know. 'Frank. Wait a moment.'

He carried on walking a few steps, until he was in the centre of the courtyard, and then he stopped and turned. It was a grey evening, and the cloud was low on the Pennines, lower on the Lakeland fells, so that Waterbeck seemed the only spot of brightness in a bleak landscape.

'I wanted to thank you.'

'You've nothing to thank me for,' he said, sticking his hands in his pockets and waiting until she reached him. 'I'm just glad you're all right. After yesterday.'

He knew. Shadows flitted about in the trees, a reminder of Jane's restless spirit, but if she was troubled by the outcome, there was no sense of it, only the fading sun and laughter from inside the house, and Blanche's tall, slender figure moving within the Hall.

'Yes. Thanks to Tom.'

'It was him, then, that killed him?'

'Yes. I met him — William — in the lane and he must have thought I recognised him. Tom was already following him and he shot him.'

'The bastard came to my cottage,' he said, without an apology for the language, 'making out he was a stranger. I don't suppose we'll ever know why he came back. Couldn't keep away from the scene of the crime, maybe. By the time I'd got to the Hall for the inspector and got back down again, he was already dead.'

'And you let the policeman take the credit?'

'Doesn't matter, does it? I don't grudge him a day in the sun. Those fellows can make life difficult for us if they want to. What matters is that justice is done.'

So it was, of a sort, but the truth about Jane's killer was the secret she'd keep for Tom's sake, even from Frank, because Tom had allowed her, and Sally, to live.

'Mercy,' he said, a sudden lightening to his tone.

'What?' Instinctively, she turned her wedding ring over on her finger as she'd seen Kitty do, a reminder that she was married, a charm against temptation.

'If I'd got there, and he'd still been alive, I'd have killed him. You know that?'

She swallowed. 'Yes.'

'You're Teddy's woman, but Teddy's my mate. I'd have done it for the both of you. I'll be there for him if he ever needs me. I'll always be there for you, whatever happens. So if you ever need me, just call.'

'Thank you. I will.'

He leaned in and kissed her on the cheek in a breath of stale beer and cigarette smoke, then strode away. She watched until he was around the curve in the drive before she turned back to the Hall, where a flicker in the hallway announced the coming of dusk and, behind her in Waterbeck, the lights of the village came back on, one by one.

THE END

Acknowledgements

TBD

FIND US ON SOCIAL MEDIA

@northodoxpress

@northodoxpressofficial

@northodoxpress

@northodoxpress

www.northodox.co.uk

NORTHODOX PRESS

SUBMISSIONS

CONTEMPORARY
CRIME & THRILLER
FANTASY
LGBTQ+
ROMANCE
YOUNG ADULT
SCI-FI & HORROR
HISTORICAL
LITERARY

SUBMISSIONS@NORTHODOX.CO.UK

NORTHODOX PRESS

FIND US ON SOCIAL MEDIA

www.northodox.co.uk

f @northodoxpress

@northodoxpressofficial

@northodoxpress

@northodoxpress

www.northodox.co.uk

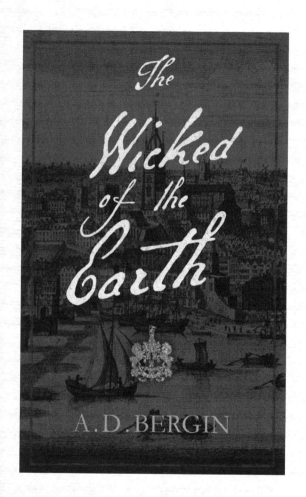

The Wicked of the Earth

A. D. BERGIN

A
DROWNING
MAN

A Manchester Noir

JOHN STOREY

Printed in Great Britain
by Amazon